JUST THE WAY YOU ARE

All Parr could think of was how irresistible Mary Beth was. She smelled of some lush, feminine perfume, a scent so enticing that he longed to see if she tasted as sweetly sensual. He had no right to touch her. She was his brother's woman.

So why the hell wasn't Bobby Joe here protecting what was his? Male instinct should have kicked in. It was for Parr.

"I want to taste you, Strawberry. I want to put my mouth on yours."

"Parr . . . I . . . Look, just don't. Please. This is hard."

"Yeah. For me too."

"Yes," she sighed. She wasn't agreeing to anything. But that softly breathed *yes* was a million miles away from *no*.

"I may be too rough," he warned. "I'm not used to good girls like you."

"It doesn't matter," she pleaded.

One big, dark finger touched her lower lip, running tenderly from corner to corner, pausing as her mouth gradually opened. "Your lips look so sweet," he murmured. "So inviting."

"Oh, Parr."

"Do you want my mouth on yours, Strawberry?"

"Yes," she begged, her body leaning into his. . . .

Books by Beverly Barton

AFTER DARK
EVERY MOVE SHE MAKES
WHAT SHE DOESN'T KNOW
THE FIFTH VICTIM
THE LAST TO DIE
AS GOOD AS DEAD
KILLING HER SOFTLY
CLOSE ENOUGH TO KILL
MOST LIKELY TO DIE
THE DYING GAME
THE MURDER GAME
COLD HEARTED
SILENT KILLER
DEAD BY MIDNIGHT
DON'T CRY
DEAD BY MORNING
DEAD BY NIGHTFALL
DON'T SAY A WORD
JUST THE WAY YOU ARE
THE RIGHT WIFE (available as an eBook)

Published by Kensington Publishing Corporation

JUST THE WAY YOU ARE

BEVERLY BARTON

ZEBRA BOOKS
KENSINGTON PUBLISHING CORP.
http://www.kensingtonbooks.com

Chapter One

Parr Weston stood just inside the wide double doors that had been left ajar, his broad shoulders practically filling the opening. He hated social gatherings, especially if the invitation specified black tie, but this was one he'd been unable to refuse. The engagement party for his younger brother, Bobby Joe, seemed to be in full swing. The enormous hotel ballroom was jammed with formally attired guests, dancing, drinking, and celebrating up a storm.

But Bobby Joe was nowhere to be seen, which was odd. Maybe he had stepped out for a smoke, something he'd sworn he'd given up long ago. Parr wouldn't put it past him.

He looked back into the crowded ballroom and shook his head, then went outside. The dimly lit patio beyond the doors was edged with benches set between manicured shrubs, but Parr didn't want to sit. The night air was warm and balmy, surprisingly pleasant for late April in Iminga, Mississippi. He leaned back against a smooth wrought-iron pillar, relaxing his tall, rugged frame for a few moments in the embrace of the soft night.

Since he'd footed the bill for this extravagant shindig, he thought the least Bobby Joe could have done was be there to greet him at the entrance to the ballroom. He was surprised Mama hadn't rushed over to introduce him to Bobby Joe's "perfect" fiancée. During the three months he'd been on the construction site in Canada, the whole family had met and fallen in love with this paragon of virtue his brother intended to marry.

True, Parr had arrived over an hour late, but the delayed flight from Memphis hadn't been entirely his fault. He couldn't help it if a last-minute problem with one of his suppliers made him miss the departure of his original flight.

He'd parked himself and the carry-on with his formal wear at the gate to wait for the next flight, and caught up on other pressing business on his laptop. Parr Weston believed in staying focused. He worked off-line, so as to avoid wasting time on the Internet, where Bobby Joe had no doubt posted scads of flattering photos of himself and his true love.

Parr preferred to skip all that and judge for himself when he met her in person.

He had figured his family and the fabulous fiancée were all mad at him. But just what did they expect him to do? His successful construction business had to come first so they could all continue to enjoy their present lifestyle. Parr had taken on the role of head of the household long ago, at the too-young age of twelve, when their old man died. It hadn't been an easy job then. It still wasn't.

A low, sobbing sound interrupted his solitude, bringing his mind away from his troubled thoughts. What was that noise? he wondered. Was someone crying?

He listened for several minutes, trying to figure out where the sound was coming from. As if in answer to his confusion, the weeping grew louder. Then he saw her. On the far side of the patio, a small form stood huddled against the wall, her face hidden by a hand that brushed away tears.

Even in the semidarkness, he could see the gleaming, fiery gold length of her hair, not quite concealing the pearly white smoothness of her bare neck and shoulders, and the womanly curves of her satin-covered breasts and hips. Before he saw her face clearly, he knew she was beautiful. Just looking at her made him ache with powerful longing. He wanted to take her in his arms. Comfort and protect her.

He crossed the distance between them without thinking twice. When his big hand came down on her shoulder, she cried out and whirled around to face him. Too late, he realized he should have spoken before touching her.

"Calm down," he said as his hand eased gently from her shoulder to rest tentatively at the small of her back. "It's all right. Really. I heard you crying. I was concerned."

She tilted her head slightly to gaze up at the towering, dark-eyed stranger, her whole body surrendering as his arm encircled her, pulling her against his hard male strength.

She clutched at the lapels of his tuxedo jacket, burying her face in the stiff pleats of his white shirt as the tears began to flow again.

"I'm so . . . sorry . . . I . . . please," she gulped helplessly between sobs.

He let her lean against him, still weeping as she snuggled closer and closer, as if wanting to lose herself in the warmth of his body. God, but she felt right in his arms.

Parr couldn't fight the wild idea that she belonged there or the strange feeling that this unknown woman was somehow meant for him.

But she didn't belong in his arms, he told himself. He sure as hell didn't believe in fate—or luck, for that matter. But he made no move away. She nestled closer.

What would it be like, he wondered, if they could act on instinct and let this unexpected closeness lead to its natural conclusion? What would her small, round body feel like naked beneath his?

Parr stiffened. That wasn't his brain talking. He had to regain self-control or this random encounter might go in an unwanted direction. The beautiful teary woman in his arms obviously needed nothing more than to be held for a few minutes. Give her that and then let her go, he told himself.

"Shhh . . . shhh . . ." His voice was deep and rough.

She moved her face up a few inches from his chest, looking into his eyes, trying to smile. "You must think that I'm crazy."

"No." He was still holding her close, so close that he

could feel the soft warmth of her breasts. "Something upset you, hurt you."

She stared into his brown eyes, eyes so dark they appeared almost black. "Yes. But I—I just can't explain. Not now. Not here."

His hand gently stroked her cascading strawberry blond hair and she rested her head on his chest again as her arms went around his waist.

To steady herself, Parr thought. Not to embrace him.

"That's all right, honey," he whispered into her hair. "You don't have to tell me anything you don't want to. Just let me hold you. It'll do you good."

Her response was a tiny, relieved sigh.

Parr wasn't sure how long they stood there hidden in the shadows. No one saw the big, dark man with a small, golden woman in his arms. Soon enough, he realized that they couldn't stay out there forever. The nearness of her was driving him crazy. He didn't even know her name, but he wanted her more than he'd ever wanted anything in his entire thirty-two years.

"Hey." His lips brushed her forehead. "You okay?"

She didn't answer. Her green, catlike gaze raised to meet his, then moved downward to his slightly open mouth. Then up again. The eye contact was as hot as a kiss. Maybe hotter.

Parr guessed that she was feeling exactly what he was. That she wanted him desperately, his lips on hers, his body on hers, his . . .

Oh God, he thought. We've got to get out of here.

"Come on," he said, putting one hand at her waist to lead her across the patio. "Let's go to the lounge and get something to drink."

She hesitated momentarily before accepting his proposal and moving into step beside him. "I don't usually drink."

He wondered if he'd heard her right. She'd sounded so prim and proper, it almost made him want to laugh. Was she kidding?

No. One look at that beautifully sweet face told him that she was sincere. "Don't drink, don't smoke, don't fool around," he mumbled under his breath.

"What?" She stopped still, her body suddenly tight as a coiled spring.

"Nothing. Just thinking out loud. I'll get you a Coke or coffee. Okay?"

She smiled with relief. "Yes. A Coke would be great. Thanks."

The entrance to the lounge wasn't far from the double doors. Parr guided her toward it, shouldering through the crush of guests as she followed until they reached the lounge, which was large, overheated, and even more crowded than the ballroom. The music was loud, the atmosphere stimulating.

Couples filled every corner, their eyes, their hands, their bodies speaking a language of sensuous longing and human loneliness. Some—too many, in Parr's opinion—were staring into smartphones, the tiny, glowing blue screens doubled and redoubled in the mirrored walls of the lounge as the phones' owners ignored the real people all around them. Parr didn't get it.

Parr kept her close, easing her through the throng until he found a table for two. He slipped her smoothly onto a chair, guarding her with his big arm as he pulled up a seat for himself.

Then he signaled a waiter, not ordering anything for himself. Parr let her finish one Coke and ordered her another before he felt she had calmed down enough to talk. The entire time they'd sat there together, she'd remained silent, occasionally glancing his way with a strangely puzzled look in those big, feline eyes, once or twice offering a thanks-for-being-here smile.

He decided she was definitely the loveliest woman he'd ever seen, and totally different from any he'd ever known. Perhaps it was because she seemed so young and vulnerable, and was obviously in a great deal of emotional pain.

She winced when she caught a glimpse of herself in a background mirror. "I need to fix my face," she sighed. "Would you please excuse me for a few minutes?"

No argument there. Parr had thought it ungallant to point out that her tears had not improved her eye makeup. A few delicate streaks didn't make her any less beautiful. But she didn't have a purse with her, something she seemed to have just remembered. Giving him an awkward smile, she rose and made her way through the crowd.

Every male head turned to watch her walk. Parr couldn't blame them, not with all that strawberry sweetness on display. Coming or going, she was a stunner.

He leaned back a little in the spindly chair, drumming his fingers on the tabletop, alone with his thoughts.

He didn't need drama, hadn't ever liked it. He wasn't remotely tempted to turn this accidental encounter into something else. The last thing he wanted in his life right now was someone with a new set of unknown problems.

Since he'd been a kid, other people had needed him, depended on him, and he'd come through every time. He'd been there for Mama, even before Kenneth Parr Weston, his dad, had been found in a motel room with a bullet through his heart. He'd been there for Bobby Joe, and for his cousin Eve and her family. He'd been provider, substitute father, as well as brotherly advisor, to the whole tribe. By the time he was grown and on his own, it was like women sensed Parr would just naturally step up and take care of whatever had to be done.

And he had. Too often.

Every woman he'd been involved with had wanted, needed, demanded—endlessly. Maybe he didn't know how to ask for what he needed, but it was still a fact that the giving never seemed to work both ways. When he'd needed to know that someone would return the favor, stand by him, have his back . . . it didn't happen.

The lounge crowd got liquored up and louder. Parr observed the interactions around him, unable to avoid listening to chitchat that sounded depressingly familiar. The more things changed, the more they stayed the same. Women wanted their freedom, their careers, their hard-won rights, and at the same time, they wanted a man's love, his money, his body, and his total acceptance of them just as they were.

Parr was thinking that he ought to stop thinking

and order a real drink, a stiff one, when the standing guests stepped this way and that to let someone through.

Her.

His cynical mood dissolved in an instant.

She didn't look right or left but straight at him. Her eyelashes were darker, her cheeks pink. She had fixed what needed fixing with a damp paper towel, he supposed. The streaks were gone.

"Thank you for waiting." Her voice was gentle, extremely feminine, just like her smile, her face, her body.

Parr rose as she reached the table. "Not a problem."

He sat down after she did. "Don't you want anything?" she asked, moving aside the glass of melting ice.

The returning waiter stopped and set down the second Coke, pausing for a fraction of a second to look down at Parr, who shook his head. "Nothing for me, thanks."

The young man moved on.

"I was thinking we might go somewhere quieter," Parr began.

"I don't mind the noise."

"I mean, if you want to talk. Would it help?"

"I don't know." She reached for the Coke the waiter had just delivered.

"Sometimes it's easier to talk to a stranger." He didn't know exactly why he was encouraging her. But he really did want her to talk, to tell him what was hurting her. Seemed like the least he could do, even though they might never see each other again.

He couldn't take his eyes off her soft, sweet mouth.

God, what a smile. Sensual and sincere. Meant for him. She wasn't checking herself out sideways in the mirrored walls like practically everybody else in the lounge, female or male. A tiny dimple appeared in her cheek. That right there was almost his undoing.

Parr struggled to sit up straight and not lean over the table to taste those full, pink lips and kiss the breath out of her.

"For some reason, you don't seem like a stranger," she said. "It's as if I've always known you."

Her frank admission surprised him. The identical thought had just crossed his mind, unbidden, but he would never have told her. "Same here," he muttered.

Before he could stop himself, he raised a hand and caressed her cheek. Her skin was dewy and cool. She must have splashed cold water on her face in an effort to regain her composure. He was getting more rattled by the second.

"I didn't mean anything by that," she said quietly. "I . . . I have a boyfriend." She took a deep breath. "Well, he's more than that."

"You're engaged?" Parr couldn't help noticing that her hands were in her lap. He hadn't noticed a ring, but then he hadn't been looking for one, mesmerized by every other little thing about her.

"We were." Two words that seemed to have been ripped from her heart.

Anger and frustration consumed him. Whoever the other man was or what his reasons might be, Parr wished he didn't exist. How could any man hurt her? The would-be bridegroom deserved to be broken in two.

"We were supposed to be celebrating tonight, in fact." Her voice cracked on a sob, her eyes pressed tightly shut to hold back renewed tears.

Parr scooted his chair next to hers and pulled her into his arms, not caring who saw. No one seemed to notice—a noisy game of beer pong had started up at the back of the lounge. Thankful for that, Parr knew his only concern was for her. He wanted to comfort her. He wanted to ease her pain. He wanted to make her happy.

Oh God. He just plain wanted her.

Seeming to draw strength from his embrace, she continued, her voice ragged and low. Parr had to strain to catch every word.

"He says he loves me, that he wants to marry me, but tonight—of all nights—he did something . . . unforgivable."

The last word was spoken with anguished determination, as if she were making a vow: *No matter what anyone says or does, I will not forgive him.*

"What did he do, honey?" The endearment seemed right. Parr couldn't take it back.

"I . . . I saw him . . . them."

"Who?"

"He was with his old girlfriend. In each other's arms, to be exact. And that's n-not all," she stammered, her face scarlet.

"Maybe she was kissing him."

"No *maybe* about it. She was all over him!" Abruptly jerking out of Parr's arms, his fire gold angel faced him. "And vice versa. Kissing. Touching. He practically had her undressed less than an hour after we announced our engagement."

"Oh." Parr wasn't sure what to say, didn't know what she wanted to hear. She obviously needed consoling, but he'd bet good money that, gentle as the woman seemed, she had good reason to take her fury out on any representative of the male sex in a fifty-mile radius. And he was a lot closer than that.

The fire in her soul shone in her green eyes. Parr was dazzled. Angry, she was even more beautiful. *And* available, because some selfish idiot had cheated on her. Parr was suddenly more than ready to volunteer for consolation duty.

It had been a long time since he'd wanted a woman badly. In all honesty, he couldn't ever remember wanting one this much.

"I knew he'd loved her once. I knew that they'd had a hot affair. But he swore everything ended when she married another man. And I believed him."

Parr nodded.

"He used to say that the love he felt for me was so different." She just about spat the words. "So much *deeper*. Then tonight . . . there they were. I caught them almost in the act."

This was no ordinary drama, not the way she told the story, in few words but with matchless intensity and good old-fashioned righteous, blazing indignation that would do a real angel proud. Even though infidelity happened every damn day, every hour, every second all around the world.

Still.

Whoever her fiancé was, he must be the biggest fool

ever to walk the earth. What man in his right mind
would mess around with an old girlfriend when he
could have this gorgeous little redhead?

"I'm sorry," she said, placing her hand on his where
it lay on the table. "You don't need to know the details.
I appreciate your patience. You've been truly kind."

"Whatever I can do." Parr forced his thoughts back
onto the gallant track.

"Thank you. But we are strangers. I can't ask you for
help—I've already presumed too much."

Her hand began a slow withdrawal. The sensation
of her soft fingertips moving over his skin was too
much for him. "Not at all." Parr captured her slender
wrist.

She gave him a startled look but didn't pull away.

Impulsively, he took her hand, brought it to his lips,
and pressed a kiss to her palm. Then he released her.
She didn't seem shocked or pleased.

"Sorry." Parr didn't know what had possessed him
to do that. "I just thought—maybe you needed—"

Her reply was swift. "No need to apologize."

"Right. But there is a question I'd like to ask."

"Go ahead. You can say anything you like. This
night couldn't get any weirder."

"What if I said that I needed you?"

Her lips parted with evident surprise. "Huh? You
need me?"

Her startled gaze met his. Parr wished there was a
surefire way to get her to understand what was on his
mind. But he couldn't quite define it himself.

"I think I do."

"Really," she said, her voice laced with wry amusement.

"The love of my life, whom I thought I knew, doesn't need me at all, and a total stranger apparently does."

"It was just a question. I'm not sure what I meant by it."

"That makes two of us. Just the two of us." She surveyed him warily.

Parr nodded. *Just the two of us.* He liked the sound of that. Maybe he hadn't overstepped the bounds of propriety or whatever rules were in effect when rescuing a damsel in distress.

"I guess—well, it seemed to me you needed a kiss, that was all."

"Is that something you do often? Find an unhappy woman and plant one on her?"

"No. And it wasn't like I was looking for you."

That tiny dimple appeared above her slight—very slight—smile. Nonetheless, Parr had a feeling she was taking him seriously, for reasons known only to herself. Maybe she was just used to men throwing themselves at her feet.

Which was all the more reason not to let her walk away. But she honestly didn't seem outraged by his impulsively romantic gesture and she certainly didn't seem scared of him.

So far, so good. But where did they go from here?

She put her fingertips to her temples and rubbed. "I think I need something to eat," she said. "I feel a little dizzy."

"Good idea." He looked around for a waiter, not seeing a single one in the thickening crush of people. The place was jammed and the music cranked up to deafening levels. "There has to be a menu around here somewhere. I'll grab one. Be right back." He stopped for a second after he got up. "What's your name? You never did say."

"No. I didn't. Just get a menu. Please."

Exchanging vital information like that would just have to wait. She was grateful for a few moments alone, which she desperately needed, to think about just what the hell she was doing here. With him.

Whatever *his* name was.

Mary Beth sipped her Coke, which had lost most of its fizz, and watched him shoulder through the crowd.

He had to turn around once to get past an entwined couple who'd just set down their cocktails to smooch and cuddle, generating the usual friendly advice to *get a room.*

None of her business. She just hoped other hearts weren't being broken.

The look on his craggy, masculine face as he eased by the oblivious pair was priceless, though.

He wasn't really handsome. More like rugged. The waitress he asked for a menu perked up when she handed him one, obviously just as attracted to his jewel-brown eyes. Even from this distance, his eyes sparkled with devilment. She felt a tiny pang of jealousy that she instantly dismissed.

But he didn't seem interested in the waitress once he had scored a menu. Good. She kept on studying him as he got closer, which was taking a while.

His features were too roughly hewn, his nose too hawkish for him to be considered classically good-looking. He was a real man in every sense of the word, hard, tough, maybe even a little too masculine.

If there was such a thing, she couldn't help thinking.

The revolving spotlights that pierced the dim atmosphere of the lounge touched his hair now and then, making it gleam darkly. She wouldn't mind doing the same thing. That thick sable hair looked extremely touchable. She suppressed a smile of admiration when several guys stepped aside, consciously or unconsciously ceding their turf to him. He was big, so very big. The kind of man who looked as if he could carry the burdens of the world on those massive shoulders.

And he'd been bold enough to say he needed her.

Hmm. Although it was possible that it was a pickup line, it actually hadn't sounded like one. More like a statement of fact.

But she was in no condition to judge accurately after the devastating discovery in suite 5-C. Or rather, in the storage closet next to suite 5-C. She had knocked on the door by mistake and heard a low-voiced *yes* at almost the same moment. And she'd opened the door.

Her fingers tightened on her cold, empty glass. All she could think was *payback time*. Someone richly deserved it. She couldn't figure out how, exactly, not just yet. But she would.

The man who needed her had stopped to talk to a pal. He didn't nod in her direction or give any indication that they were together, for which she was grateful.

She was still somewhat numb, basically unable to form a coherent thought. Or maybe stunned was a better word. The intensity of her attraction to this well-built stranger was affecting her ability to reason, on top of everything else.

Raw emotion was no balm for her hurting heart.

Unless she was just experiencing a powerful physical reaction and nothing more.

She did want him that way. The feeling was new and wild. She'd never wanted a man just physically before in her whole life.

At the moment, he seemed to be unable to extricate himself from an unwanted conversation. He finally did manage a reassuring glance at her over his friend's shoulder. He was coming back.

He cared. Good enough. If this encounter lasted a grand total of an hour, start to finish, he still cared enough to treat her right.

Mary Beth was all about doing right, first and foremost. Above all, she believed that you took care of your family and loved them best. Next to that was her work. She genuinely cared for the young students who came to talk to her in confidence. As a school social worker, she knew a lot about life that she hadn't personally experienced.

She had convinced herself that she loved her fiancé and that she was ready to take the huge step of starting a family of her own. At least she was sure she hadn't accepted his proposal for any of the wrong reasons.

She didn't need him to be financially secure. She didn't have to have a man around the house just because she'd been so close—and still was—to her widowed father, Harold Caine.

No. She'd gotten engaged because it was the logical next step in her orderly life, a perfectly reasonable idea that had shattered into a million pieces when, by mistake, she opened the closet door next to the suite the guys had used to change into formal wear.

In seconds, her whole damn life had changed. There was no going back.

If one of her girlfriends should dare to tell her to get over herself, that men were just teenage boys at heart who could be expected to fool around one last time before they got dragged down the aisle—well, so much for that friendship. Mary Beth drew the line at cheating.

Though this was the first time she'd been cheated on. She amended the thought. This was the first time *she knew for sure* she'd been cheated on. It felt horrible.

Any woman so lacking in self-respect that she put up with crap like that even once would be doomed to a lifetime of it.

No way. Not her. But she had no Plan B. And now here she was in a noisy lounge staring at a man who made her feel like she actually mattered. And feeling flummoxed.

He'd come to her aid instantly. And held her as if he knew what had just happened when he didn't know a thing. Tried to help. Been a gentleman the entire time, including that funny, old-fashioned kiss. She'd felt like a lady.

In that roughly tender voice, he'd claimed out of nowhere that he'd needed her and seemed as surprised by his confession as she had been.

It was impossible to tell why or how it had all happened so fast, but she still wanted him to hold her, to caress her, to love her. By all rights she should be afraid of him, but she just wasn't. Her barely restrained desire ought to have been a warning not to get involved, but she didn't hear any alarm bells.

Mary Beth didn't think anyone had ever really needed her, not even her lovingly protective father. Being a widower with a growing child who was only four years old when he'd had to learn to do for himself after his wife's death in childbirth, Howard Caine had become a very independent man who did it all, including cooking and cleaning.

It was only natural that his daughter grew up to be a strong, independent woman taking care of herself too. She had a BA and a master's in social work, and a career she loved. She invested her own money and had been saving for a house even before she met her soon-to-be-former fiancé, that rat bastard. Life skills were par for the course: she could change a tire, and she could even hem a dishcloth, although she never did, considering that the dollar store sold perfectly good dishcloths every day of the week for ninety-nine cents plus tax.

But more than anything she wanted a real family of her own, and especially a mother-in-law who could substitute for the mother she'd lost.

She'd been so sure that her fiancé and his wonderful mother would help make her dreams a reality. There was plenty of family on his side—he was always after her to check out zillions of photos online, what with all the cousins and a big brother who lived out of state but was still the head of the family somehow.

Mary Beth had never gotten around to it. Social media wasn't her thing and she didn't even have a Facebook page. After long hours on the job, solving problems right and left for so many people, she wasn't interested in posting and instant messaging or photos of what anyone'd had for lunch and carefully posed selfie shots.

Outside of meeting a few individuals at various get-togethers, she really didn't know much about the family she'd wanted so much to be part of. Perhaps she had instinctively been aware even then that reality would never live up to her girlish fantasies. After tonight, she realized that her unfaithful boyfriend was hardly the man of her dreams.

There was no doubt whatsoever in her mind that he had secretly reconnected with his former flame on some damn Web site designed for people who wanted to do things like that. She didn't spend a lot of time online but she had a general idea of what was out there.

Betrayal was just a click away.

Lesson learned. She wouldn't be so naive next time.

Chapter Two

"A silver dollar for your thoughts," Parr couldn't resist whispering in her ear.

She jumped a little. The sound of his voice seemed to snap her back to reality. From where he'd been standing, buttonholed by his long-winded pal, she'd looked like she was a million miles away.

"I didn't know thoughts were going for such a high price these days."

"I'd pay more than that for yours, Strawberry."

Her cheeks pinked slightly. "Is that my new name?"

"Until you tell me your real one, yes." She seemed to like the sound of it. As far as he was concerned, it was definitely an endearment.

"Why?"

His huge hand lifted hesitantly to touch her hair. "This, for one thing. Beautiful. Never saw anything like it. If you don't mind a mixed metaphor, it glows like strawberry blond fire."

"Oh. No. Mix away. I don't mind."

"And I know it's natural."

She nodded. "My mother's hair was the same color. She had all-over freckles to match. I only have them here." She pointed to each shoulder.

The innocent gesture got to him, big time. His black eyes caressed those creamy, sun-kissed shoulders while his hand moved ever so slowly over the red gold curls to the bare beauty of her neck.

He stopped.

They were still in a public place, for all that the boisterous lounge crowd paid no attention to them. An unseen someone who controlled a light board picked her out of the crowd with a traveling spot. Inside the glowing circle, she was luminous for several unforgettable seconds. Parr was riveted.

The spotlight moved on.

He longed to trace her collarbone, then delve downward to the cleft between her breasts where they swelled above the strapless gown. Just to vary the fantasy, he imagined stroking upward to her shoulders with utmost gentleness. Like stroking a soft little cat until it purred with pleasure.

She sighed.

"I love the freckles too." He wanted to kiss the copper-colored sprinkles, tease each and every one with his tongue. They were beautiful. Like all of her.

"Blatant flattery. But keep talking."

Without hesitation he replied truthfully. "I'm not good at making pretty speeches. When I look at you, I say what I feel."

"Oh." Looking at him took her breath away. Unless it was the stuffy atmosphere of the crowded space that was doing that. But she knew it was him. The depth of emotion on his harshly handsome face rendered her pretty much speechless.

"I want us to get to know each other," he said. "I want tonight to be only the beginning."

Big, bold, romantic words. Sometimes you had to take a chance. She trembled just a little when he rested his hand on her shoulder. God, how he wanted to do more.

He wanted to kiss her but he couldn't. Not here. Something very special was happening, though, and he wasn't going to let her go until he was sure they could find each other again. If she wanted to. That was far from a sure thing.

"Yes. I mean no. Sooner or later, I have to go back to my"—she cleared her throat—"my fiancé. He has no idea where I am."

"He doesn't deserve to know."

Mary Beth pressed her lips together for a few seconds. "I know he must be worried." She didn't want to face the two-timing rat, but she knew she had no choice.

"Do you really have to? Tonight?"

"Yes, I'm afraid so. He probably has his whole family and my dad running around looking for me."

Parr absorbed the information. If that was so, her father must have worked up quite a head of steam. The man had to be outraged by what had happened to his daughter.

"So go tell your dad that you found a better man and you're going to run away with him tonight," Parr said jokingly. In his heart he meant every word.

"Of course. Why didn't I think of that?" She studied him, trying to suppress a wry smile. "Sounds like a plan."

"With all due respect, you need one."

"And if we ran away, which is the last thing I would do, because I'm not that crazy, what would happen?"

"Anything you wanted," he said bluntly. "I'd make it unforgettable. You'd never have to tell anyone. Just one night. You and me."

She looked into his eyes. Whatever she saw there was something she desired.

"I probably shouldn't say this, but the idea is tempting."

The urge to kiss her consumed him. He reached out to get her on her feet. Moving toward him. Her first, tentative step made his heart race with joy.

As if in a trance, she followed him outside into the shadowy moonlight of the patio.

Someone in the lounge closed the heavy glass doors in back of them and the loud music and din of voices were shut off as if by magic.

She led the way down a narrow path just wide enough for the two of them and turned to face him in the enfolding darkness. His arm stretched across her back and his large hands began to move caressingly up and down. He looked down at her beautiful face.

"Are you sure this is something you want?" He tried to control himself. He knew this was a woman who could not be rushed.

"Yes," she replied honestly. For some reason, she seemed to trust him completely. Silently and passionately, Parr vowed never to take advantage of that trust.

"I want to kiss you."

"Then do it."

The soft command made him smile as he lowered his head and claimed her lips in a tender kiss. After several seconds they both abandoned any pretense of caution. She moaned deep in her throat as she swayed against him when his tongue explored the silky wetness of her sweet mouth. His hold tightened as her pale, slender arms encircled his neck.

"You taste so good," he murmured, savoring her, pulling her more closely to him.

"Don't talk." Her supple body was yielding and pliant but she was still giving the orders. Parr was secretly delighted. Whatever she desired, however she had to have it, he was ready to give.

"You want more, don't you?" His tongue feathered a line across her pretty chin. "So do I. Much more."

And then his mouth was on hers again, hard, hot, and demanding. His tongue pushed its way between her lips, thrusting with a need so great they were both shaken by the intensity. Expertly, he explored, retreated, plunged, and conquered as she clung to him, her entire body alive with carnal vibrations.

She was woman. He was man. It was as simple and as complicated as that.

The sudden sound of flirtatious laughter not far away broke the spell that held them. Some other couple had left the lounge and ventured outside. Parr couldn't see them or hear the words of their low conversation. He and the beautiful strawberry blonde were safe enough from discovery for now. He held her quivering body in his arms, shielding her from view, almost angry that their solitude had been intruded upon.

"I want to make love to you," he whispered. "But this obviously isn't the time or the place."

"I . . . I don't know what to say."

He had the feeling that she'd never done anything like this before, for all that she seemed so willing. As for himself—Parr realized that he had never been so ready to initiate an encounter that they might both regret by morning.

Fiercely, he pushed the thought away. The time was now. And if now was all they had, he would make the most of it.

Her hand rested on his chest, over his heart. Just the sensation of that was something he found wildly erotic. He wanted there to be nothing between them at all. Bare skin, bared souls.

"Is there something wrong with me?" she asked hesitantly.

"No. Good God, no," he muttered.

"But I've never reacted to a man like this before."

"You've never been with me before." He wasn't bragging. He'd never felt like this either.

"Please. I should go back inside."

He stiffened visibly, seeming even taller as she stepped back, breaking his close hold. "I'll go with you."

She stared at him, puzzled by his statement.

Parr smiled reassuringly. "I don't want that idiot fiancé talking you into forgiving him."

She blew out the breath she'd been holding.

"There's not much chance of that. I wish I never had to see him again."

Parr was gratified to hear her say it so emphatically. "My offer to take you away tonight is still good."

She laughed, as if she was suddenly feeling very giddy. "Hmm. Thanks. But I'm afraid I can't. You see, there's always tomorrow."

"Things won't be any different then. We're still going to want each other." Even as he spoke the words, a sense of foreboding came over him. There was trouble ahead. He'd gone too far and said too much. But at least he hadn't lied.

"There are other people besides my fiancé waiting for me. People that I care about. People who shouldn't be left to worry."

"I suppose so."

Their voices were low but the feelings were running high again. The fiery look he loved shimmered like an aura around her when she spoke again. The woman he'd kissed so ardently was no one he ever wanted to cross.

"That black-hearted cheater ran to my father, I just know it. And Dad's probably called the police by now."

"You didn't do anything wrong," he said. She was so upset, she could be imagining the worst. Best to let her just talk, even if it didn't make perfect sense. It would help to ease her mind some, Parr thought.

She frowned and stepped forward, but Parr didn't move. There wasn't enough room on the narrow path for her to get around him without snagging her lovely dress.

"And I'm going back with you."

He wanted to add that she was his now, but wasn't sure how she would react to such undisguised possessiveness.

She shot him a disbelieving look. "Promise not to hit anybody?"

It was clear to Parr that her instincts were excellent. She might as well have read his mind. "Ah—as long as he—your fiancé, I mean—doesn't touch you, I promise."

"Be good and I'll introduce you to my father."

Parr was thinking that if she was able to envision that scenario his kisses had done her good. But even so. Hell of a way to meet the man who'd produced this goddess. She'd said nothing about her mother.

Oh Lord. What had he gotten himself into?

"Move," she instructed.

He did, but his eyes twinkled with mischief. "Just tell me what you plan to say. 'Dad, I want you to shake hands with this man I just met outside in the dark. He's been trying to make mad, passionate love to me, and I haven't even tried to stop him.'"

The dimple flashed above her smile. "If I said anything like that, then Daddy would hit you."

"Then by all means, introduce me some other way. I'm leaving it up to you."

She couldn't seem to hold back her laughter. "Hey, how about I tell him how very kind you've been, considering the circumstances, and how much I like you?"

"Do you, Strawberry?" He wanted her to. More than anything.

"Very much."

Parr said nothing, but he felt like he'd been shot by

the sharpest arrow in Cupid's quiver. Even if she'd never really loved her good-for-nothing fiancé, it was too soon for her to trust her own emotions.

You're not *her* big brother, he reminded himself. So skip the good advice.

"If you want me to stand by you, I will. But let's get it over with."

Parr hoped that the fiancé would be too ashamed to show his face, because he wanted nothing more than to knock him senseless.

He extended his arm for her to take and they went back the way they'd come—and then made a turn, once inside, toward the doors leading to the main ball-room.

His gut tightened. Now that he wasn't looking into her luminous eyes, a few reasonable questions kicked in. Could she and her fiancé be friends of Bobby Joe? Holy cow. Were they attending the engagement party? He'd never reviewed the guest list, figuring he wouldn't know the names since he didn't live around here but in Tennessee. There seemed to be countless guests by this point on the other side of the French doors.

Just as Parr was about to guide her in, the doors swung open. A stocky older man in formal wear came through.

"Daddy!"

"Mary Beth!"

Parr stepped back. The gray-haired man and the strawberry blonde stood stock still for a moment, staring at each other.

"Where have you been, girl? We've been worried

sick over you. I was about ready to call the police." His handsome face glowed a heated red.

"I'm fine, Daddy. I needed to get away from my ex-fiancé."

"Ex?"

"I gave him his ring back tonight. Actually, I threw it at him."

Her father was momentarily at a loss for words. Then he finally noticed the tall stranger behind his daughter. Parr was clearly with her, though he no longer had an arm around her.

"Daddy, I want you to meet someone."

Her blithe tone didn't match the agitation Parr knew she was feeling. That sense of trouble ahead grew stronger.

The two men exchanged assessing glances before extending their hands.

"This is . . . this is . . ." She glanced desperately at Parr, who took the initiative. At least he would finally learn her full name. He had the first two, common enough in the south—Mary Beth. The ticklish introduction taking place distracted him from wondering why the name rang a bell.

"I'm Howard Caine. She only ever calls me Dad, of course."

"Parr Weston, sir." He gave a particularly hearty handshake to make up for her memory lapse.

"I ought to have recognized you!" Howard exclaimed in relief. "And here I was thinking that Mary Beth was with some stranger."

There were a few minutes of manly small talk that

she didn't seem to hear. They stayed off the subject of the ex.

It was Mary Beth's turn to step back. The man who had kissed her *was* a stranger. What on earth was her father talking about? She met Parr's dark eyes across the little distance she'd put between them.

He had just said his name was Parr Weston. . . .

It couldn't be. It just couldn't be.

"Thank the Lord you found her." The country-southern voice belonged to the plumply attractive woman who joined them near the doors. "Bobby Joe's half out of his mind. We couldn't make head nor tails out of anything he said."

"It seems your other son found her, Alma," Howard told Parr's mother.

"Now, how did that come to pass?" Alma Weston asked, her shrewd brown eyes jumping from Parr to Mary Beth.

Mary Beth offered no explanation. She looked like she wanted to run away for real. And not into his arms.

This couldn't be happening, Parr thought. She couldn't be his brother's fiancée. She just couldn't be. "Where the hell is Bobby Joe?" He growled the question.

"He's searching everywhere for Mary Beth!"

"Is he now? Well, he has a few things to answer for," Parr told his mother, the rough edge in his voice conveying his fury.

"What's going on?" Howard asked.

"I caught Bobby Joe with Luellen tonight," Mary Beth practically screamed at her father.

"You caught him? Doing what? How did Luellen get mixed up in this?" Howard seemed stunned, even though he'd been tipped off only minutes ago. The unfolding drama needed only a few more sordid details and they would all know what had happened.

"Need you ask?" Tears misted Mary Beth's eyes. She dashed them angrily away.

When Parr pulled her close against his side, she melted into the solid strength of his big body. Even knowing he was Bobby Joe's big brother didn't change the fact that she wanted and needed the protection he offered.

She closed her eyes, wishing she could make everyone but the two of them disappear. A familiar voice made her open them again.

"Just what's going on here?" Bobby Joe Weston demanded when he stormed through the doors and saw his fiancée wrapped in his brother's arms.

Ignoring his mother and Howard Caine, Bobby Joe strode to Mary Beth and reached out to her.

"If you touch her, I'll kill you," Parr said.

Chapter Three

Bobby Joe sat rigidly in the dinette chair, his long, lean fingers clasped together on the maple tabletop in the center of Alma Weston's rambling ranch-style house. He ignored the cup of coffee Parr had just set in front of him.

They hadn't bothered to get dressed all the way. Parr was shirtless. His mother tended to be thrifty with the air-conditioning and didn't turn it up all the way. Sometimes he forgot how humid Mississippi could be after living in Tennessee for so many years and getting used to a cooler climate. Where he lived now, in the foothills of a scenic mountain range, suited him fine. He had never been that happy here. Most of the family had stayed on, set in their ways, once Alma had moved to Iminga with her boys years ago.

The sunny yellow tiles that framed the sink and appliances cast a golden glow all over the kitchen. But even that didn't do much to brighten the mood between the brothers.

"I do love Mary Beth," Bobby Joe argued. "She's the most wonderful woman I've ever known."

"You sure have a strange way of showing your love." Parr felt entitled to criticize his sullen brother if he wanted to. But one of these days, he was going to get out of the business of taking care of Bobby Joe. Just not right yet.

"That's not for you to judge."

"Says who? How in hell could you hook up with Luellen at your engagement party? What were you thinking?"

"I didn't mean for it to happen." The younger man seemed eager to justify his actions. He ran his hand nervously through his short brown hair. "I had no idea Lue would show up. I told her I was marrying someone else."

"Really."

Bobby Joe nodded, missing the sarcasm in his brother's one-word reply. "Yes. Even though her divorce is final, I'm not taking her back."

"Is making out with her in a damned storage room your idea of discouraging her?" Parr demanded as he poured himself a cup of the strong black coffee and sat down across the table from Bobby Joe.

His brother's sad-eyed expression seriously irked him. Not to mention his insincere avowal of "love."

"We went in there for privacy," Bobby Joe asserted. "I didn't want Mary Beth to know that Lue was even there."

Parr took a scalding sip and grimaced. "So how did she find you?"

"Beats me. She must have been watching me on the sly." Bobby Joe drummed his fingers on the tabletop. "My guess is that she saw everything from the minute Lue came up to me and started talking. That's all it was at first. Just talking."

Parr was unimpressed. "She told me that you had Luellen nearly undressed."

"Hell," Bobby Joe mumbled. "Maybe I did. But you know what a hot little number Lue is. She could always heat me to the boiling point in minutes."

"Yeah. Next you'll be telling me little Lue knocked you down and wouldn't let you go."

"She practically did, Parr."

There were several seconds of charged silence.

"How could you?"

"I'm a man."

Parr shook his head. "A lowdown, no-account excuse for a man is more like it."

"Could have been you. Don't tell me you never heard of a guy going for one last fling just before—"

"Yeah, I know it happens, but that doesn't give you a free pass to be a total jerk. If you love a woman enough to want to marry her, you wouldn't be quick to give in to a hot little number. Isn't Mary Beth passionate enough in bed to keep you cooled off?"

Parr hated even asking the question. His reasons were partly personal. If he knew that she went wild in Bobby Joe's arms, then maybe it would be possible to forget about the way she'd responded to him last night. Bonus points if Parr could also forget about how desperately he had wanted her.

"Ah—that's part of the problem." Bobby Joe rubbed the sparse, light-colored stubble on his chin, his milk-chocolate eyes thoughtful. "Mary Beth doesn't satisfy me . . . I mean, sexually. She's a different sort of woman entirely from Lue. But in every other way, she's the best thing that ever happened to me."

Parr barely believed what he was hearing. His brother couldn't possibly be talking about the woman Parr had encountered last night. That woman had clung to him, had responded passionately to his advances, and had clearly craved more.

Maybe foreplay was what got her going. Parr knew well enough that some women preferred that to actual sex, per se. He couldn't blame them. So many men rushed the whole business and didn't care if their women froze up during the act of making love, as long as they got their jollies. He took his time. A skilled buildup to a sensual explosion was worth it.

His body began to react against his will to the thought of her naked body moving seductively under his in the throes of ecstasy. Parr distracted himself by focusing on the calendar, a tractor company handout. The photo for the month had monster wheels and a bright green paint job. He calmed down again.

Bobby Joe was pouring sugar in his coffee and stirring it rapidly.

"Tell me something," Parr asked. "Why do you want to marry her then?"

"Like I said, I love her. She'll be a perfect wife, a perfect mother."

"Listen to yourself, Bobby Joe. A perfect wife

everywhere except in the bedroom? That's not going to get you bouncing babies."

"All it takes is one time per baby," Bobby Joe cracked. "And besides, sex isn't everything." He gulped down his sugared coffee.

"Maybe you're the wrong man for her," Parr suggested. If he could make his brother see reason, Mary Beth just might see the light as well. Parr would be honored to be the man for her. But as long as Bobby Joe claimed to love the woman, Parr knew he could never make her his.

He was a proud man, loyal to friends and family. He would never betray his brother, even after what Bobby Joe had done, not even to satisfy a need so overwhelming that it scared him.

"Look, Parr. I admit I made a big mistake, but I honestly do love Mary Beth and I still intend to marry her. Luellen had her chance and she blew it last year. I can't forgive her for jilting me to marry that big dumb jock."

"And now that she's been dumped, you look good again. So was it payback for you? Or are you really hot for her?"

"Maybe both."

Parr heaved an angry sigh and finished his coffee, which had cooled to lukewarm. "You're a piece of work. Sometimes I can't believe we're brothers."

"Me neither."

"Do you still love Luellen?"

Bobby Joe dodged the question by asking one of his own. "Why should I? Even before the stud of the century came along, I knew I wasn't the only man in her life. She's probably made it with a dozen guys before me, maybe more. She liked to act all fluttery and hard to get, but I can assure you she was no virgin."

A thought struck Parr to the core. "Was Mary Beth?" He had to know. A lot of things would depend on it. If his brother could bring himself to be completely truthful for once . . . Parr felt as if a huge, cruel hand were grasping his heart, preparing to jerk it brutally from his body.

"What?"

"Were you the first with Mary Beth? She's younger than you."

"Yeah. By a few years. So?"

Parr persisted. "You didn't answer the important part of that question."

"Of course I was first," Bobby Joe boasted. "These days, no one cares though, right?"

Parr didn't take up that argument, if it was one. "But you just said that you prefer Lue's sexual experience to Mary Beth's cool innocence. I'm asking you again, do you still love Luellen?"

"Yes, damn it!"

"Then how can you say you love—"

Bobby Joe didn't let him finish. "Oh man. Am I on trial here?"

"No, but—"

"Then just shut up. I love them both, but it's Mary Beth that I want to marry."

"What kind of husband will you be if you're always hankering after other women?"

"A good one. Good as I can be, I guess." Bobby Joe quickly amended his statement at Parr's withering glare. "Back off. I don't understand how any of this got to be your business."

"I'm simply judging you on past performance."

"That's what I get for trying to explain," Bobby Joe grumbled. "But hey, is it news to you that we're living in the twenty-first century? Things that used to matter a whole lot don't anymore. The rules of relationships are just different. Do you have a problem with that?"

"Yeah."

If his brother didn't give a damn about using women however he wanted, Parr did. He couldn't bear the thought of Mary Beth being hurt again. He remembered how fragile she had seemed last night, although he would bet anything he wasn't wrong about the streak of steel underneath all that tenderhearted emotion. No matter what, she would be devoted to the man she chose to love.

Neither man heard the kitchen door open. Neither saw Mary Beth standing in the doorway, her jade eyes moving from one to the other before resting on Parr's bare chest. A dusting of fine dark hair was just enough to delineate the muscles. His arms were strong and thick, traced with a few barely visible veins under the tawny skin.

It was a pleasure to look at the real man, now that the formal wear was off and stashed somewhere in a garment bag. And he had thought she was beautiful. He wasn't the first man to say so, but she'd never believed any of the others. How could she when she didn't see herself that way? Parr had made her believe she was a gorgeous goddess for a little while. That, and the way he listened and his gentle touch and scorching kisses made her dizzy, in fact. Mary Beth still didn't know what to make of their moonlit encounter.

She stayed put. The brothers' argument seemed about to escalate.

"You're so self-righteous." Bobby Joe, weighing in.

Parr didn't respond to the jab. A lot of folks, not just him, thought his brother had been indulged too much over the years. Parr wasn't to blame and he couldn't fix it now that he was thirty-two. His brother wasn't much younger but he didn't act his age, that was for damn sure.

"You've got no sympathy for us lesser mortals. I don't measure up to your lofty standards anymore than Dad did."

That made Parr wince. Mary Beth didn't miss the way his face paled under his tan.

"Why bring up the old man? He's been dead for twenty years."

"Yeah, and we both know he'd be alive and well and still with us if it hadn't been for you."

Parr refused to take the bait. This was an old quarrel between the brothers, one that he could never win without destroying Bobby's illusions about the man who had fathered them.

"Excuse me." Mary Beth had decided it was time to make her presence known.

"Sweetheart!" cried Bobby Joe, jumping to his feet and attempting to hug her. She didn't push him away but she wasn't falling for the phony act either. She stood there rather stiffly until he quit.

"How are you, Parr?" she said quietly, stepping a short but decisive distance away from his brother.

"I'm all right. Yourself?"

She gave a faint shrug. For a few seconds, Bobby Joe didn't seem to know what to do with himself. Then he stuck his hands into the pockets of his track pants and stayed standing, as if that would give him some advantage over his brother. "Well. Here we all are. Mary Beth, I wanted to thank you for accepting my mother's invitation to stay here for a little while."

"I'm very fond of your mother," she replied in a matter-of-fact tone, folding her arms over her chest. "Daddy's talking to Alma now, in fact."

"Don't be like that," he pleaded with her. "I know we can work things out." He reached out to try and take her hand, then dropped his at his side.

Nothing doing. She refused to allow him the privilege. She was thinking that she hadn't looked him straight in the eye since he'd acknowledged her presence. About all she could see was his bare-chested brother.

Parr stayed sitting, legs sprawled in a too-small chair, his heavy jeans worn down to white over his thigh muscles. He was so big that he seemed to dwarf everything around him, especially his younger brother. His coal black hair was unkempt, as if he hadn't combed it this morning, and there was a dark shadow of beard on his face that proclaimed his need for a shave.

He knew she was staring at him, but wouldn't give himself the pleasure of feasting on her beauty this morning. She was still his brother's woman, and even if she was looking at him like a hungry cat eying a dish of fresh cream, he could not reciprocate. Being in the same house with her was agonizing without being able to let her know—or even hint at—how much he still wanted her.

"If you two will excuse me," Parr told them, "I'll leave you alone to patch things up."

His words caught her by surprise, making her gasp. "Thanks," she hissed.

"Don't mention it, honey," he retorted as he rose from the chair and quickly exited the kitchen.

Bobby Joe breathed a sigh of relief.

Chapter Four

"Please sit down, Mary Beth. Let me explain about last night."

Needless to say, the big, expensive party had ended sooner than expected. The guests were probably still trying to figure out why.

Without speaking, she took the seat left warm by Parr's half-naked body. The way the jeans fit his muscular legs, he might just as well have not been wearing them at all. Mary Beth brought her attention back to his brother, who'd launched into a speech that sounded rehearsed.

"I didn't ask Luellen to come to the party last night, you know. That was all her idea."

"Then how did she know where it was?"

"The whole town of Iminga knew. We invited just about everybody. You saw how many guests there were—"

"That's beside the point," she snapped. "What I want to know is whether what I saw in the storage room was all her idea."

Mary Beth fumed when Bobby Joe didn't answer right away, her observant gaze directly meeting his. Her tension showed in her hands, flattened on the tabletop as if she had to fight the urge to smack him. She waited for his answer.

"Oh Lord. I'm not sure I know how to say this so you don't misconstrue my words," he began.

"Just spit it out."

"I took her in there, hoping to avoid a scene. Her divorce is final now, and she has—had—this crazy notion that I might dump you and take her back."

"Oh?"

The monosyllable hung in the air between them.

"She couldn't be more wrong. And what you saw— well, that was her last-ditch effort to persuade me."

"It was effective." The memory of Bobby Joe caressing the girl with the unbuttoned blouse and no bra popped into Mary Beth's mind. Anger consumed her. "You looked very persuaded."

"I made a mistake." He reached for her hand, grasping it hastily before she pulled away. "I want you to be my wife. Give me another chance, baby. I love you."

Bobby Joe looked pitifully sincere. He brought her hand to his lips and kissed it tenderly. Mary Beth wondered cynically if he had stolen that move from his older brother's playbook. She felt nothing, absolutely nothing. When Parr had kissed her palm last night, tingles of pleasure had spread through every nerve in her body.

Her remorseful fiancé delved into his pocket to retrieve her diamond engagement ring. Without asking, he slipped it onto her finger.

She stared at him briefly, then gazed down at the sparkling gem in its exquisite setting, remembering when Bobby Joe had formally proposed and placed this token of his love and symbol of their betrothal on her finger for the first time. She had been happy. Bobby Joe Weston was handsome, fun, made good money what with one business deal and another, and he had seemed to adore her. What more, she'd thought at the time, could any woman want?

After meeting Parr Weston, she knew.

"I . . ." She hesitated, unsure of her reply. "I can't give you the answer you want. I can't simply forget about last night."

He started to move closer, frowned at her instant retreat as she pushed her chair away from the table. "Sweetheart?"

"I need time."

She wanted to see Parr—alone. To talk to him, to find out how he felt. She'd spent a restless night reliving every awful moment of the disastrous party, from when she'd opened the storage room door on Bobby Joe and Luellen until her father had whisked her out of Parr's arms and away from the hotel.

Her dad had been understanding when she had refused to discuss what had happened, but he'd insisted that she take Alma's phone call this morning.

Mary Beth loved Alma Weston, and he knew it. Though the two of them had little in common. The older woman was past sixty, with no more than a grade-school education, a bawdy laugh, and a taste for polyester pantsuits. Mary Beth at twenty-four had two college degrees, a soft laugh, and a love for silk, linen, and cotton. She knew that Bobby Joe was often ashamed of his mother's shortcomings, as he called them, and his shame had hurt the woman who had given him life.

But Mary Beth admired Alma, who had struggled to raise two sons without a husband, and had taken in a runaway niece into the bargain, at a time when she could barely afford to feed her own children. Howard Caine thought the world of her, and his esteem had gradually increased until Mary Beth was sure her father was considering a serious relationship.

"How much time?"

Bobby Joe's question forced her to look at him.

"I can't say," she replied. "Not right now, anyway. Don't push me. You've hurt me terribly. How do I know if I can ever trust you again?"

"Baby, you have my word."

"Don't make vows you can't keep, Bobby Joe. You've already broken a solemn promise."

Mary Beth toyed with her engagement ring, twisting it this way and that. Granted, forgiveness was a virtue, but not to the point of making a fool of yourself in the process.

Bobby Joe had the sense to shut up while she thought for a bit. He even looked a little shamefaced. As well he might. She was still angry.

She wondered what kind of ring Parr would give the woman he loved. She knew from Alma that he had never been married or even engaged. And she knew from Bobby Joe that his big brother was quite a ladies' man, moving quickly from one to another, generous to a fault but never promising anything in particular before moving on to the next conquest.

"I made a mistake." Bobby Joe was beginning to repeat himself. "Don't make us both pay for it by giving up our chance for happiness together."

There was some truth to that, enough to make her relent.

"We'll see." She slipped the diamond ring from her finger and set it on the table. "If I can convince myself that you're right about that, I'll put this back on. Understand?"

"Excuse me," Alma called out loudly as she buzzed into the kitchen. "I hate to disturb you children, but I've got to check on that roast beef in the oven."

"It's all right," Mary Beth told her. "We're done talking for now. Where's Daddy?"

"Howard's glued to the wide-screen in the den. There's a ball game on. The Atlanta Braves," Alma laughed.

"Uh-oh." Mary Beth smiled, surprised by how relieved she felt, free of Bobby Joe's ring. "We'll never get him to the table for dinner."

In their part of the South, that was served in the afternoon. The meal was more than lunch and not as formal as supper. Alma still cooked some things but she was no stranger to good prepared food to save work.

"Oh dear. And I got his favorite peach cobbler for dessert," Alma told her.

Her younger son interrupted the food discussion. "Mother," he said. "Talk to this woman. Make her believe that I love her and will never let a repeat of last night happen."

"Lordy," Alma sighed, her warm brown eyes looking misty. "I love you both. Mary Beth, you're a dear girl. My baby here isn't a bad boy, just a mite misguided. I was so sure what he needed was a strong woman."

If anyone was counting, Mary Beth thought, he now had two strong women in his life. Her and Luellen. Make that three, with his doting mother.

"You are so right." He patted Alma's shoulder. "Mary Beth is perfect for me."

"Are you sure?" his mother asked anxiously. "And are you the kind of man she needs?"

Bobby Joe's expression turned sour. "Just whose side are you on, anyway?"

Howard Caine came through the door. "Alma and I are on the side of our children's happiness." He paused and fixed a stern look on Bobby Joe. "You've got to know how disappointed I am in your callous behavior, son."

Mary Beth knew her father was being somewhat tactful for her sake and Alma's. And he didn't know everything that had happened and he might never know. But if he had his druthers, he'd probably knock some sense into Bobby Joe the old-fashioned way.

"I promise it'll never happen again, sir."

"You're damn right it won't," Howard guaranteed the young man. "Your brother and I aim to see to that."

"I don't see how this is any of Parr's business," Bobby Joe fretted.

Mary Beth changed the subject. "So why'd you

come in, Daddy? There must be a commercial on."
Her intention was to keep Parr out of it any way she
could. The circumstances were complicated enough,
what with him visiting from Memphis and no return
date mentioned. She hadn't seen any packed suitcases
by the door when she'd let herself in.

No one in this room needed to know what had
transpired between her and Parr—at least, not until she
knew exactly how things stood with the two of them.
Parr knew plenty: that she had been his brother's girl,
that she hadn't accepted the ring back, and that Bobby
Joe still wanted to marry her.

The blare from the next room told her that a new
type of dish detergent was the key to a woman's happiness. Wouldn't it be nice if it were that easy, Mary Beth
thought wryly.

"You guessed it, Mary Beth. Can't stand those loud
ads." Her father grinned. "I wanted a cup of coffee
before dinner."

Alma quickly filled a mug at the coffeemaker and
handed it to Howard, a girlish smile brightening her
slightly lined face. "Now then. All of you clear out of
my kitchen so I can get dinner on the table soon."

Mary Beth took the opportunity to get away from
her persistent ex-fiancé. Bobby Joe had always made
a point of sticking to an argument, however minor,
until she gave in, even if only just to shut him up. And
this one had been major.

As little as she cared for baseball games, she preferred joining her father in the den to continuing a
useless conversation with a man whom she doubted

she had ever loved. You could not be in love with one man and yearn for another's touch the way she had.

When Howard and his daughter had disappeared into the other room, Bobby Joe turned on his mother. "You could have defended me."

"I'm not sure you deserve it."

"You too? Is anyone going to cut me some slack on this?"

His peevish tone made Alma shake her head. She gave him a weary look as she placed the roast on the counter and began unwrapping the foil covering.

"Get Parr to talk to her," Bobby Joe continued. "For some reason he's decided to be her champion. She might listen to him."

"That's a thought," Alma said. She moved the roast to a platter and poured the drippings into a saucepan to start making beef gravy. "I'll ask him after dinner."

"What's on your mind, Mother?" Parr handed his mother the large platter that had held the sliced roast.

"Nothing," Alma answered. "Why do you ask?" She was busy loading the dishwasher.

Too busy to look up, apparently.

"Stop hedging," her son demanded.

"All right." She straightened and frowned at a stack of plates before she met his gaze. "I want to ask you to do something for Bobby Joe."

Parr nodded, which wasn't a yes. She would have to tell him more.

He watched her scrape the plates and fit them into the rack. He'd offered to hire a maid for her several years ago when he was financially secure at last, but she had adamantly refused and continued to refuse. She'd said that she didn't want strangers in her house being paid his hard-earned money for doing things she enjoyed doing.

Alma seemed to be stalling. Parr cleared his throat. "Okay. What is it?"

If her request had anything to do with his brother's beautiful redhead, he did not want to help.

"Talk to Mary Beth," Alma implored, her dark eyes searching his. "Ask her to give Bobby Joe another chance. She seems to be . . . well, hesitating about forgiving him."

"Can you blame her?"

"No, of course not. It's just that I think she ought to be concerned about more than Bobby Joe's little sin."

"Meaning?"

Parr suspected what his mother was thinking and knew she was right. He, Parr, could not allow what had happened between him and Mary Beth to go any further. He had no claim on his brother's woman, even if she were willing.

Yeah. *If* was not the operative word. She had been more than willing.

"Mary Beth lacks experience." Alma rinsed her hands and briskly dried them with a dish towel. "Your brother is her first serious relationship."

"She confides in you, huh?"

"Sometimes. But never mind that." She hung up the towel and looked straight at him. "You're a powerfully attractive man, Parr. It would be hard for her to resist you if you decided to turn on the charm. Your brother does not need competition from you."

Parr got the point. "All right. I'll talk to her."

"Today?"

"Right now."

Mary Beth hadn't joined her father in the den after dinner and had refused to take a stroll with Bobby Joe. She wanted to go home, to escape the Weston brothers.

Dinner had been a strained affair with Howard and Alma creating most of the conversation. When Parr had joined his mother in the kitchen, Mary Beth headed for the backyard, where a small pool, still concealed by its winter cover, took up the middle of a concrete patio and manicured flower garden. By April in Mississippi, everything that bloomed was reaching for the sun.

She snapped off a tiny leaf from a fragrant herb and crushed it in her fingers, feeling low.

Why had Parr been ignoring her? He must know how badly she needed to talk to him. She was so confused, so utterly bewildered by the sudden changes in her orderly life. She had planned everything so carefully: her engagement party, her bridesmaids' get-togethers, her huge church wedding to come.

She and Bobby Joe had even decided to live in the big, rambling, ranch-style house with Alma until they could build their own dream house once they found the perfect plot of land.

If only Luellen had stayed married.

If only Parr had never kissed her, held her, touched her. But he had, and nothing would ever be the same again. Now she understood what other women meant when they talked about wanting a man. A *real* man.

One look from his onyx eyes and she was lost. The spark of fire in their dark depths had ignited an answering blaze in her soul. Bobby Joe didn't make her feel like that. Parr's powerful masculinity was very different. It defined him in every detail. He was gallant in an old-fashioned way that melted her resistance.

Bring that back, she thought to herself. When had women gotten into the habit of putting up with overgrown boys?

Parr Weston was a man with a capital *M*. And while she was on that subject, he was drop-dead sexy. That deliciously dangerous quality was heightened by his physical confidence. All the same . . .

It was possible that Parr was just as emotionally confused as she was. Certainly it had to have been a shock, finding out that the woman you'd been passionately consoling was your brother's fiancée.

Ex-fiancée.

She had to get used to the sound of that. Mary Beth had to be honest with herself too. She had no intention of marrying Bobby Joe now. For all she cared, he could go back into that storage room and spend the rest of his life locked inside with Luellen Simpson and a dozen brooms.

A worrisome thought stopped her pacing for a moment. What if Parr hadn't been completely honest with her? Mary Beth headed for a small bench tucked between two flowering shrubs and sat down.

From what she knew about him—before she'd even met him—he went through relationships with women as fast as he could. Did she mean any more to him than a new challenge? Granted, the circumstances were unique, but that was even more reason for her to be cautious. There was no happy ending to a fling that would pit brother against brother, and the older generation against the younger.

The situation was impossible.

But there it was. However, she could do without either brother, without a man at all, and certainly without sex. She couldn't miss what she'd never had.

Mary Beth had never planned to be a virgin for this long. For some reason, she hadn't questioned Bobby Joe when he'd wanted to hold off on sex with her, saying all the while that he loved and respected her too much. Now that she knew the real reason—because the town tramp had her polished claws in him again—she should feel better. But she didn't.

Whoever said that love is a many-splendored thing had never peeked into that storage closet.

Mary Beth stayed on the bench, feeling cold all over but not inclined to go in. Knowing that she would be returning to her routine and making the rounds of county schools for her social work assignments didn't cheer her up. If she was lucky, there would be only a few tactless questions from colleagues and acquaintances. But, oh Lord, spare her the sympathetic looks. Someone out of all those people had to have seen Luellen at some point. The big announcement hadn't been a surprise anyway, and that part of the evening had been, well, finessed. Even so. Rumors got started over the least little things. If she could avoid the inevitable murmured comments as well, that would be a plus.

Did you hear . . . ? Yes, but I don't understand why Luellen was even invited. . . . She wasn't! And there's more. . . .

The whispered words she dreaded most: *Poor Mary Beth . . . poor, dear Mary Beth.*

Parr stood just outside the door, scanning the backyard until he spotted Mary Beth inspecting the tulips blooming brightly near the gate. She looked so beautiful, so fresh, like a piece of ripe fruit, ready for the picking. A luscious strawberry.

What was he going to say to her? How could he ask her to go back to his brother when he wanted her so badly for himself?

He knew his mother was right. She was Bobby Joe's fiancée. Love was patient, love was kind, love forgave.

But Parr still thought his brother didn't deserve all that much love. Or her. Still, he had to acknowledge that her strong reaction to *his* loving had been triggered by the hurt and frustration of sudden betrayal. The angel who'd cried in his arms—and turned sweet devil at his kiss—had no special desire for him. He'd been there at the right time, that was all. Pure coincidence.

It wouldn't be fair for him to take advantage of the situation. Even if Bobby Joe was emotionally torn between two women, he still had to figure it out on his own, young as he was. Parr had to step back. The fact that Mary Beth might yet become his brother's wife changed everything.

Maybe she was what his brother needed. Parr couldn't predict the future. Bobby Joe could shape up into a decent man under the right circumstances.

Trying to make that happen had taken a toll on both his mother and Parr. Ever since they'd been kids, he had watched out for Bobby Joe, helped him, tried to keep him out of trouble. When things had been tight financially, Parr had done without to see that his baby brother had whatever he needed.

And when money was no longer a problem, he'd made up for the hard times by getting Bobby Joe a head start in business, fronting the money for the first foreclosed home his brother had bought, fixed up cheap and sold for a healthy profit.

He'd been taking care of Bobby Joe all his life; why should things be any different now? But they were. He had never wanted one of his brother's women before. Not even remotely.

Mary Beth's slender hand briefly cupped the tallest flower in the tulip bed. It swayed on its stalk as if enchanted. She had to be about the only person he knew right now who could walk in a garden and be fully present. She wasn't staring into a smartphone or catching up on texts. She was *there*.

But not for him. He felt a pang when she looked up and turned away.

Stay here or go to her? Parr hesitated.

* * *

Mary Beth was reluctant to face him. So much depended on him, on what he would say and do. Her desire for him could change her life, and the thought of anyone having that power over her was frightening.

She had always been in control of her life and the people around her. Since her mother's untimely death twenty years ago—the newborn, a boy, had died at birth—her father had doted on Mary Beth, granting her every wish. When she was little, her Grandma Lloyd watched over her. Once she'd started kindergarten, her father, as a school principal, spent as much time with her as his schedule allowed. They had the same days off and shared the long stretch of weeks in the summer months. Howard Caine let nothing come between him and his only child.

Her Grandma Lloyd had been a strong-minded, highly moral woman who would have a few things to say about her current predicament, Mary Beth thought ruefully.

Love for her grandchild had often overruled her grandmother's better judgment, though. She had spoiled Mary Beth shamelessly while at the same time managing to instill character by dint of her own example.

But sometimes Mary Beth wished she could be a little less responsible. Being a good girl meant you didn't take chances. Sometimes even she forgot that she was an emotional person, as vulnerable as any other woman when it came to love.

"Mother's flowers are beautiful." But not as beautiful as you, Parr thought as he spoke.

Facing him at last, she replied, "Yes, they are. Alma and Mr. Mays put a lot of work into this garden."

"Would you believe that she had a fit when I first hired Mays to help her?" He began walking steadily in her direction. "She didn't want a gardener any more than she wants a housekeeper."

"I can just imagine." Mary Beth smiled, her eyes finally making contact with his. What she saw in those obsidian depths startled her, but before she could respond, his expression quickly changed from desire to concealment.

"That rosebush over there," he said, pointing to a large, healthy shrub, "was moved from the old house. I helped her plant it again when I was about ten. It was one of the few things the old man ever gave her."

"It's hard to hate a rosebush."

Even nature was a loaded subject. She knew that Bobby Joe was the only one in the family who ever mentioned Kenneth Weston without any trace of bitterness. Even Alma, who seldom spoke of her late husband, couldn't hide the hostility in her voice whenever she said his name.

"Guess so."

"Alma certainly has a green thumb." She wanted to start running to him, to meet him halfway, but she couldn't move. There was something odd about the way he was acting that made her uneasy. "I'm the opposite. Every plant I buy seems to keel over within a week. Hands of death," she joked, wiggling her fingers at him.

He was suddenly right beside her, his rugged six-foot-three frame towering over her, his big, rough hands reaching out to take hers. "No way."

She couldn't breathe. Which was probably due to the fact that her heart was racing. Throw in dizzy. Parr Weston had a powerful effect on her.

He raised her hands to his mouth, running the tip of his tongue across her fingertips. She quivered, inside and out.

"I can't believe these pretty hands could kill anything." He enfolded them warmly in his. "But they might make a man die from the pleasure of their touch."

"Over the top, Parr." There was a warning note in her voice. She didn't want to complain too much. She loved his touch. She knew his banter was meant to please her. Secretly, it did.

Her green eyes studied his face, as if she were about to question his intentions. She ought to. She wanted to speak, tell him she was too inexperienced for games like this, but she couldn't say a word. Still, there was nothing one-sided about the seduction. Her body language conveyed her willingness to play along just fine.

"Have you been thinking about me, Strawberry?" He hated himself for starting something he didn't intend to finish. Even though Bobby Joe had wanted Parr to believe that he'd helped himself to her virginity, it seemed to Parr that her essential innocence was intact. However, he found it hard to believe that a twenty-four-year-old woman could be so fundamentally naive about men.

"Yes," she answered honestly. "I've been thinking

about you and me and Bobby Joe and even Luellen Simpson."

"And have you come to any conclusions?" Parr released her hands but held her gaze with his.

"A few. What about you, have you been thinking about me—about us?"

Please let him say yes. Let him tell me to forget his brother and all the foolish plans I made. Let him ask me to go away with him like he did last night.

"Hell yes." He ran a thick, hard finger over her lower lip, nudging it downward. "I can't stop thinking about how we'd be together."

"Parr?" If he didn't stop touching her, she would have to step back. The contact was intensely distracting.

"You're very different from my usual women," he informed her as he took her by the shoulders and pulled her close. The sensation of Mary Beth's soft, sweet body against his made him rock hard. She was a born vixen, even if she was vulnerable right now. The combination could be his undoing.

He had to stay in control if he was going to pull off this charade and send her flying back into Bobby Joe's waiting arms. He had to be careful not to let his real feelings about her ruin this act.

"Your usual . . ." Mary Beth wondered exactly what he was implying. Did he know she'd never had actual sex? How much had Bobby Joe told him? She didn't dare ask and was too busy wondering desperately about other things. Was he saying that he wanted her to be his woman? *One* of his women? Absolutely not. He had to know she would never consent to being another notch on his bedpost.

"You know how much I want you." His lips brushed against her ear, his warm breath fanning the tendrils of red gold hair curling around her face. "If we were alone, I'd take you right now. I'd ease you down in that chaise by the pool and slowly strip you. You wouldn't be cold with me, would you, my sweet Strawberry?"

The sound of his voice was intoxicating. His words wove a sensual web about her, confusing her mind and endangering her heart. "Parr, don't. You shouldn't be . . . we shouldn't be . . ."

He had to wait for the right moment before he made his move. He had to time it just right or she might not react the way he hoped she would. He didn't want to hurt her, but he had to think of Bobby Joe and of getting the two of them back together. Even if it ripped him apart.

"Bobby Joe wasn't thinking of you last night. Why should you worry about him today?"

"You don't think I'd do something wild just to get back at him, do you?"

In the heat of the moment, she had thought about payback. But her heart really wasn't in it.

"Of course not. But getting a little revenge along with a lot of pleasure wouldn't hurt, would it?" He smiled, a smirky, self-satisfied smile meant to convey his cocky pride.

"How can you say that?" She refused to believe that Parr meant what he'd just said. He couldn't be that insensitive or that uncaring about his brother's feelings.

"Are you trying to tell me that you wouldn't like to hurt that spoiled baby brother of mine the way he hurt you?"

"No. No."

Did Parr secretly despise Bobby Joe? That was news to her. She'd understood that they were close. Was there some reason he wanted her to seek revenge? This conversation was just plain weird and getting weirder by the second.

"I don't think he meant to hurt me," she said at last. "It was something that got out of hand, something he didn't intend to happen. He's sorry about it. Genuinely sorry."

"And you believe him? All Luellen has ever had to do is crook her little finger and he comes running." Parr was watching her closely for a reaction. "She's quite a woman. The kind a man can't get enough of once he's sampled her charms, or so Bobby Joe tells me."

"What?"

Her incredulous question didn't faze Parr a bit. Her eyes narrowed, searching his smug expression. How could he be doing this to her? He had to have some idea of how inadequate his revelation made her feel. Maybe he did know more than she'd ever wanted anyone to know about her.

Mary Beth was stunned. And seething with fury.

"I have a feeling there's a hidden fire in you that my brother can't find."

God, how he wanted the words to be true. He wished he could be the only man to satisfy her, now and forever. But he had to forget about what he wanted. He had to remember and remind himself constantly that Mary Beth Caine did not belong to him.

"Shut up, Parr."

"Don't you want to find out what I'm talking about? I'm a man, honey, not a boy."

"I don't understand."

"You've been playing around in the minor leagues with my little brother," he taunted as he kept her within his arms, his head lowering to her neck. "Are you woman enough to play in the big leagues?"

"Don't be ridiculous—*oh*."

He feathered kisses along the slender column of her throat. Before she could protest again, he took her mouth in a kiss so hard and hot that her knees buckled beneath her. She had to cling to him for support. She tried not to respond but she couldn't help herself. She had never been so consumed by passion, so completely overtaken by sexual need. The kiss seemed to go on forever as they made love with their mouths, in sensual imitation of stronger and deeper pleasures.

Finally he broke the kiss, struggling to gain control of his own body, knowing that he had to do it now or he would never be able to.

"I can't believe a hot little honey like you hasn't been able to satisfy Bobby Joe," he growled.

She jerked abruptly out of his arms, her emerald eyes blazing with rage.

"How dare you say something like that?"

Parr gave an arrogant shrug. "It's the truth, isn't it? I know for a fact that he had you . . . and didn't come back for more. Luellen takes care of his, um, needs."

Her hand flew to his face, anguish powering her

move. His big hand grasped her wrist, stopping the slap before it landed.

"Never hit me, honey. I'm no gentleman when you get right down to it. And if you intend to act like a brat, I just might turn you over my knee and spank that cute little backside of yours."

Hurting inside as she had never hurt in her life, she lashed out verbally. "I wouldn't waste my time touching you ever again."

"I don't know about that," he sneered. "You lose control pretty quick. A few minutes I could have had you right here in my mother's backyard."

"You're right," she cried, trying desperately to hold back tears. "You're not a gentleman. You just pretend to be one at parties. How could I be so stupid? You're a crude, sneaky, lying, oversexed—"

He laughed at her. "Why, Strawberry, you do have a way with words. I'd say that description fits well enough. But I still think you're interested in some of that last part. I have a feeling you wouldn't disappoint me the way you did Bobby Joe. I wouldn't allow it."

Instinctively moving in retaliation, her open palm took aim at his face.

His warning voice stopped her immediately. "Uh-uh, Strawberry. Remember what I just said."

"You—you—I hate you! And I'm running out of bad things to call you!"

"Doesn't matter," he jeered, grabbing her around the waist. "Just don't lie to yourself about what you really want. You and I both know what it's like when I touch you." He deliberately pressed himself against her, not stopped by her braced hands. "You're practically on fire for me right now."

Mary Beth was so agitated she was panting. What did she have to do to get him to back off? Bite? In a frenzy, she opened her mouth, half ready to do just that, and he shut her up with another spectacular kiss. Why did it have to feel so good?

Hell and damn.

She pushed him away with all her strength but she was still inside the circle of his arms, breathing hard, trying to think. What was happening here? She hated herself for being so deluded in the first place. She must have temporarily lost her mind the night before— or been so emotionally overwhelmed that she'd imagined he was Mr. Perfect.

"I can't believe I thought you . . ." Her voice quivered and broke.

"What did you think?" he goaded her. "That you were something special? That I heard wedding bells and the patter of little feet when I looked at you?"

"Don't . . ." she pleaded.

"I'd like to get you into bed, honey. Nothing more, nothing less. I guess I went a little overboard myself. Seemed like it was worth it at the time. I never expected you to take me that seriously. You didn't know me from Adam."

Smirking bastard. She had to put an end to this. How exactly, she didn't know. She couldn't tell Alma and break her heart. Let the woman find out for herself someday what her oldest son was all about. She wouldn't hear it from Mary Beth.

She pushed at him again. This time he let her go.

Parr watched her run toward the house, her burnished gold hair swaying across her shoulders. He remembered the satiny smooth skin covered up now and all those kissable freckles. He hated himself more than he ever had, more than he had the day of his father's funeral when a seven-year-old Bobby Joe had hurled accusations at him, creating a barrier of guilt and blame that time had not erased.

He knew he had hurt her, but like the old saying, he had done it in order to be kind. Kind to her, to Bobby Joe, to his mother, and in the long run, even to himself. What he'd said to her hadn't been all lies. He had acted and spoken to achieve a desired effect and it had apparently worked, but some of what he had said and done had been true. He did want to bed her. She did catch fire in his arms.

He told himself that he had done the right thing. He wasn't the marrying kind and Mary Beth was. Bobby Joe loved her and wanted to marry her. He'd made an incredibly stupid mistake but he deserved a chance to make things right. Mary Beth was probably just what his brother needed.

But damn it all, she was probably just what Parr needed too.

He waited a few minutes after she entered the back door before following. He stopped just inside the entrance hall and stood by the kitchen door, watching as she marched straight to the table where Howard and Alma sat enjoying after-dinner coffee. Bobby Joe was at the counter filling his mug.

Mary Beth reached down, picked up the diamond ring from the table, and put it on her finger. All eyes were on her. The mug slipped from Bobby Joe's fingers and hit the floor with a resounding crash.

Alma looked at Howard and then cocked her head to see her older son hovering in the doorway, his rugged face etched with pain.

"I've decided to give Bobby Joe a second chance," Mary Beth announced. "We're engaged again."

Chapter Five

Parr drove the rented Thunderbird into his mother's drive, parking the classic car behind his brother's red Mercedes convertible. He hadn't returned to Mississippi in over three weeks and wouldn't be here now if he hadn't flown to Muscle Shoals, Alabama, this morning on business.

"Are you sure your mom won't mind me just dropping in like this?" asked the brunette sitting beside Parr.

"Of course not." He smiled at her.

Her answering smile was dazzling. His assistant was pretty enough to be a model and nearly as tall as he was. They had stayed friends after their brief affair, but they'd both moved on, romantically speaking. The chemistry had fizzled out fast. But, capable and bright as she was, Gail Cash was the best assistant he'd ever had, and much more valuable than a girlfriend at this point in his life.

He paid her well. They got along fine.

She opened the passenger-side door and unfolded

her long legs, stepping out into the driveway and looking around curiously. "Nice. Very leafy. Look at all those flowers. And are those tomatoes I see around the side?"

The entire garden was in full, glorious bloom. The southern sun had done its magic now that it was May.

"Still green." Parr joined her. "You must be hungry. We're probably just in time for supper." He looked around too. "I wonder what Bobby Joe's car is doing here. I was sure he and his fiancée would be out and about."

Something in his tone made Gail turn around. "Don't you like this girl Bobby Joe is planning to marry?"

"What makes you say that? I hardly know her."

"Sorry." Gail studied his closed expression for a few seconds, a puzzled look on her lovely but heavily made-up face.

"Did I give you the impression I don't like Mary Beth?"

Parr didn't want anyone, least of all this ex-lover of his, to suspect the truth about his feelings for his brother's fiancée.

"The few times you've mentioned her, your voice was different. Like you were angry with her or something. Maybe *upset* is a better word."

"You're imagining things." He gave her a playful chuck under the chin. "And hey, I had no idea you ever listened to me that closely."

"You still haven't answered my question."

Parr moved toward the house. "Mary Beth Caine is a wonderful woman. She's perfect for Bobby Joe. Now come on. I want you to meet Mother before I take you to the motel."

Gail caught up with him. "Gee whiz," she teased. "Sounds like old times."

"Keep it down."

"Oh, all right." She stayed close to Parr as they walked toward the front porch.

Before they entered, he stopped and smiled into the sapphire blue eyes of the woman whose striking height nearly equaled his. "We made an agreement, Gail."

"I know. I know."

"I couldn't run the business without you, but let's not blur the boundaries, okay?"

Before she'd ever set foot in his construction company's office, he'd set the terms. Flexible hours, excellent pay, no fooling around—ever. It had to be that way. If either of them couldn't handle working together, she would have to go. Of course he would help her find another, similar job. But he didn't want to lose her entirely.

"I'm over you, boss man," she assured him. "I haven't been lonely since we split up."

Parr nodded. That had happened four months ago. He'd had an inkling at the time that Gail's feelings for him could become serious, even though she wasn't the marrying kind either. He hadn't wanted to lead her on with false promises when his heart wasn't in it. And that was well before Mary Beth had stumbled into his arms at the engagement party.

"It's just that you were fantastic in bed," she added slyly.

Parr grinned, his male ego expanding momentarily from the feminine praise. "I appreciate the compliment, but let's leave things the way they are. We're both better off."

She couldn't seem to resist speculating about him all the same. "There has to be a new woman in your life."

Parr didn't answer. They'd gone up the stairs and stood on the welcome mat. He unlocked the front door and walked into the foyer, Gail on his arm, poking at him.

Muted laughter and cheerful talk echoed down the hallway from the back of the house.

"They must be in the den," Parr said.

"Sounds like a party going on."

"Probably my cousin Eve and her family."

He led the way quickly down the hall and into the den, which was filled with a small group of jovial people. Parr stopped so abruptly that Gail almost stumbled. The laughter suddenly ceased as all eyes turned toward the intruding couple.

"Parr." Alma Weston jumped up from the couch where she was sitting next to her blond niece, Eve Ross. "I had no idea you were coming in this weekend."

To the left of Eve, Bobby Joe reclined in a huge easy chair, a startled Mary Beth sitting stiffly on his lap. Her long, fiery hair hung loosely from a ribbon-tied ponytail and her luscious body rounded out her white jeans and ecru lace top. Casual but vaguely bridal. To his eyes, anyway.

His name was on Mary Beth's lips, unspoken. She seemed thunderstruck. Her troubled gaze moved to Gail and back to Parr.

"Somebody get them soft drinks," Bobby Joe commanded from his cushy throne. "Hello, you two. How was the trip?"

"Fine."

His mother reached out a hand to her oldest son. "Make yourself at home, boy. We're just having a little birthday celebration for Mary Beth."

"So I see." Parr was certain his mother had told him that next Monday was Mary Beth's twenty-fifth birthday. He'd even bought a present for her and had Gail wrap it perfectly. His assistant, of course, had no idea what was inside the sealed box and he'd refused to answer her curious questions. The gift was still in the rented car. He'd planned on leaving it with his mother tonight.

He'd convinced himself that it was quite proper to buy something for his soon-to-be sister-in-law, even though doing the proper thing had never mattered to him before. But in a way, he hoped the gift would ease some of the pain he'd seen in her glorious green eyes the day she'd stormed out of his life. Women liked presents, or so he had reasoned as he'd handed over his credit card without flinching at the price. Expensive trinkets could soothe hurt feelings.

* * *

Mary Beth mingled with the other guests after a while but she kept a safe distance from Parr and his assistant. If that's what Gail actually was. She had her doubts.

Seeing him again wasn't easy. She had spent three weeks trying to forget him, not wanting to think of him, praying that she would never see him again. The anger he'd provoked spurred her to try even harder to make things right with Bobby Joe.

She had even tried, unsuccessfully, to seduce her fiancé. It had been a total disaster. She simply didn't respond to the younger Weston the way she did to the older. Humiliated, in retreat, she was ashamed to admit even to herself that her dreams had been filled with erotic images of Parr. Big. Dark. Uncompromisingly male. How could an intelligent woman, in her right mind, fantasize about a philandering, disloyal heartbreaker?

Who couldn't seem to take his eyes off her at the moment, even though his mother was bustling around him. He still hadn't sat down and neither had the woman with him.

"Let me make you each a plate," Alma offered. "We've already eaten, but there's plenty of food."

"Don't worry, Mother. Relax." Parr insisted that Alma sit down. "We'll get a bite to eat later before we head out."

"How long will you be here? And why didn't you call?" Alma plopped back down beside her niece as Eve scooted over to make room again.

"We flew down to Muscle Shoals on business. I put in a bid to build a small office complex."

"Isn't that nice." Alma beamed at him.

"Anyway, we decided to drive back so we could stop by and see you, and stay overnight. I've got a dinner appointment tomorrow back in Memphis."

Parr tried not to look at Mary Beth, who was now sitting on his brother's lap, but he couldn't resist, his black eyes glancing her way just in time to catch her staring straight at him. His heartbeat accelerated and he suddenly felt too warm.

"Who's that with you, Parr?" The pert question came from a plump bundle in a polka-dot dress sitting cross-legged on the floor. Carrie Ross, four years old and as blond as her mother, Eve, scratched her nose with the pointy foot of the skinny fashion doll in her hand.

"Hello, sugar pie." Parr reached down to pick up his cousin's little girl and toss her playfully into the air. When his strong arms caught her to him in a hug, she rewarded him with a wet kiss right on his jawline. "That happens to be my assistant, Ms. Cash, if you really need to know."

"Oh." Satisfied with that answer, the child kicked her chubby legs as Parr set her back down on the floor.

"Hey," Bobby Joe called out teasingly to Gail. "You're looking good. So how do you like working for my hardheaded brother?"

"Never a dull moment." She fended off his flirtatious interest with a wave of her hand. "Does that pretty lady on your lap know what a hopeless flirt you are?"

The sudden silence was deafening. Everyone seemed to be waiting for Mary Beth's reaction to the unintentionally tactless comment.

Parr's voice broke the tension. "Bobby Joe doesn't do that anymore, Gail."

Relief spread through the room like the smell of honeysuckle on a warm spring night.

"Unlike his big brother." All heads turned, surprised by Mary Beth's caustic remark.

Parr responded after a slight pause. "I'm not engaged to the girl of my dreams."

Mary Beth squirmed on Bobby Joe's lap, putting an arm around his neck. "Is that what I am to you?" she asked her fiancé softly. Irrationally, she wanted Parr to envy his brother, to still desire her. Would he try again to persuade her to do wrong and cheat on Bobby Joe somehow if he got her alone?

"Baby, you're every man's dream." Bobby Joe gave her an affectionate peck on the cheek.

"I wish AJ still said things like that to me," a very pregnant Eve Ross sighed. She rested a hand on top of her belly, her topaz eyes moving from the engaged couple cuddling in the recliner to the couple still standing.

There was a murmur of masculine protest from elsewhere in the room. Parr realized that his cousin-in-law, AJ Ross, was attending the party via video when a male voice came from a computer screen and AJ's face appeared.

"And I wish he didn't have to work so much," Eve added wistfully.

"Good Lord, girl," Alma said with fond scorn. "Is that the biggest problem in your life? Some women don't know when they have it good."

Eve's husband did his duty and assured her that no other woman had ever looked so lovely in her eighth month. Then he blew her a kiss and said good-bye to all. The screen faded to black.

"Sit down, you two," Eve said to Parr and Gail. "Aunt Alma and I—if I can get up and that is a big *if*— were about to bring in Mary Beth's birthday cake."

"Me too," Carrie squealed. "I get to help Mary Beth blow out the candles!"

"Parr and Gail may want to eat first," Mary Beth suggested.

"Cake and coffee is enough for me." Gail finally took a seat.

"Same here," Parr agreed. "Go ahead with the celebration."

Alma gave Eve a hand up and they went into the kitchen. Mary Beth longed to join them. She felt uncomfortable snuggled in Bobby Joe's lap while Parr and Gail sat watching them.

Parr's dark gaze still stayed mostly on Mary Beth, so intensely that she blushed. If he didn't stop staring, somebody was going to start wondering what was going on. She wasn't quite sure herself, but she knew she had to get away from those ebony eyes. When she pulled away and stood up, Bobby Joe shot her a questioning look.

"I think I'll look at my gifts again," she explained as she went over to the corner desk where several opened presents lay. She fingered the delicate crocheted collar

Alma had made by hand for her, then picked up a bottle of very expensive perfume from Eve's family. The pale yellow peignoir set that Bobby Joe had presented to her in front of everyone, much to her embarrassment, stayed in its box. He had assured his mother and cousin that it was something he expected his bride to wear on their honeymoon.

Parr watched the beautiful birthday girl as she inspected the fine silk of the gift he knew his brother had chosen for her. God, he could imagine exactly what she'd look like in the soft, lemon silk gown. When would she model it for Bobby Joe? Tonight? Pain shot through him like a razor-sharp blade, cutting to the bone. It shouldn't matter to him that she might very well be sleeping with his brother, but it did.

"If you're here overnight," Bobby Joe asked lazily, "where is Gail staying?"

Parr had been so distracted watching Mary Beth that he barely heard the other man speaking. "Huh?"

"Your assistant. I believe her name is Gail," his brother said. "Where is she sleeping? Not in your bed, I know that. Not in Mother's house."

"Hell no," Parr muttered. But his reply came out louder than he'd intended. Several of the others pretended not to hear.

Mary Beth's hand dropped to the boxed gown and clutched it so tightly it wrinkled in her hand. The last thing she needed was to hear about Parr's current sleeping arrangements, on the road or anywhere else.

Gail only laughed at Bobby Joe's remark. "If it's any of your business, I'll be staying at your local motel."

"Not alone, I bet."

One more snotty comment from his brother, and Parr would have to ask him to step outside. "Cut it out," he growled.

He wasn't sure why it mattered, but he didn't want Mary Beth to think for one second that he would be making love to Gail tonight. Was he foolish enough to subconsciously want to bargain with her? *You don't with Bobby Joe and I won't with Gail.*

"What's wrong with you?" his brother snapped, eying Parr suspiciously.

"What's wrong with who?" Alma asked. She held open the door for his cousin to enter, carefully carrying a huge cake adorned with numeral candles. The little flames flickered as Eve walked in.

"Blow them out, Mary Beth," Carrie begged excitedly. "Please. Pretty please."

"After we sing 'Happy Birthday,'" Alma said. Aware of the tension between her sons, she looked from Bobby Joe to Parr, whose expression betrayed his agitation.

"Gather round, everybody," Eve suggested, and began to sing.

One by one the others joined in. Mary Beth turned, forced herself to smile, and sat down in front of the coffee table where Eve had placed her cake. "I think I'm going to need help. Carrie, could you blow them out with me?"

"Yes, yes!" The delighted child moved close to Mary Beth, placing a chubby arm around her neck. "I'm ready."

The candles were blown out to applause and cheers, and the cake cut into slices and served with coffee, but the strained mood in the room didn't improve. The only one who dared to speak was Alma.

"I do miss your dad," she said to Mary Beth. "But I know he's enjoying the game up there in Atlanta."

"Oh yes. He definitely is," Mary Beth replied. She filled in the others in the room, who seemed grateful that the party had returned to something like normal. "He and Uncle Louie go to Atlanta two or three times a season to see the Braves play, and he always comes home with a new ball cap and a week's worth of heartburn." She knew that her father had considered asking Alma to accompany him on this trip instead of his brother, but that hadn't happened.

"Well, Carrie and I need to head home," Eve announced. "It's past our bedtime. Can someone find the tote bag for her dolls?"

"Oh, it's early yet. What's your hurry?" Alma was the type who hated to see visitors leave.

"Do you three need a lift home?" Parr asked, eying his cousin's pregnancy. They would fit in the Thunderbird if he slid the front seat back.

"We came with AJ on his way to work, but we live so close, we can walk."

"It won't take a minute for me to drive you." Then Parr frowned. "I don't have a booster seat for Carrie, though."

"Aunt Alma has one in her car."

"Then we're set. Carrie might go to sleep on her feet and you don't need to be lifting her."

"Okay. Thanks." Eve gathered her child, then located the tote bag stuffed with dolls, and an oversized handbag, then kissed and hugged her aunt and Mary Beth. "See you all later."

"Why don't you drop me by the motel after you get back?" Gail asked Parr. "Just honk. I'll run out."

"You know you're welcome to—" Alma began the invitation.

"She can squeeze into the backseat. Carrie doesn't take up much room and Gail's bag is in the trunk," Parr instantly interrupted.

Not another word was spoken as Parr picked up Carrie and, with Eve and Gail, started toward the door.

Wide-eyed and innocent, Carrie stared at Gail now that they were eye to eye. "How come you got so much stuff on your face? Can you wash it off? Does it—"

"Carrie!" her mother scolded.

Everyone laughed, even Gail, good-naturedly enough but with an understandable touch of annoyance.

As soon as the others left, Alma began tidying up the room, leaving her younger son to entertain his fiancée. But Mary Beth's solemn expression left no doubt that the party was over as far as she was concerned.

"There must be a full moon tonight," Bobby Joe mused.

"What?" Mary Beth had been so preoccupied with thoughts of Parr that she didn't understand the comment.

"Everybody, including you, was acting strange. Parr especially. I wonder what's on his mind."

Mary Beth chose to ignore that. She began helping Alma. "Let me do this. You sit down and rest."

"Why? I'm almost done. Tell you what. You just enjoy being with your man," the older woman recommended. "When I finish up, I'm going to go watch that Jimmy Fallon and figure out if I like him better than Jay Leno. But I have to say, neither of 'em is a patch on Johnny Carson."

"He's gone," Bobby Joe reminded her.

"But not forgotten."

Alma was nothing if not loyal. Mary Beth had to smile. She tried to collect the cake plates, but Alma shooed her away.

"I'm in charge here. And no arguing. You two need time alone. The way Bobby Joe's been so busy at that real estate office of his lately, you're becoming strangers," Alma declared, walking out before any objections could be made.

"She's right, you know." Bobby Joe came up behind Mary Beth, slipped his arms around her, and nuzzled her neck. "I'm sorry if I've neglected you, sweetheart."

"I understand," she assured him. "You're trying hard to close some deals. I'm proud of you. I want you to succeed."

"Me too," he agreed. "I'd like to show Parr that I can make it just as big as he did."

"You will." He sure seemed to love being praised. She might as well lay it on thick. "You're smart, determined, good-looking, and very smooth. You don't have any rough edges, unlike Parr."

"You think?" He turned her in his arms, prompting her smile. "It's true he can be pretty crude sometimes. I'm glad you don't like his type. A lot of women seem to go for the rough guys."

"Not me," she lied. "Now stop wasting time talking about Parr. Why don't you kiss me instead?"

Just as he lowered his head and touched her lips with his, the shrill ringing of a telephone stopped the kiss before it began. Alma wouldn't dream of giving up her old landline. It was awfully loud.

Hesitating briefly, Bobby Joe answered it. After saying hello, he simply listened, mumbled a few words in reply to the caller, and turned to Mary Beth.

"That was Jack Quinn. You're going to kill me, but I've got to go. He wants to talk business in person."

"At ten o'clock on a Friday night?"

"I'm sorry. He insisted." He looked at her imploringly with puppy dog eyes, genuine regret in his voice. "If it weren't important, I wouldn't go. I can drop you at home on the way."

Where she would be completely alone, what with her father in Atlanta. The prospect wasn't appealing. But she didn't really have a choice.

"That won't be necessary," she snapped. "I'll call a cab."

"Don't be like that. This is something I have to do. Not only for me. For us."

"Please. Just go."

"Mary Beth . . ."

"We'll talk about it tomorrow. Just go on and get rich. Let business take over your life the way it has your brother's."

"This could turn out to be something big," he insisted. He brushed her forehead with a quick good-bye kiss before he rushed out. "Take Mother's car. Don't call a cab," he ordered from the hallway. The door slammed behind him.

"And you can go to blue blazes," Mary Beth grumbled to the silent, empty room. During the three weeks of their reconciliation, they had gone on exactly two dates alone, and caught moments here and there surrounded by other people.

She went upstairs to the guest bedroom and found the bag with a change of clothes she'd brought with her. Always prepared, she thought resentfully. But not for a last minute business meeting. She pulled out a rolled blouse in a soft, neutral color twill that zipped up the front. Thinking ahead, she'd checked the weather report, which said it would turn cooler, in which case the lace top might not do and she had this for backup. Unromantic. Practical. It suited her mood.

Mary Beth went back downstairs, dawdling on each step with nothing to do and nothing to look forward to.

She knew Bobby Joe had a burning desire to succeed, driven to do so largely because of his intense rivalry with his brother. Confiding in her was about Bobby Joe's only way to let off steam on the subject. He resented the fact that Parr had supported him almost all his life, had paid for his college education, and even backed his fledgling real estate enterprise. At twenty-seven, Bobby Joe seemed to think time was running out. Parr had founded his own company, a diversified construction business, and turned a healthy profit within months. And he'd been the same age. In the ensuing five years, Parr had done very well indeed.

She wanted to be supportive and helpful as his

fiancée, and later as his wife, but she couldn't help resenting the insane schedule Bobby Joe was trying to adhere to. She didn't want to be neglected or forgotten. If things were like this now, would they improve or worsen after marriage?

She wanted children, but not if their father was never around to share their lives. What kind of dad Bobby Joe would be was an open question. He was a gentle, loving man who had a genuine affection for little Carrie.

But when Mary Beth imagined her own baby cradled in its father's arms, those were the strong, muscular arms of Parr Weston. As hard as she tried, she could not shake the image.

"What are you doing all alone?" A deep, masculine voice erased his image with the reality of his presence. "Where's Mother and Bobby Joe?"

Taken off guard by his unexpected reappearance, Mary Beth gazed longingly at the big man silhouetted in the doorway. His dark eyes drank in the sight of her soft, receptive face. She looked happy to see him, almost eager to welcome him.

"Ah—hello. Your mother's gone to her room and Bobby Joe got an urgent business call from Jack Quinn." The part of her brain that was functioning told her to run as fast as she could, to get away from the danger facing her.

But the dreamy, unreasoning part was listening to her fantasizing heart. "You didn't stay with Gail."

"Never planned to," he hastily responded. "There's nothing between us. I had no reason to stay. She works for me. We're friends."

The thought of the gorgeous brunette in close contact with Parr most of the week was disheartening. "Is she, um, a friend with benefits?"

"No."

"Your lover?"

"Definitely not."

Mary Beth persisted. "But she was once?"

"Strawberry . . ."

"She was, wasn't she?"

Reluctantly he admitted the truth. "Yes. But it was nothing special. I didn't love her."

Mary Beth watched him come into the room, his tall, virile body clad in faded jeans and a plaid shirt. She wondered where he'd ditched the sport jacket he'd worn earlier. His shirt, unbuttoned by a few, stretched tautly across the massive muscles in his broad chest. A sexy dusting of black hair curled where she could see it, tempting her fingers to explore.

He was nothing like his more sophisticated younger brother. Bobby Joe prided himself on his conservative, preppy image. He was an up-and-coming businessman and did his damnedest to impress. In contrast, Parr Weston dressed only to please himself and didn't give a plugged nickel about his image or anyone else's.

"Have you ever been in love, Parr?" The question was presumptuous, the answer absolutely none of her business, but she asked it anyway, instantly dreading his reply.

"Nope. I love 'em and leave 'em."

"I didn't expect to hear that corny line from you."

He jammed his hands in his jeans pockets. "But

you knew what I meant. I don't choose my words that carefully."

His self-assurance was irritating. Did he know he made her nervous? Did he realize that despite her fear and anger she couldn't stop herself from wanting him? All that rampaging emotion was useless when he didn't give a damn one way or another. She decided to tough it out and see where the conversation went.

"Don't you ever want to fall in love and get married?"

He shrugged. "Maybe someday. I'd like to have some kids." He walked up to her, taking her hands in his.

It was a brazen move, but what else had she expected? She couldn't have predicted his next question though.

"Why didn't you stop Bobby Joe from leaving?"

Taking a deep breath, then slowly exhaling, she controlled her reaction to him enough to explain. But first she let go of his hands.

"He said something came up that couldn't wait. Jack Quinn needed to see him tonight. He hated leaving me, but . . . but I understand how important it is to him to stay on track and jump at opportunities."

"You're starting to talk like him."

His observation piqued her temper, in part because he was right. "Is that a bad thing?"

"I don't know. Anyway, Quinn could have waited until tomorrow. Nothing could be that urgent."

Parr knew for a fact that Jack Quinn had taken his wife and kids to Opryland in Nashville this weekend. Eve, being Bette Quinn's best friend, had mentioned the fact in casual conversation. Why had Bobby Joe lied? Who had been his mysterious caller?

Mary Beth launched into a defense of her fiancé's actions. "Bobby Joe's trying very hard to follow in your successful footsteps. Business always comes first. You taught him that back in the day."

"Yeah. When I had a widowed mother and a kid brother to support," Parr reminded her, his impatient stance making her think that he might just bolt. "But I didn't have a beautiful strawberry blonde. I'd never leave a woman like you to tend to business that could wait until I got around to it."

"Okay. What do you want me to say?" His compliments unnerved her.

He took a few steps closer. She took the same number of steps, in reverse. His nearness was doing a number on her self-control.

"One of us ought to remind my brother to keep his priorities straight."

"Go ahead," she challenged him.

"Why me?" His question had a bitter edge.

"Because you're family," she answered simply. "Isn't that enough?"

Parr's glowering look told her that she'd crossed some invisible line. The problem was that she didn't know which one.

All he could think of was how irresistible she was. She smelled of some lush, feminine perfume, a scent so enticing that he longed to see if she tasted as sweetly sensual. He had no right to touch her. She was his brother's woman.

So why the hell wasn't Bobby Joe here protecting what was his? Male instinct should have kicked in. It was for Parr.

"I want to taste you, Strawberry. I want to put my mouth on yours."

The outrageous statement took her aback. She tried to swallow but couldn't. A huge knot had formed in her throat, almost cutting off her breath.

"Parr . . . I . . . Look, just don't. Please. This is hard."

"Yeah. For me too." Some unseen force held him back, still not moving any closer, still not touching her.

"Yes," she sighed. She wasn't agreeing to anything. But that softly breathed *yes* was a million miles away from *no*.

"I may be too rough," he warned. "I'm not used to good girls like you."

"It doesn't matter," she pleaded.

One big, dark finger touched her lower lip, running tenderly from corner to corner, pausing as her mouth gradually opened. "Your lips look so sweet," he murmured. "So inviting."

"Oh, Parr."

"Do you want my mouth on yours, Strawberry?"

"Yes," she begged, her quivering body leaning into his.

His finger moved from her lips, drawing a line down her chin to her throat, ever so slowly easing inside the collar of her blouse to stroke the upper swell of her breast. He was tormenting her with his sensual, patient lovemaking. She wanted him madly. Not even her erotic dreams had made her feel so wanton.

"Your heart's wild," he whispered. "So is mine. Feel." He took her hand, placing it on his pounding chest. "Feel what you do to me."

"Please . . . please . . . I can't bear this."

"You want me, don't you?"

"Yes." Why should she lie? He was already well aware of her half-crazed desire for him.

"Isn't it about time you took her home, Bobby Joe?" Alma's voice came from the doorway, instantly freezing them to the spot. Neither spoke as his mother entered the room, but Parr removed his hand from Mary Beth's body and stepped aside before they were caught in the act.

"Good Lord. It's you. Where's your brother, Parr?"

"He got a business call," he replied. "Something about a late meeting or so I understand. I was just about to take Mary Beth home."

"No . . ." Her voice was so faint that only Parr heard her, but his quick warning glance silenced her refusal.

"My goodness, that boy," Alma fussed. "I'm sorry, Mary Beth. You're going to have to take him in hand and make him remember what's most important."

"She isn't Bobby Joe's keeper," Parr reminded his mother.

"Of course not," Alma agreed with a yawn. "Well, go ahead and get her home. I'm going to bed."

"Good night." Mary Beth hoped her future mother-in-law hadn't realized what had been going on when they were interrupted.

"Good night to you both." Alma disappeared down the hall.

"Come on. I really do have to get you home now." Parr reached for her but she dodged his hand.

"I can take Alma's car and drive myself. There's no need for you to go out again."

Parr didn't touch her again, but his tone of voice demanded compliance. "Let's go."

The drive to the gable-roofed, redbrick house where she had lived all her life took less than fifteen minutes. She had helped her father plant the rows of shrubbery that lined each side of the narrow paved driveway. At this moment, she wanted nothing more than to escape inside the safe harbor of this welcoming abode.

Parr killed the engine and turned to her. She sat huddled on the passenger side, her hand on the door latch. "Thanks for the ride. Nice car, by the way."

"I always wanted a classic T-bird. Got lucky at the rental desk."

"Oh. What do you usually drive?"

He snorted, as if the answer should be painfully obvious. "A pickup truck."

Mary Beth could imagine it. New, dominatingly large, and polished to a high dark shine. "Right. Of course."

The conversation was low-key but the undercurrents weren't.

When she moved to open the door, his big hand reached out to stop her. "You're in an awfully big hurry."

"I want to go in," she told him, nervously reaching for the door latch again.

"What are you afraid of?" He cupped her chin with his hard fingers. "I'd never hurt you, Mary Beth."

"You already have," she admitted, pulling free. "I'm afraid of you."

"Stay just a minute," he requested. "I have a birthday present for you."

"No. Oh, Parr, why?"

"Please take my gift." It was suddenly very important to him that she accept his present.

When she didn't respond, he opened the glove compartment and took out a small, gift-wrapped box. He held it a moment before offering it to her. She sat staring at the gift as if it were a time bomb ready to explode. Her hand trembled as she reached out. When her fingers made contact with his, she had to bite her lip to keep from crying out. Taking the box from his hand, she turned toward the door.

"Open it first," he appealed.

"Parr—no."

"Please."

Her nervous fingers clumsily removed the bow, unwrapped the paper, and peeled the tape from the outer box concealing a small jeweler's box. She lifted it out. Nestled on a bed of white velvet was a flawless ruby strawberry, glowing like a crystal flame.

"Do you like it?" He wanted to touch her, hold her, and never let her go.

"It's beautiful," she gasped as she gently lifted the delicate gold chain, the jeweled fruit suspended daintily from it. "Where did you find this? I've never seen anything like it."

"I had it made just for you. A perfect strawberry for my . . . for the most beautiful strawberry blonde in the world."

"I can't—I shouldn't accept it. What will Bobby Jo think?"

"This is something between us. It has nothing to do with my brother."

"Oh? But I'm going to marry your brother eventually."

"I know," he acknowledged, trying desperately to control the sensual yearning that threatened to consume him.

"I have to go in now."

He leaned toward her. She didn't move. She wanted to encourage him but knew she didn't dare. He desired her. That was obvious, but he'd made it very clear that an affair was all he offered.

"One sweet strawberry kiss," he implored. "Just a good-bye kiss that won't mean anything to either of us tomorrow."

She didn't say yes or no to his request, and thus allowed him to decide for her. He took her face in both of his huge hands and looked at her in the shadowy darkness. His lips brushed her forehead, her cheeks, her nose, her chin. A wild, overwhelming desire coursed through her body like liquid gold into a waiting mold.

"I've never wanted a woman so badly in all my life."

He knew it was wrong to admit even this much of his true feelings, but passion overcame his better judgment.

"Then kiss me. Really kiss me," she breathed.

His lips touched hers gently, coaxing a response. She wanted him, body and soul. Wanted him in a way she had never known existed. He swallowed the sound of her moans, his tongue sliding between her lips,

seeking entrance. He pulled her against him and she
clung to him, wanting more.

"Open your mouth for me. Let me in." His voice
persuaded her.

His tongue plunged into her moistness, taking,
giving, sharing in an adventure so intense that their
bodies pulsated with pleasure too long denied. He had
to touch her. *He had to.*

He covered her breast with his warm palm, caressing gently. "Please let me look at you."

She moved his fingers to the front zipper opening
of her blouse, inviting him to seek his pleasure. When
the zipper stopped just below her waist, he eased his
hand inside, touching the satiny smoothness of her
skin beneath bra and panties.

"Oh God," he groaned.

The halogen glare of a passing car's headlights
flashed briefly into the Thunderbird's interior, breaking the sensual spell that had clouded Parr's judgment. Realizing what he had done, he redid her
zipper, holding her tenderly in his shaking arms a few
minutes before releasing her.

"Forgive me, Mary Beth." He never wanted to hurt
this special woman, but he could already see the bewildered pain in her green eyes. "That was all my fault.
I let things get out of control."

"Parr . . ."

"You're so damn beautiful and it's been months
since I've had a woman. I'm sorry."

Her throbbing body stiffened in defiance. She
jerked out of his arms, opened the door, and bolted
from the car.

He called out to her, but she ran up the sidewalk without looking back. He slammed his large fists against the steering wheel.

Mary Beth fumbled in her pocket for the keys, tears blinding her. Her closed fist beat against the front door. Suddenly she felt something inside her curled fingers. Opening her hand, she saw the gleaming strawberry necklace she had been clutching without knowing it. Warm, anguished tears dropped onto her palm. The fiery ruby glowed brighter.

Chapter Six

A brilliantly sunny day chased away the lingering memories of last night. As it turned out, Mary Beth and Bobby Joe hadn't even argued about his leaving her to meet Quinn. He'd gotten home at a reasonable hour, even though she hadn't been there. Still, Mary Beth knew exactly when because he'd called her from Alma's house on the landline, trying to reach her on her cell phone first. It had occurred to her that he'd used the landline deliberately instead of his cell, as if he was trying to establish an alibi or convey the fact that he had returned to his mom, who always bragged about not sleeping soundly until all her chicks were safely in the nest.

Even so. Bobby Joe had been there and he'd tried her dad's number next. She hadn't picked up either call, still shaken after what had happened with Parr.

Had he planned the encounter? It hardly seemed possible. But he had to have gone to considerable trouble to find her a ruby strawberry after the engagement party. To think that he'd never seen her before that night, let alone given her the nickname—every time he said it in that low voice of his, Mary Beth felt a thrill.

Bobby Joe never addressed her by anything other than her full name. That wasn't quite true. He did call her *baby* sometimes. It was just a word. It didn't register as an endearment.

Mary Beth turned the key in the ignition and started the engine. It usually took a little while before the air-conditioning got going, and the warmth inside her car was making her a little breathless. Unless that was her memory of Parr's sensual embrace and hot kisses kicking in, she thought, rolling down the window. She held a hand in front of the dashboard vents, feeling the first faint stirrings of cool air.

It's been months since I've had a woman. How could she have taken a line like that seriously? Far from flattering, when she thought about it. But then Parr had said something else first. *You're so damn beautiful.*

Was she really that hungry for masculine attention? Apparently so.

Bobby Joe had come over in the morning and taken her out for an early breakfast. The subject of his unexpected absence had been studiously avoided by them both. Why fight, she had thought—and still thought. She couldn't take the moral high ground, not after that encounter with Parr. Today it seemed like a dream. She rolled up the window and leafed through a manila folder, briefing herself before her next stop, a meeting with the principal of one of the local elementary schools.

Mary Beth was making the rounds of the county

while Teacher Days were in progress. Thousands of kids had most of the week off while teachers and staff from principals on down brushed up their skills in workshops and conferences. Part of her job as a social worker was to track various initiatives put in place by the state and community boards, and Teacher Days were ideal for that purpose. Plus it was an opportunity to catch up with friends and colleagues that she looked forward to each year.

There were bound to be curious questions from some about her wedding plans, now that the engagement party had happened. But Mary Beth had always preferred to keep her personal life separate from her professional aspirations.

Good luck with that in the South. She closed the folder. There was only one other stop she had to make in her hometown and then she could drive off to other assigned areas, where no one really knew her.

Even though Iminga had grown rapidly in the last five years, what with an influx of well-heeled retirees and affluent young couples buying second homes in this unspoiled corner of Mississippi, it was still a small town in many ways. Mary Beth knew it—and felt like privacy was a luxury granted only to those who guarded it fiercely. The older generation kept to boundaries set by church pews and front porches where just about everyone was made welcome. Alma in particular was a stickler for hospitality if not discretion.

But even Alma didn't discuss the most personal matters.

Mary Beth was aware that something had happened

to the Westons years ago, before they'd moved to Iminga—the kind of scandal that nice folks didn't talk about. Just about everyone else's business got covered at town gatherings, though, when people turned out in droves for Fourth of July picnics and fund-raising barbecues and the like.

When he'd started going places with her, hand in hand, lovey-dovey as could be, Mary Beth could tell he was being sized up by some in a way that said they didn't think a Weston was worthy of a Caine.

Like most of the South, people had relatives and friends in distant communities who traded juicy tidbits, old and new, from far and wide. Gossip was a regional obsession. A family might move away and it would be as if they had never left to those who remained.

She didn't want to ask him about what she had only sensed, and never dared to bring up the subject with her dad, who no doubt knew as much as anyone. Every family, she felt, was entitled to keep the past in the past.

She couldn't help thinking, though, that maybe that was why Bobby Joe's behavior at the engagement party had been hushed up so fast. The flow of friendly phone calls requesting updates from Alma had stopped even before Mary Beth's family-only birthday party, as far as she could tell.

Which didn't mean that people wouldn't talk if a rumor got started about her and Parr. Mary Beth was running a risk by wearing the ruby strawberry. But no one could see the gem nestled between her breasts, not with her blouse done up to the collar on what promised to be a sultry day.

The necklace was hers, after all, a unique gift that Parr had chosen with care, and she didn't see why it should languish in a dresser drawer. However, even though Bobby Joe hadn't seen it, she'd taken the precaution of lengthening the fine gold chain with a shorter, plainer one clipped to each end.

If she were wiser, she would hide it away but keep it as a warning to herself that she and Parr had gone as far as they could go without tempting fate. He hadn't been wrong when he'd muttered the words that described her to a tee. *Don't drink, don't smoke, don't fool around.*

No. She didn't. And hadn't, not even as a teenager. She'd gone to an exclusive prep school away from Iminga, girls only, where they didn't have time to gossip, let alone get in trouble. So she hadn't known a thing about the legendary charm of either of the Weston brothers until she'd come back home after college.

Kind of a shame. If she'd known more, she might have been prepared for Parr. Bobby Joe lacked the powerful attractiveness of his mysterious older brother. But that was probably to her advantage.

Mary Beth slowed the car for an upcoming stoplight and waited for it to turn green. Absently, her fingers traced the chain. If she was honest with herself, the little gem was also a memento of those precious hours when Parr had been nice enough to rescue her and make her feel cherished and desired.

She had loved the feeling. But that was all it was. She couldn't throw over Bobby Joe and run to Parr like a giddy schoolgirl. The wild rush of emotions he triggered in her with such ease was beyond comprehension. It wasn't something she'd ever experienced. All that overwhelming sensation couldn't be allowed to erase the serious commitment she'd made to his younger brother. It was natural enough to have second thoughts, she supposed, and even crave one last fling before the walk down the aisle.

Which, she reminded herself, was probably a long way off. She and Bobby Joe were still only engaged. Not married. Nonetheless, common sense demanded that she had to steel her heart against her wayward, impulsive attraction to Parr.

Apparently he'd left town early this morning. Alma hadn't mentioned it and Mary Beth hadn't wanted to ask his brother what Parr was up to. But Bobby Joe had offhandedly passed on a little information as he salted his scrambled eggs: Parr had put in a bid on a project near Memphis, something that was bigger than anything he'd ever done. Nothing more specific than that.

She drove on for several more blocks, then turned into another school parking lot. Jill Cameron, her high school pal who now taught second grade, had practically begged her to stop by, without saying why.

Mary Beth maneuvered into a parking spot by the wide glass doors of the low brick building. The paper cutouts the kids had made for window decorations, bright-petaled flowers that heralded spring, were still up, a little faded but cheerful.

She flipped down the visor and checked her appearance, applying a dash of pink lipstick and running a brush quickly through her hair. Then she gathered up her papers, stuffing them into the tote with the laptop.

Maybe Jill had something she wanted to discuss that would take precedence over Mary Beth's current problems. If so, excellent. She had every intention of encouraging Jill to pour out her heart to avoid talking about Bobby Joe. Jill was in love, therefore she had problems. The two went together.

Mary Beth pushed open the door and entered, her footsteps echoing faintly on the hallway floor. She went to a classroom on the right, looking through the open door and spotting Jill. The petite brunette was bent over and peering into a rectangular glass tank.

"Hello," Mary Beth called.

"Come on in." Jill straightened. "I was just talking to the lizard."

"You really do need a few days off." Mary Beth laughed as she walked to the tank and looked in. Tiny, beady eyes glanced up at her as the little reptile flicked its tongue in and out.

"Don't I know it," Jill replied. "I'm heading out to the lake now that I'm done with my workshops. Kev and I rented a waterside cabin and a powerboat. It's going to be a blast."

"Sounds like it. Get going. It's a beautiful day."

"I can't. Not just yet." Jill threw a pleading look at Mary Beth. "How do you feel about babysitting our hamster?"

Mary Beth raised an eyebrow. "Is that why you called me?"

"Yes," Jill said hopefully. "It's not like you have to walk it or anything. The cage has an exercise wheel."

Mary Beth just wasn't a fan of rodents, but that didn't keep her from feeling guilty. "Am I your only option?"

Her friend sighed. "No. I guess I can take the hamster with me. And the custodian will feed the lizard. Unless you could."

"Maybe." Mary Beth almost relented. "What does he eat?"

"Crickets."

Mary Beth shuddered. "I take back the offer. Sorry. Anything else I could volunteer for?"

She had to ask.

"You bet," Jill said quickly. "There's the science project on the growth rate of plants." She pointed to a group of plastic drink cups filled with dirt. "Baby beans. You don't have to walk them either."

"Sign me up." Mary Beth decided not to explain her lack of a green thumb to Jill. "Do you have something I can put them in?"

Waiting at the railroad crossing for the bars to lift, Mary Beth tipped the rearview mirror to check on the plants in the backseat, tucked into a cardboard box that she'd managed to get a seat belt around. So far, so good. They were all upright.

The kids' names were written on the plastic cups and most had named their plants as well. There was Sprouty and Beanster and, for some inexplicable reason, Ed, a single leaf on a wobbly stem that belonged to a girl named Janey. Mary Beth felt a strong obligation to take care of them all, but that one in particular. It wouldn't do for little Janey to come back after the break and find out that Ed had keeled over.

The caboose clattered past and the bars slowly rose.

Next stop, another elementary school three miles away. Then she could return to her father's house. Since Howard spent more time than ever with Alma, Mary Beth had had the big brick house to herself for the last few days, which suited her fine.

Without her dad and without the Weston brothers, she could focus on work, something she needed to do. With the wedding plans undecided for the time being, she might as well. Besides, she had vowed to slog through the hefty textbook that was keeping the paperwork on the passenger seat—and her mind—from flying away. *Community-Based Modalities in Educational Systems*, Fourth Edition. A major yawn but required reading. What she wouldn't give for a paperback romance.

Mary Beth stepped on the gas.

Two hours later, the last meeting of the day was over. She walked briskly to her parked car and checked the bean plants in the back. All of them had keeled over. Mary Beth swore under her breath. She never should have left the car in the sun. It was hotter than blazes in the back.

She pulled out in a hurry and drove straight to Alma's house.

"Don't worry. They'll perk right up." Alma found a shady place and filled a watering can, pouring a little into the first row of plastic cups. "The soil was fairly dry and they got too hot. All they need is a drink and a shady place to recover."

"Thanks so much."

"Happy to help. How about you? Would you like some lemonade?"

"If it's not any trouble."

"Don't be silly, girl." Alma handed her the watering can. "Here. You can do the rest. Not too much, now. You don't want to drown them. That's as bad as drying them out."

Mary Beth concentrated on the task while Alma went into the house via the screen door on the porch. She could hear the sound of hammering from somewhere nearby but thought no more of it. In another minute, Alma came back out with a tray holding a frosty pitcher of lemonade and glasses.

"Where should I put the box?"

Alma set down the tray on a wicker table between two chairs. "Right there. We can find a spot for them around the back in a little while."

She poured the lemonade and the two women chatted for a bit. The hammering kept up and they had trouble hearing each other. But it didn't matter. The late afternoon sun relaxed them both.

"That was refreshing," Mary Beth said, putting down her glass. "But I should get going."

"All right. Let's get those little baby plants squared away before you go, though. How long do you have them for?"

"Not sure. I forgot to ask when the kids come back." Mary Beth rose and picked up the box, waiting for Alma to lead the way. "But I think it's in four days."

The older woman went down the stairs and walked down a flagstone path. Mary Beth followed her but not too closely. Alma disappeared around the corner of the house as she paused to get a better grip on the box.

The loud hammering stopped suddenly. Mary Beth caught up with Alma. And stopped in her tracks when she saw Parr. Shirtless. Wearing thick jeans that were faded and a little ripped, and heavy, scuffed work boots. He wasn't looking at her as he shoved the handle of the hammer into a low-slung tool belt around his lean hips. Lengths of lumber lay on the grass around him as if tossed down in frustration. Others leaned against the house.

"Wha—what are you doing here?" she gasped.

"Building a greenhouse from a kit." He looked just as startled, though he answered matter-of-factly. He obviously hadn't been able to hear her and his mother talking on the porch. His expression said as much.

"If he gets done right quick, we can use it for the bean plants." Alma stooped to pick up a stapled booklet. "Are these the instructions?"

"Yes. Which are worthless," Parr growled. "And half the hardware is missing. Not to mention that the two-by-fours are either one-sixteenth of an inch too short or too long." He snapped out a section of metal measuring tape and checked another one. "Okay. Some are all right."

"And I was about to ask you how it was coming along," his mother chirped. "Do you want to return it?"

Parr set the good piece next to the others leaning on the house, his back to Mary Beth. The rear view was even better. She was hypnotized by the interplay of muscle in his broad shoulders as he rearranged the lumber, his biceps rising and rounding. He lifted several two-by-fours at a time, as if they were as light as pencils.

"No. That would mean getting it all back on the pallet in order and strapped down again. It's easier to slam it together."

He put his hands on his tool belt, studying the lineup of precut lumber without turning around. "Might have to replace that warped one, though," he said to himself, crossing his brawny arms over his bare chest.

Mary Beth gulped, staring at the way he stood, with one hip cocked to the side and long legs apart, rocking back on his heels. He seemed so different from how he'd appeared on the night they'd met by chance: the gallant gentleman in evening wear who'd kissed her tears away had morphed into a hands-on guy who could swing a hammer and build things without looking at the plans. She wasn't sure which Parr she preferred. Right now, this one, all man and all muscle, blocked everything else from her mind.

"I feel bad," Alma said. "Maybe I shouldn't have ordered it. But you know what happens with online shopping. It's too easy."

"Next time read the customer reviews," Parr muttered, bending to lay out the longest lumber in the approximate shape of a wall frame. He squatted, using a small tool to check a corner angle.

"I did, son. They were all five-star."

"Dead giveaway right there. The manufacturer paid for those."

"Oh dear. I am sorry," Alma fretted.

"I'll manage, Mom. At least the foundation is ready," he said to Mary Beth, nodding to a rectangle of concrete framed by planks as he rose. "All I have to do after the basic framing is set the uprights in those holes."

"Oh." She just stood there, transfixed by the sight of him so close, stripped to the waist. His musculature, something she'd only guessed at when he was clothed, was fully displayed, his bare skin burnished by the late afternoon sun to a deep gold.

He moved with athletic ease, stepping through the pieces of the project to face her. "What's in the box?"

She'd almost forgotten she was holding it. "Bean plants."

"Why, Mary Beth. Are you starting a farm?" A glimmer of amusement lit up his dark eyes.

"No. It's a school science project. A friend of mine— a teacher—asked me to, um, babysit the plants during the break."

"I see."

She shifted position, wishing she could put the box down somewhere, afraid she would knock down or trip over the scattered lumber.

"Mary Beth, you can set that over there." Alma took charge, pointing to the dense shade under an old chinaberry tree. "How long do you think this will take to finish, Parr?"

"About a day. Then I have to get back to Memphis."

Mary Beth made her way over the uneven lawn to the spot Alma had indicated, setting down the box.

She stood up and brushed bits of dirt from her skirt as she straightened.

The sound of a ringing phone from inside the house got Alma's attention.

"'Scuse me, you two. Be right back."

His mother went back around the corner of the house, leaving them alone. Mary Beth had forgotten how long a landline could ring. Seemingly forever. The ringing stopped but Alma's voice carried through the windows as she picked up with an exuberant "Howard! Well, hell-oo!"

She'd only just seen him yesterday. Mary Beth was getting the feeling that the relationship between her father and the lively widow was more than a friendship, or would be soon. In any case, the phone call would take a while. Alma never rushed a phone call from a friend or relative.

Self-consciously, Mary Beth put her hands in the pockets of her skirt. Parr's dark gaze locked on hers, then moved down for a few seconds. He met her eyes again.

"There's dirt on your blouse too," he said.

She brushed it off, then let her hand drop to her side, uncomfortable under his steady gaze.

"You're so buttoned up." His mocking voice was low and a little rough.

"That's because . . ." She trailed off. He could guess why if he wanted to. She didn't have to tell him.

"Are you wearing the necklace I gave you, Strawberry?"

Her lips parted as she mouthed a yes. The ruby pendant hidden between her breasts might as well be glowing. How had he known she wouldn't be able to resist wearing it?

"Let me see it."

Mary Beth didn't have to go that far. She raised her hand again, touching the button over her heart, with no intention of opening it. "Trust me. It's right here."

The sound of footsteps, followed by a different male voice, not as deep, saying hello, made her whirl around.

"Hey, Parr. Mary Beth." Bobby Joe crossed the lawn to her, stepping over the lumber in his way. "Mom said you were out here. She's glued to the phone, waved me away. How's it going? Need my help?"

"Nope. I don't need anything from you," Parr muttered. He picked up the stapled instructions and studied them.

Bobby Joe slid a hand around her waist and squeezed a little too hard. "I got you something," he whispered into her ear.

"Oh?" Her answer was distracted. With Bobby Joe's lips staying on her ear, she didn't have to look at him. Her gaze never left Parr, who had turned his back to both of them.

Bobby Joe captured her left hand and held it up so the diamond ring caught the last rays of the fading sun. "Something for the other hand," he whispered. He slipped a small box into it, laughing softly into her ear. "Go on. Open it."

Mary Beth shook her head, turning to focus fully on him. "Not here. Let's go inside."

"I don't care if Parr sees."

"Well, I do."

"He's not even looking." Bobby Joe maneuvered her against the chinaberry tree. He uncurled her fingers to take back the box and opened it for her. Another diamond ring, not as elaborate as her engagement ring, sparkled inside on a nest of white satin.

Mary Beth hardly knew what to say. The ruby strawberry felt hotter than a burning coal against her skin. She was on fire with guilt, even though she hadn't done anything to be guilty about. Not really.

"It's—lovely," she choked out. "And it looks expensive. But why?"

"I don't have to have a reason to give you a present, do I?"

Mary Beth wriggled free. "I assume you haven't done anything else that would cause a scandal." She wondered if he would even notice that she'd left herself out of it. The emotions he'd evoked in her before—jealousy, suspicion, anger—didn't seem to be in play. She felt nothing.

For him.

"Of course not," Bobby Joe answered her impatiently. "I happened to see the ring in a shop window and all I could think of was how it would look on your pretty little hand."

Mary Beth managed a smile. "Okay."

Bobby Joe pried the ring from its satin nest and slipped it onto her right hand. "Look. It's perfect." He kissed the tip of her nose. "Like you."

"Please don't say that."

"Why not?" He tucked the empty box in his shirt pocket and clasped her around the waist. She was more uncomfortable than ever.

"Because it isn't true. But thank you for the ring. And the thought." Her expression of gratitude was no more than duty required. There was very little feeling in the words, even though her emotions were in utter turmoil.

Bobby Joe sighed and let her go. "You're welcome. So long as you like it, I'm not taking it back."

She nodded, distracted again by the noise of Parr's work boots clomping up the back stairs into the house, looking his way out of the corner of her eye. He grabbed the shirt he'd slung over the railing and threw it over his shoulder before he stuck the instructions into an empty flowerpot.

"What's his problem?" Bobby Joe wanted to know.

"The greenhouse kit. He's having trouble putting it together."

Bobby Joe glanced indifferently at the pieces of the project. "Beats me. He's the expert. I actually don't know much about construction." He walked a few steps away from her, picking up a two-by-four and inspecting it, then tossing it back on the ground.

"Put it back where you got it." Mary Beth's reply was tart.

Bobby Joe gave her a look of mild surprise. He kicked the piece of wood into approximately the right place. "Is that where it was? I guess there's a method in his madness."

"Looks to me like he knows what he's doing."

Defending Parr to his brother might not be the best idea under the circumstances. Mary Beth came out from under the overhanging branches and moved toward the house.

"He knows how to get on Mother's good side."

"Don't be like that. She ordered the kit online. My guess is that she didn't ask his advice."

Bobby Joe stretched out his arm and captured her, resuming his possessive hold. He pulled her back against the front of his body, pressing his chin against her cheek as he breathed his reply. "He's not in charge of the world, even though he acts like it. But never mind. Even he's happy that you're going to be part of the family."

She swallowed hard, hoping that wasn't true.

"And by the way, I have another surprise for you. Something really big. Our future is looking bright. Very bright."

Mary Beth fell silent. He swayed a little, trying to get her into his rhythm.

"Aren't you curious?" he whispered.

She still didn't answer. Bobby Joe didn't have the smarts or sensitivity to figure out that she was wondering about Parr.

Parr yanked open cabinet doors and slammed them shut again, quickly finding what he wanted—a mixing bowl, a jar of mayo, sweet pickle relish, and a can of tuna—and making the maximum amount of noise in the process.

"What's all that racket?" Alma called from the hallway. She peered in through the doorway.

Parr slammed a hand down on the lever of the electric can opener. The whine of metal cutting through metal made his mother jump. "I'm making a sandwich."

"Sounded like you just decided to remodel the kitchen. With a sledgehammer."

Parr dumped the tuna salad ingredients into the mixing bowl and mashed them up aggressively, taking out two slices of bread from the wrapped loaf on the counter.

"Is that a hint?" He gave the walls and flooring a professional glance. "Could use it. Maybe this summer."

"You're too good to me."

Parr cut the sandwich on the diagonal with one swift stroke and put it on a plate. "Want some?" he asked.

"No thanks. Strictly speaking, I'm still on the phone. My friend had to go get something she wanted to read to me."

She left him to his meal. He ate alone, chewing slowly, not interested in what he was eating. Bobby Joe had to be still out there pawing Mary Beth. He wasn't going to look out the window and get accused of checking up on his younger brother.

It was a damn shame that the engagement was on again. But it wasn't Parr's place to say it shouldn't be. He hardly knew who he was when Mary Beth was around him. He hadn't expected her to show up here, but then neither had Alma, obviously. His mother would have mentioned it in advance.

Maybe he should have put his shirt on when Mary Beth came around the corner with that box of bean plants. But it had been hot out there and he'd been unwilling to sweat any harder than he already was sweating. He'd felt the effect of her admiring gaze, had to turn away to hide his reaction, practically pretend he couldn't bang together a cheap kit.

And then Bobby Joe had showed up. Parr rose from the table and fetched himself a cold beer from the fridge, cracking the top off with his thumb.

He hadn't seen the ring. Bobby Joe had probably intended for him to come over, act impressed. Hell of a thing, how sweet Miss Mary Beth was keeping so many jewelers in business.

Parr didn't finish the beer or the sandwich. He cleaned up after himself, fast. He needed to get out of here. On his way out, he bent to give his mother a kiss on the cheek, bumping into the phone receiver stuck to her ear. Her raised eyebrows and avid *mm-hmms* left no doubt that the gabfest was a juicy one. Parr didn't wait for a hug, even though Alma Weston was an expert at talking nonstop and doing anything else you could think of simultaneously.

"Bye," she called after him. But the door was already shut. Parr headed to the truck he'd parked in the garage, out of sight. He had to return it to the builder's supply store where he'd rented it and get the Thunderbird back to the rental place too. Wouldn't be long before he was back in Memphis.

Chapter Seven

"Only the best. I wanted fourteen-karat gold lettering," Bobby Joe said. "With the business name below mine—'Real Estate Investing for Select Clients.' What do you think?"

"It'll be nice when it's done, Bobby Joe."

Mary Beth smiled through the wavy old glass of the front door at Pete Corlear, a local sign painter who still did everything by hand. He was inside, carefully scraping off names in gilt. The attorney who'd once owned the vintage brick building with his long-dead partners had left it to an out-of-state heir. A discreet FOR SALE OR RENT sign was tucked in the corner.

Pete stopped scraping and gave her a wrinkly smile in return before he resumed his meticulous task.

The balmy afternoon air carried the scent of honeysuckle, brought into full bloom by the scorching temperatures during Teacher Days. Tomorrow the schools would reopen and she would be back at work. Right now she was simply enjoying some quiet time with Bobby Joe.

Pretending to write his name on the glass, he underlined it with a flourish. "Robert Joseph Weston. It fits just fine."

The sign painter scraped away on the other side.

The glass reflected the county courthouse right across the street, a proud but somewhat faded relic that was undergoing restoration. Its once white columns supported ornate architecture and protected a statue of blindfolded Justice holding up a scale. It was probably a good thing the statue couldn't see the pigeons sunning themselves at her marble feet. One flew up into the scale and settled there with a flutter of gray wings.

"Can't beat the location." He gestured to Mr. Corlear to let them in and waved her through the open door with a flourish.

The courthouse was still used for civil case trials but that was about it. She wasn't sure what he meant. "You're not an attorney."

"No." Bobby Joe took her elbow and guided her into the next room. "But all the mortgages and deeds and claims and property tax files are going to be moved back here from the new facility out on the highway."

"Are you sure?"

Mary Beth vaguely remembered that truckloads of documents had been transferred to climate-controlled storage in a new facility out on Route 37 when she'd been a kid. The joke had been that a century-old clerk had to be coaxed out of the nursing home to make sense of it all.

Bobby Joe might be overly optimistic about his

chances here. The other storefronts and old offices clustered around the courthouse were beginning to find tenants, but the center of town wasn't a hive of activity.

"Sure as I can be," he said breezily. "There are two upscale boutiques about to open, so it's not like I'm flying solo. We're all going after clients with money."

"Are there that many around here?"

"It'll happen." His confidence wasn't contagious. Mary Beth gave him a dubious look but didn't argue.

"With an office here, I'll know the clerks and county officers and find out useful information ahead of the competition."

"Okay. Go for it then."

Her flat statement made him frown. "I intend to. Connections are everything in real estate."

The cell phone in his jacket pocket chimed. Bobby Joe excused himself to take the call. Mary Beth welcomed the chance to drift through the empty rooms on the lower floor. The echoing coolness was a relief after the sultry day, and the shadowy dimness calmed her. It would be nice if Parr had no claim on her imagination. But every second she had to herself, she thought about him.

Maybe he was in on this deal. Bobby Joe hadn't mentioned it if so.

A bare lightbulb in a ceiling fixture snapped on, breaking her reverie.

Bobby Joe caught up to her and slid his hand through her arm, gesturing with the other one. "Imagine this when it's all fixed up. No more cracked plaster, fresh paint. Mahogany desk there. Maroon leather sofa here."

"I assume you're not buying anything secondhand. So where are you getting all this money?"

They were engaged. She was entitled to ask, even though they hadn't gotten to the planning stage of meshing their personal lives.

"What?" There was a trace of indignation in his voice. "You sound like we're already married."

Mary Beth just looked at him expectantly.

"Baby, if you really have to know, I cleared fifty grand on that house I just flipped."

"There's taxes. There's expenses. Wouldn't it be easier to do business online like you are now?"

"Look, I started out on the Web," he conceded. "And I'm not giving that up. But I want an office too. When your name is on a door in gold letters, you're somebody."

She acknowledged that with no more than a nod.

"Iminga is coming back. I want to be part of that."

Mary Beth hoped so. It was her hometown, after all. But she still had questions about exactly what Bobby Joe was up to. "So . . . how much is the rent?"

"Reasonable. Very reasonable." He had dodged the question. Before Mary Beth could point that out, he dropped a bomb. "Actually, I, uh, made an offer to buy. Still waiting to hear."

Her eyebrows went up. The revelation had the potential to turn into an argument she wasn't in the mood for. But she couldn't let it pass without comment. "Oh. So . . . I guess we'll be living with our folks for a while longer."

"It's worked out so far." Bobby Joe pulled her into a close embrace. "Come on, baby. I'm on the verge of making serious money. Don't fuss and fight. I did this for you. For us."

"That's nice. But it doesn't explain why you never told me one thing about it." She stiffened in his hold and he relaxed his grip on her.

"I thought it would be fun to surprise you, that's all." He took her hand and led her into the hallway. "Here we are. That photo is the first thing I put up. My real estate license will be the second."

A framed photo of her and Bobby Joe hung on a wall that needed painting. It had been taken weeks before the engagement party. Mary Beth was laughing with him, as if she didn't have a care in the world, gazing up adoringly into his handsome face.

Things changed awfully fast sometimes.

"My mother e-mailed it to me last night," he said.

"I remember her taking it." Her answer was soft, almost self-directed. She wouldn't for the world disappoint Alma, who'd been nothing but kind to her, welcoming her into the Weston family as if Mary Beth were the daughter she'd never had. And her dad had been just as grateful for Alma's good-heartedness. However, it was clear to one and all that the widow and widower had formed a bond that went beyond friendship by this point.

Mary Beth pressed her lips together, vowing to ride out this rough patch as best she could. For Alma's sake, if nothing else. Every engaged couple fought, she told herself. Bobby Joe wasn't the first and only man who'd ever strayed on the eve of a lifelong commitment.

And he hadn't strayed that far. Just far enough to get caught and look foolish.

And he was doing the best he could to build a future for both of them. That was what she wanted. Security and stability. If both were first and foremost in his mind, she ought to be grateful.

She turned to him and let him take her in his arms once more. His embrace was warm and comforting.

Bobby Joe pressed a chaste kiss to her lips. She drew back, unsatisfied. His indicating nod puzzled her for a second, until she realized that Pete Corlear was right in the next room, scraping diligently away at the window. "We shouldn't. Not now," Bobby Joe whispered. "Besides, I think I know a better way to make you happy."

He took her outside again. They stood on the sidewalk, reflected in the old window glass. Bobby Joe smiled down at her and took her by the shoulders. "I think it's time you figured out what you want for us."

"What do you mean?"

"You should start thinking about what you want for our wedding registry. I don't know the first thing about tableware or china patterns or cooking sets. That's going to be all up to you."

"Bobby Joe, we haven't even set a date."

He shrugged as he dug into his pocket, removing a wad of cash and peeling off several big bills. "Doesn't matter. Go look around. Buy yourself something nice." He pressed the money into her palm and made her curl her fingers around it. The diamond band he'd given her yesterday sparkled under the streetlight.

"You already went all out on this ring," she said. "It

wasn't necessary." The understandable flash of irritation in his eyes made her add a hasty, "Although I love it."

"Consider it a small token of my affection. Now head out to the mall and have some fun."

"By myself?"

Bobby Joe looked at his watch. "Yes. Sorry. I have another meeting. And I promise you this is the last time I'll go. I'm not going to be at Quinn's beck and call."

Mary Beth stepped away from him. "Tell him I said hi."

"I will," Bobby Joe said firmly. "I want him to feel guilty."

"Good. Someone has to." She sighed. "All right. I'll go look at china."

"I'll walk you to your car," he said. The cell phone in his pocket chimed in but he ignored it this time.

Mary Beth circled the mall lot, looking for a parking space. Judging by the vehicles occupying every available one, the summer sales must have already started. She hadn't even bought anything new for spring.

She pulled in between an SUV and a minivan, reaching for her purse when her cell phone rang.

Somehow she assumed it would be Bobby Joe, checking in to make sure she was taking his advice. "Hi. I'm here."

"And where would that be?" The deep voice that asked the question made her sit up straight.

"The mall. Hello, Parr. What's up?" Keep it casual,

she told herself. *Stay cool, no matter how hot he makes you feel.*

"Just making a duty call. I got the greenhouse done and the bean plants have their own shelf. Mother says you can herd the kids over to collect them anytime."

"Oh, I'll bring the plants back to the school myself. The last thing Alma needs is a bunch of second-graders running around her garden."

"Never a problem. She loves kids. But however you want to do it is fine."

"Okay then. Is that all?" Every word he said in that sexy baritone made her risk lingering on the phone just to hear him talk.

"Nope. She said she has lots of empty flowerpots for when the beans outgrow those plastic cups and for you to just go ahead and help yourself to as many as you need."

Mary Beth switched off the ignition when she realized that she'd left the car running. Even as a disembodied voice, Parr was able to distract her with ease. "That's very nice of her. But if you don't mind my asking, how come you're calling and not her?"

She could just about see him grin. Alma didn't have ulterior motives, but Mary Beth couldn't say the same for Parr. Still, the topic was safe and not remotely flirtatious.

"She took off for a few days. Going to visit a riverboat casino with the gals, I believe."

Something Alma liked to do now and then. Mary Beth's dad, Howard, stayed home, but he always gave Alma fifty dollars for the slots and told her to play for him.

"Sounds like fun." She cleared her throat. "So. Are you back in Memphis?"

"Yes. I have business to attend to. Maybe Bobby Joe told you."

"Nothing specific. He mentioned that there's a big deal in the works."

"That's correct. I'm reviewing the contracts right now. Just wanted to get this call out of the way before I forgot."

His matter-of-fact tone piqued her temper. He had relayed his mother's message with efficient courtesy. As if he hadn't ever kissed her, hadn't caressed her, fully clothed, until she felt naked, hadn't given her a little gift that could cause big trouble for both of them.

She was still wearing the ruby strawberry for reasons she couldn't begin to explain, not even to herself.

"Oh. Well, now you can check it off your list."

"Yup."

"Parr, I really have to get going."

"I won't keep you. Just so you know, I'll be back in Iminga within a week."

"Why?"

"I'm looking forward to seeing you, Strawberry." His velvety voice dropped still lower, sending a quiver through her whole body. "Be good till I get there."

She started to protest, then realized he'd ended the call. Mary Beth stayed in the car, not seeing what was around her, lost in thoughts that verged on anger. Who the hell did Parr Weston think he was? Was he expecting her to swoon backward into his manly arms?

What had happened between them couldn't continue. She had to see to that.

Frowning, she tossed the smartphone into her purse.

* * *

The mall was a cheerful place, brightly lit and filled with strolling shoppers. A few scattered groups of teenagers eyed each other and were watched in turn by security guards. It wasn't the kind of place where they could run wild, though. The customers were mostly families out bargain hunting and couples wandering hand in hand. She saw a few young women like herself who seemed to be there for retail therapy, however they defined it.

Once inside the doors, Mary Beth stopped for a few seconds at the bridal shop that dominated the entrance. Stiffly posed mannequins stood under spotlights in different gowns of lace or satin or silk. Something for everyone, she thought idly. But nothing she liked.

The billowing tulle that draped the window was parted by a sales associate, who peered at her curiously through the display. Mary Beth smiled awkwardly and moved away.

She entered a large department store, pausing for a moment to get her bearings, then headed toward a sign that said TODAY'S KITCHEN. A dazzling array of goods filled the glass-shelved aisles. Idly, she inspected the displays, not ready to choose anything. The decisions to be made were overwhelming in number.

After a while, she began to feel depressed. The silverware patterns and gleaming china were all nice. But the thought of picking out items she would supposedly look at for the rest of her life was getting to her.

The colorful pot-and-pan sets endorsed by celebrity

chefs had even less appeal than the tableware. Mary Beth cringed at the sight of pricey toasters and waffle makers, walking away quickly through an endless array of glasses of different types.

Some other time, maybe. Not now.

She wandered through the clothing department, seeing what was new for summer this year. Mary Beth chose a few items and headed for the dressing room, closing the door and stripping down to her underwear.

White, plain, boring underwear. The same brand and style she'd always worn because . . . well, just because. She'd breezed through the Intimates section on her way in without pausing to look at the bras and panties on beribboned hangers. Maybe she should get dressed again and go back. She could spend Bobby Joe's money on black lace and scarlet satin.

She decided against it, considering he never got lower than the second button from her neck unless she threw herself at him. The few times she'd been brave enough to suggest going further, he'd been skittish. Truth told, she hadn't known whether to feel insulted or relieved.

But she had promised herself to him. Twice. She didn't have to hide the diamond rings he'd given her. Without her willing it, her fingers brushed the chain around her neck and slid down to the ruby. The overhead light made the gold-set pendant glow red. Her body heat had made it warm to the touch after being nestled between her breasts for so many hours.

Mary Beth looked more closely at her reflection. The pendant had marked her skin with a tiny, strawberry-shaped impression, as if Parr Weston had secretly branded her as his own.

After today, she told herself, she would never wear it again. Parr would never know. But she didn't unclasp the fine chain.

Her thoughts raced as she looked at herself, the clothes still on hangers forgotten for the moment. What if Parr ever saw her like this, her nearly nude body captured by his ardent gaze? She already had the feeling he undressed her with his eyes every time they met. And strange to say, she didn't mind. In fact, she craved it, with bad-girl intensity. Just hearing his voice during that brief call had sparked her imagination. Being angry with him only made the flame leap higher.

She collapsed on the small bench provided in the dressing room, giving in to a sensual fantasy of him caressing her elsewhere, anywhere with a door that locked, slipping off her bra straps one by one, taking his time about unhooking the front closure, pleased beyond measure to see his gift to her worn over her heart. Kissing her lips while he fondled her bared breasts, then bending to nip at her arched neck, moving lower to kiss the swelling flesh his large hands cupped so firmly, teasing her peaked, throbbing nipples with expert fingers until he lifted her breasts to his mouth and suckled each in turn. The imagined pleasure was so intense she bit back a moan.

It was only a waking dream. But it was a powerful one that made her ache with forbidden desire. Mary

Beth let her head loll back, willing away the sensual fog that had enveloped her mind. She got dressed again without looking at herself and grabbed the items on hangers.

"How did those fit? I can get you different sizes," a sales associate said brightly.

"Fine. I think I'll take them. But I'm going to look through the racks some more."

"No problem. Take your time. My name is Kim, if you need help with anything."

"Thanks."

An hour or so later, she ended up at the food court, needing a snack after a second go-round with different dressing room mirrors and a couple of summer outfits. The skimpy cuts in style this season showed too much. She'd settled for fitted, scoop neck tees in ice cream colors and a new pair of jeans.

Shopping on Bobby Joe's dime didn't make her feel guilty. He did know a thing or two about female psychology. Besides, there was plenty of money left over. She'd make him take the rest of it back.

She chose a chain with restaurant style service and slid into a table behind a leafy fake tree, ordering from a busy waitress. Mary Beth sipped from her glass of water, grateful for the chance to sit. She bent to the side to get her shopping bags straightened out, looking into them with a feeling of returning happiness. Retail therapy worked, if only temporarily. It had been ages since she'd bought herself clothes as pretty as these.

Her salad was served up in minutes and she dug right in, contemplating the fresh-baked roll that came with a pat of butter on the side. Single-serve sin. Not that she was dieting.

But . . . Mary Beth hesitated, then split the roll with her knife and slathered on the whole pat, spreading it slowly before she took a bite. Mmm.

She'd finished her meal and was chasing a few toasted almond slivers around her salad bowl when a familiar voice stopped her cold.

"Trudy, this'll do." A clatter of paper shopping bags hit the floor as the speaker scraped a chair away from the table in back of Mary Beth. "Hell, do I ever need a drink. Where was I?"

The fake tree rustled as the woman sat down first.

"You're not going to get one here, Luellen," her friend said irritably. "And what I need is a chair. You were telling me about him and his fiancée."

Him being Bobby Joe and *his fiancée* being her. Mary Beth didn't know if she should cover her ears while she waited for the check or just throw down a twenty, pick up her shopping bags, and run. Her back was to the tree. By the rustling, Mary Beth guessed that Luellen was sitting with her back to it as well. Bobby Joe's secret squeeze wasn't the shy type and wouldn't be talking to the leaves.

The friend's voice was louder than Luellen's. But no less unpleasant.

"Let's order," Trudy squawked. "Two Cokes to start."

The unseen twosome hailed a waitress, selected their entrees, and got that over with. Then Luellen got started. "Bobby Joe told me that his fiancée is a little too inexperienced. It was obvious that he was desperate for some female attention."

Mary Beth cringed inwardly.

"Which you were kind enough to provide," Trudy said archly.

"Yes indeedy. In the storage closet." Luellen giggled. "What a place for a rendezvous. Although nothing much happened."

Her friend had nothing to say to that. Mary Beth wondered if Bobby Joe knew Trudy too. What would he think if he knew Luellen was dishing the dirt on their clandestine encounter out in public where anyone could hear?

Mary Beth almost didn't care. She just wanted to get out of the restaurant, but that wasn't possible at the moment. She heard a double thunk of two soft drinks being set down. The other women sucked noisily through straws and refreshed themselves before the gossip really got started. She listened with burning ears. Not all of it was about her.

"So my lawyer said that adultery is still a crime in Mississippi," Luellen said, laughing. "I was amazed. But turns out that he's right."

The second woman rattled the ice in her glass, slurping the last of her Coke. "You mean you can go to jail for what you did?"

"Technically. But since DH—my darling husband— was cheating on me way before we separated and Bobby Joe isn't even married, I don't think it's going to be an issue. Someone would have to sue for

alienation of affections. It's not going to be me,"
Luellen cooed.

"Remind me why you married DH again. Were you
crazy in love or was it just the bulge in those football
britches?"

Luellen leaned back. "That's a protective cup, as if
you didn't know. Basically an optical illusion."

"I never got to investigate. Jocks didn't like me."

"Oh, you did all right, Trudy."

The fake tree rustled as both women laughed. Mary
Beth scooted forward away from them, holding on to
the little table and moving it with her.

"He was hot while it lasted," Luellen said without
much interest. "But between you and me and the lady
in the beauty parlor, I get bored fast."

"No kidding. So now what?"

"We eat."

Mary Beth heard the plates being set down. At some
point, the waitress who'd served her was bound to
notice that she'd finished with her meal and come
over with the check. Unless the other table wasn't her
station.

In self-defense, Mary Beth nibbled on the last
chunk of buttered roll without really eating it. She
could go back to chasing almond slivers. She looked
around without turning around, fixing the location of
the exits in her mind. There really was no way to leave
unseen except by dashing through the restaurant
kitchen.

And Lord forgive her but she had to know what
Luellen would say next about Bobby Joe.

Mary Beth didn't have long to wait. What she heard
filled her with fury.

It took all her willpower to stay and not storm out. But she was damned if she would make a scene. Luellen had seen her cry once already, a memory that made Mary Beth feel deeply ashamed of her weakness. Today, though, Bobby Joe hadn't been the direct cause of her renewed pain.

But once she made her escape, she was going to find him and they were going to talk with a capital T, for what it was worth.

"It's not my fault, baby. I had no idea Luellen was scheming like you say," Bobby Joe insisted. "I haven't seen or talked to her since that night."

He raked a hand through his hair, which had been and was no longer as immaculately groomed as the rest of him when he'd walked into the restaurant that evening. The place was a lot nicer than where she'd eaten lunch. And just look at him. Nice suit, nice shirt, nice tie. And what a nice lie he'd just told. Mary Beth looked daggers at Bobby Joe.

"Can you prove it?"

"Sure. Just look at my smartphone. Not one single call to Luellen, made or received, since our engagement party. Go ahead. Look at it." He dug it out of his pocket and handed it over.

"There are pay phones." Mary Beth waved it away. "Calls can be deleted."

"True, but I never did, because I didn't have to. Hell and damn, Mary Beth, you can look at the bill online. Shows everything. My mobile carrier doesn't delete anything they can charge me for."

She gave an infinitesimal nod. But she didn't take

the phone from his outstretched hand. Bobby Joe gave up and put it back into his pocket.

A moment of angry silence stretched out to more than a minute.

"Are you going to tell me what she said?"

Mary Beth folded her arms across her chest. "I guess I have to." She glared at him. "Feel free to check with her and confirm everything, by the way. I may have missed a line or two of her declaration of undying love."

"Luellen said that?" He stared incredulously at her.

"Not exactly. But words to that effect. Specifically, that she has no intention of giving you up. Which concluded her conversation with some unknown female friend that began with Luellen saying that she gets bored easily."

"Oh no—"

"So." Mary Beth leaned over the table and gave his tie an unfriendly tug that made the knot tighten around his crisp collar. "My guess is that she likes yanking your chain at the very least. What are you going to do when she comes around? Or calls?"

"Tell her the truth. I'm taken. She's history."

Mary Beth let go of his tie. "I wish I could believe that."

Chapter Eight

"I keep forgetting to ask. What did your sister-in-law-to-be think of her birthday gift?"

Gail didn't miss a thing, Parr thought uneasily. Everything looked the same back at the Memphis office but he felt different about being there, away from Mary Beth.

She'd posed the offhand question without looking at Parr as he walked by her desk, keeping her eyes on her computer screen. Her fingers were flying over the keyboard as she inputted cost estimates for the big new project.

For a few seconds, Parr tensed. Then he remembered that he'd asked Gail to wrap the small box and that she hadn't seen what was inside it. "She seemed to like it. It was just a little necklace."

"Oh." Her tone was casual but Parr knew her well enough to sense her curiosity. She had stopped typing but he could see that she was not quite done with the task.

"I thought about looking up their wedding registry, but they're not that far along yet. So I got something nice."

"Isn't jewelry kind of personal?"

"She's family, right? Okay, not yet, not quite," he conceded. "But I couldn't really think of what else to get her. And I didn't want to ask you to pick out something."

"Why not?"

"You have enough to do."

Gail nodded, concentrating on the spreadsheets again. "Whatever. Anyway, if they've only announced the engagement, they can't hit up folks for presents until they send out save-the-date cards for the wedding."

"Is that how it works?" Parr gave an indifferent shrug. "Well, I guess that's next then. Hard to imagine Bobby Joe preferring one china pattern over another. He'll probably leave all that up to her."

Gail hummed tunelessly. "Men usually do. There." She hit save. "That's done. Bottom line looks good. You're going to make a lot of money on this new development."

"Good. I still should get him something to commemorate the engagement." Parr knew that Gail was a catalog fiend. "Any ideas for the man who has everything?"

Including the woman Parr wanted with all his heart and soul. Bobby Joe better not screw up again. But Gail knew nothing of that.

"He seems like the playful type. Would he go for, hmm, something like a Remote Control Indoor Helicopter?"

"Nothing doing. My mother has a world-class collection of china knickknacks."

"How about a Little Black Book Incinerator?"

Parr's dark eyebrows went up. "They have those?"

"For gag gifts, yeah. Saw one somewhere. Although no one has little black books anymore. The incriminating evidence is all on smartphones."

Parr shook his head. "Still, he'd think it was funny."

"But Mary Beth wouldn't," Gail said thoughtfully. "So scratch that idea. Give me time, I'll come up with something." She rose from her swivel chair, smoothing her pencil skirt over her slim hips. The womanly gesture attracted his gaze but only fleetingly. She hadn't done it to turn him on, as far as he could tell.

"All right. Do I have enough frequent-flyer miles to get to Mississippi for free?"

She returned to her desk and pulled up his travel file. "I know, I know. The checks haven't come in and you're not rich yet. Let me see. Yes. You do. How long are you staying this time?"

"A few weeks. The contracts are signed but the demolition at the site will take about that long. So that's a window of opportunity."

Gail narrowed her eyes at him. "To do what?"

"Remodel my mother's kitchen, among other things. I'm going to call around, see if any of the guys want overtime pay to do the job. I could use locals but I prefer a crew I've worked with. Maybe they could drive down in my truck and one of theirs, and I'll fly."

"I'm sure you'll find takers. And while you're gone . . . well, leave me a list of things to do."

"Of course. I trust you."

She twirled in her chair. "I intend to take full advantage of that trust, Parr Weston."

"Yeah?" He shot her an amused look. "Just don't do anything I wouldn't do. And pay the bills as soon as they come in."

"Yes, boss."

Parr was in his pickup truck, balancing a take-out cheeseburger on the dashboard to pick up a call with a Mississippi area code.

"Mom. I was just eating."

"Hope it's a balanced meal."

He almost laughed out loud. "As a matter of fact, it is. But never mind that. How are you?"

"I'm all right."

They exchanged small talk long enough for the cheese on the burger to congeal. Parr sensed that his mother wasn't ready to divulge the real reason for the call, but he wasn't impatient. Finally she stopped and took a breath.

"Are you really coming down here?"

"Of course. You have my flight information, right?"

"Yes, I got the e-mail. But, Parr—"

"What?" He selected a french fry and bit off the end. Stone cold. Oh well.

"Look, I'll be straight with you. I certainly appreciate your offer to redo the kitchen, but can we postpone it for now?"

"Took a lot of money to convince my best guys to travel to Iminga. Exactly how long do you want to put it on hold?"

"Just for a few days," Alma hastened to say. "I cleaned it out beforehand just like you asked me to. So they could get started. But something's happened. And it may need your full attention."

Parr groaned under his breath. He propped the cell phone between his shoulder and ear while he collected the fast food to throw it out when this unwelcome call was over.

"What did Bobby Joe do now? I almost don't want to know."

She rattled on. "He and Mary Beth had a fight about something. They're not speaking."

"Whatever happened, they have to figure it out for themselves. I can't interfere."

"I know. But couldn't you just talk to him? Find out what's going on?"

"If they aren't sharing the details, then let it alone."

His blunt advice kept her from going on and on about it. Parr meant every word. Especially since he was thinking that Bobby Joe might have asked some questions about Mary Beth's new necklace, if he'd happened to see it.

Yet she'd kept it hidden. Parr had gathered that her sexual relationship with his brother wasn't all that intense. It didn't seem likely that Bobby Joe had ripped off her blouse during fun and games. No, Parr thought sourly. Bobby Joe saved that for other men's wives, not his beautiful fiancée. Still, she might have been caught unawares. But Mary Beth wouldn't have blurted out the truth: that Parr had given her the ruby strawberry as a memento of an affair that wasn't going to happen, motivated by feelings he couldn't allow himself to have.

Gail hadn't been wrong when she'd characterized

the gift of jewelry as personal. But she had no idea of its deeper meaning and never would.

Hell. Even though he was deflecting Alma's concerns, Parr knew he had to get back home sooner rather than later.

He ended the conversation with his mother on a lighter note as he rolled out of the take-out place, on his way home.

Alma quietly replaced the receiver and turned to Howard, who was reading the newspaper in an easy chair.

"Parr says to leave them alone."

"He's right." Howard carefully folded the sports section for later reading and set the newspaper aside. "You have to butt out, Alma, if you don't mind my saying so."

"I want this to work for Bobby Joe. He needs Mary Beth. It's time for him to settle down."

"Hmm. Seems to me you ought to be saying that about Parr. He's older."

Alma made a face at him. "And tougher than Bobby Joe, by a lot. I never could boss him around. But I wish he'd find someone too."

Howard rose from the chair and came over to where she stood by the window, resting his hands on her shoulders. "Didn't you say Parr had more female attention than he knew what to do with?"

"Goodness, yes. He kept all that so quiet though. He only ever brought one or two around, and both those girls married other guys ages ago."

Howard turned her around to face him and tapped the tip of her nose. "Keep out of it."

Alma heaved a huge sigh. "I guess when he finds someone with lifetime potential, I'll be introduced. But I just don't know. He's more the type to elope and show up with a brand new bride."

"Everyone's different."

Alma leaned against Howard's comfortably broad chest. "Parr is that. Never had to show off like Bobby Joe. He was always trying to outshine his older brother."

"They're grown up now, Alma." He stroked her hair. "Consider yourself lucky to have two such fine sons."

Parr seemed more solid than Bobby Joe, to be sure. But the older Weston brother was somewhat of a cipher. And Howard still had reservations about the younger one, but it didn't seem like the time to share any of that.

"I know, I know," she said wistfully. "But you would tell me if there was anything seriously wrong between Mary Beth and Bobby Joe, wouldn't you?"

"My daughter hasn't said a word to me on the subject. Don't go making something out of nothing."

Alma grumbled a little but she gave in, returning his hug.

"There's much more important things to think about," Howard said. "Your niece Eve is about to have her baby, for one."

Alma grinned. "Just in time too. Spring's about over. She's lucky." She poked Howard's round middle. "You men don't know what it's like to be pregnant in the summer."

"That's true. Now quit worrying. Go crochet some itty-bitty booties and let us men be."

Alma laughed good and loud. "Never."

"So this is your new headquarters. Nice." Parr wasn't sure the space quite fit the definition, what with it needing so much work before it could be used as an office or anything else. But he wanted to get on Bobby Joe's good side. Now that he was back in Iminga, why wait? Might give him an advantage when it came to getting the real story of the fresh quarrel with Mary Beth.

His younger brother stayed ahead of him, pointing out the fine old woodwork and high ceilings, and where furniture could be placed over sagging floorboards.

"Gotta get those shored up," he said nonchalantly, as if such a complicated repair could be done with a hammer and a few nails. "And the walls replastered and the ceiling cracks smoothed out—shoot. You name it, it needs fixing. Plus old wiring and antique plumbing and all that to deal with too. Gets expensive. But I don't have to tell you that."

"No." Parr's expertise told him what the renovation would cost. A lot.

"Going to be worth every penny, though," Bobby Joe said. "They don't build 'em like this anymore. I want to be able to make the right impression on the right people."

"Are you up for this kind of commitment? You were doing all right without any office at all."

Bobby Joe stuck his hands in his pants pockets and paced nervously. "I guess. Flipping houses made me money but it's not what I see myself doing for the rest of my life."

Interesting comment, considering he still hadn't repaid the thousands of dollars Parr had staked him. Or even mentioned it.

"You know best." Parr moved to a window whose deep, low sill was wide enough to sit on. The sunlight pouring in felt good against his back. He clasped his hands together and rested his arms on his knees, leaning forward.

"Which brings me to the big question," Bobby Joe said.

Parr's dark gaze followed him as he paced. When his brother didn't look directly at him, he took that as a warning.

"Ask away," Parr said quietly.

"I gotta borrow more money."

That wasn't a question. More like a statement.

"I'll have to look over my finances. I'm not sure I'll be able to help you right now."

Bobby Joe's jaw set in a hard line. "Why not?"

Parr gave a low laugh. "Listen, Bobby Joe. You don't get to question how I run my business or if I can swing a personal loan for you out of my cash reserve. If you need money, it's going to be the other way around. Full disclosure."

"We're brothers. Don't you trust me?"

"Business is business. You'd do well to remember that."

Bobby Joe's face showed his anger. Parr kept a lid

on his—just barely. He should have known that he was going to be hit up for major money the second he saw the gold lettering and fancy script that spelled out his brother's full name on the window glass.

There were other reasons he didn't want to fight about this. Not here and not now, anyway. He rose and looked into the next room. "Can we continue the tour?" Parr asked. "I haven't seen the second floor."

"Sure," Bobby snapped. "It's the same layout as the ground floor, but why not. I know you're thorough."

Parr followed him into the hall, staying calm. "Maybe you could rent out some of the space to bring in extra income, while you get yourself to the next level."

"Yeah. I could do that. Excuse me." Bobby Joe headed for a door all the way down the hall and closed it behind him. Parr could just make out the word GENTLEMEN on the old wood.

He strayed into a connecting hall and stopped cold in front of a photo of Mary Beth and Bobby Joe, framed on the wall. She looked blissfully happy, her eyes lit up with adoration as she looked up at Bobby Joe.

The sight made Parr's heart stop for a second. How long ago had that been taken? There were leafless trees behind the couple, so maybe in January or February. Something clicked in his mind. It had probably been Valentine's Day. That could be a red card in her hand—the lower part of the photo was blurred. And she was wearing a lace blouse.

Parr turned away. Their happiness seemed genuine. He hadn't known the first thing about her then. And now, even after all that had gone down, he knew he had no right whatsoever to come between them.

His brother returned from the end of the hall, banging the door. Parr snapped out of it.

"What's the matter with you?" Bobby Joe asked irritably. "You look like you've seen a ghost. As far as I know, the building doesn't have any."

"Just thinking."

Bobby Joe took the stairs two at a time, as if he was eager for this meeting to be over with. "Okay. Second floor." He gestured to every room from where he stood on the landing. "Like I said, pretty much the same. Want to go up?"

"There's more?"

"Yeah." Bobby Joe went up the last staircase. "A couple of small offices."

Parr entered the first one behind his brother. The room was small but nicely proportioned, with an old-fashioned skylight for illumination. Across its glass fell shadows of scaffolding.

"Is someone fixing the roof?" Parr asked.

"No. That's in decent shape. I asked Pete Corlear to do a bigger sign for me and he set up a rig to hang on to when he installs it."

"So the gold lettering isn't enough," Parr said dryly. "Mind if I ask how much all this is costing?"

"I paid him in advance, Parr. No sign, no business. People won't know I'm here without one on top of the building."

"If you say so." Parr walked around the room and looked out the window, spotting the sign painter's truck. The older man was in the cab, organizing his tools. He looked about ready to leave.

"I was thinking maybe Mary Beth would want this space," Bobby Joe continued. "As it is now, she drives from school to school. She would make more as an educational consultant and this could be her office."

"Nice idea. Is it hers?"

Bobby Joe shot him a sarcastic smile. "No. Mine. I haven't suggested it to her yet. But we have to start saving for a down payment."

"Oh. So you actually aren't doing that well."

His younger brother's quick temper flared again. "I'm sorry I ever asked you for money, ever. Just forget it, Parr."

"You signed a promissory note to repay my loan within a year." His brother could consider himself reminded. "And now you're asking for a second. That's not how it's done."

Parr wouldn't be doing Bobby Joe any favors if he let him slide.

"Didn't you just close some great big deal? You must be rolling in dough."

"I put in the winning bid for a new office complex outside Memphis. But no one's showed up with wheelbarrows full of cash yet. Takes a while. You know that. Anyway, that is a done deal. What you have here is nine-tenths imagination and one-tenth obligation."

"What's that supposed to mean?"

"Get your cash flow going on your own. I'm not bankrolling you this time."

"What if I pay you what I owe?"

"No. It's painfully clear that you can't unless you

borrow from someone else to do it. I can wait. I just wanted to make sure that you hadn't forgotten."

Parr sure as hell hoped that Mary Beth found out about Bobby's freewheeling approach to finance. She could end up bankrupt and broke before she saw it coming. However—Parr silently gritted his teeth—he couldn't tattle on his brother.

"Great," Bobby Joe snarled. "Just great. I'm trying to get ahead and you get in my way."

Parr had had enough. "Getting into debt is what you're talking about, not getting ahead. And how come you always have to do that on someone else's dime?"

Bobby Joe bristled and took a step toward his big brother. The warning fire in Parr's dark eyes was enough to make him think twice. Bobby Joe stood in the middle of the empty office, clenching his hands.

"We're not going to fight, Bobby Joe," Parr said finally. "At least not with fists. But I think you owe Mary Beth an explanation."

"Leave her out of this!"

Parr shook his head. "Sorry. This must be—"

"What?"

"Mother said you two weren't speaking to each other."

"She's wrong."

Parr studied his brother's expression. He did know when Bobby Joe was lying as a general rule. This would be, in his estimation, one of those times.

"What's going on? You didn't—"

"I don't have to tell you a damn thing. You think

you're in charge of the Westons and me most of all, but you're not."

"I wouldn't say I was in charge. I'm just trying to keep the family together. That seems to be dead last on your list of priorities."

Bobby Joe, stoked with anger, crossed the short distance between them and pushed his brother in the chest. Parr stood strong, not retaliating, unmoving as a statue.

"Goddamn it, Parr, you're the one who broke this family and you know it!"

"You're wrong." A muscle ticked in Parr's resolute jaw. "That was long ago and you never remembered it right in the first place."

"Doesn't matter how many years ago it was, brother." Bobby Joe's voice scaled up with frustrated rage into a near scream. "You know what you did!"

Bobby Joe never had fought fair. But Parr felt no obligation to defend himself. His younger brother *was* wrong—completely wrong. But there was no undoing the horror and shock of the day his father had died, shot by a jealous stranger. The memory never went away, and the rift between the Weston brothers had never truly healed.

Yet their mother had forgiven him. Bobby Joe never had.

Parr straightened his spine and began to walk out of the room.

Bobby Joe clutched at his arm. "Where are you going?"

"Out. I'm done with you," Parr said. "But here's some more unwanted advice. The stronger man knows when not to fight."

"Oh yeah?" Bobby Joe jeered. "You used to knock me around plenty when we were kids. I swore I'd do the same to you someday."

"Don't even try to hit me. I'll finish what you start and you know it," Parr said ominously. "And by the way, you'd better be good to Mary Beth."

"You going to talk to her?"

"I'm not talking to anyone. About anything. The war's over."

Bobby Joe rushed out after him as Parr went swiftly down the stairs. "Is it?" he called. "So who won?"

Parr had reached the first floor. "Not the truth."

Chapter Nine

"Can't we just kiss and make up?"

"That didn't work too well the last time we tried it." Mary Beth's voice was controlled and calm, but inside—hell. If she gave vent to what she was truly feeling, she'd break the car windows.

He turned the ignition key in the parked car and found some forgettable music, humming along to it while she seethed.

How could he still be so casual about what she'd overheard? His take on the situation hadn't changed. He'd explained over and over that Luellen would say and do anything to get attention. Which might be true, but it didn't answer a whole lot of burning questions. Such as why Luellen had used the word *rendezvous*, which implied a certain amount of planning on both sides. The encounter hadn't been all that impulsive. Mary Beth knew far more than she wanted to know about it at this point, thanks to Luellen's big mouth. But Bobby Joe had continued to stonewall.

"I did my best, baby. And you know I only want the best for you." Bobby Joe sighed. "Don't you?"

He stroked her hair and let his hand drift to the nape of her neck, rubbing it. The halfhearted attempt at a soothing massage only made her more tense.

Her reply caught in her throat when his fingers traced the chain that held the hidden pendant. His mind was elsewhere—most likely on his guilty memories, she thought with renewed anger. She knew how contrary Bobby Joe could be. If she told him to stop what he was doing, he'd only keep on.

He tugged gently at the delicate chain, as if he had hit upon something that might distract her. Mary Beth stayed motionless, frozen with sudden fear.

In a few moments the ruby strawberry dangled from his finger, glowing red in the light from the street lamp, still attached to the chain. "Pretty," he said absently. "Is that new?"

"I've had it a while." She slid the necklace from his finger and dropped it back inside her blouse. "It was a gift."

"I don't remember ever seeing it." His tone was indifferent. Maybe she could finesse this.

Mary Beth shrugged uncomfortably. "I don't wear it often."

Her other responses were only evasions, but that was an outright lie. Since Parr had given it to her, she wore it every day.

Bobby Joe pulled his hand away and rested it on the steering wheel, drumming with his fingers. Then he laughed under his breath, not with amusement. "Guess I'm supposed to ask questions, right?"

"What for?"

"You're being so cagey, Mary Beth. That's not like you."

"Bobby Joe, I'm beginning to think you don't know me at all—"

He interrupted her by snapping off the radio before she could brazen it out. She had to. Bobby Joe was immature but he wasn't stupid. If he eventually guessed that Parr was the giver, the brothers would be at each other's throats.

"That works both ways, doesn't it? Now, if it was a gift, go ahead and tell me who gave it to you. We have to be honest with each other."

Stinging tears filled her eyes. She brushed them away before he turned his head to look at her. "Let's just drop it," she said.

He let go of the steering wheel and placed his hand on her thigh, caressing her through her jeans. Mary Beth shifted in the passenger seat but she couldn't escape his unwelcome touch.

"Poor you," he murmured. "Still a virgin. You can't cheat. The whole idea is ridiculous."

She wasn't sure if he was being solicitous or sarcastic. Mary Beth took a deep breath and let it out slowly. "Bobby Joe, we can't go on like this."

He used the button to recline his seat slightly. "I get the feeling I'm in for a lecture. Like what?"

"I'll keep it short," she said tartly. "I mean like being so suspicious of each other. Fighting over things we can't resolve. Alma's so worried about us. And I'm worried about her."

"Leave my mother to me," he said in a dull voice

that nonetheless held a trace of genuine concern. "I'll talk to her."

"That's better than nothing. But it still doesn't fix the fact that you and I aren't getting along, Bobby Joe."

"What exactly do you want me to do?"

"Tell the truth." She bit her lip, knowing what he didn't: that she no longer had the moral right to make the demand. But she was bent on protecting Parr at all costs.

"I generally do." He wouldn't look at her.

Bobby Joe seemed to have lost interest in whatever she'd been up to for the moment. That right there was a sign, one she didn't quite want to acknowledge. If they were going to end the engagement, she clung to the idea that they should do so as honorably as possible, for a reason that would be understood and accepted by all.

If that happened—and they sure seemed to be heading in that direction—she would be free. But the thought didn't cheer her. If and when she and Bobby Joe split up a second time, she couldn't be with Parr.

"Can we get this over with?"

"I just want to know one thing once and for all, and then I'll never ask you again."

Bobby Joe coughed. "I'm holding you to that. Fire away."

"Are you still seeing Luellen?"

"No. For the last time, whatever you overheard was her fantasy."

Mary Beth fell silent. She'd asked to meet him here tonight in the empty parking lot near his new office because she'd sensed something different about him after her disastrous day at the mall. She could not, for the life of her, define it precisely. There was no way she could get him to admit fault a second time or trick him into revealing more.

But an odd, purely female instinct told her that something was going on in his life. She'd never admit to him that she'd snooped when she could, finding no clues whatsoever in the call log on his phone or anywhere in his room at the Weston house. Mary Beth had replaced the phone exactly where he'd left it and gone through his things looking for—she didn't know what. He wouldn't leave incriminating items around for his mother to find.

It was more the way he acted. Cool and careless. The same overconfidence that had her nerves on edge after he'd showed her the office building had intensified.

Why? Was he getting what he needed elsewhere? Mary Beth thought ruefully that she was far from the ideal fiancée. Another thought occurred to her. His rakish good looks seemed a little frayed around the edges, like he wasn't getting enough sleep. She didn't dare ask Alma when he came in at night.

"I want to believe you, Bobby Joe," she began.

"But you don't. Go ahead and play detective."

She studied his profile. He was handsome to a fault and always would be. Cocky too, but that might fade as he got older. There was something weak in Bobby Joe that she hadn't fully understood before. She could no longer ignore the fact that he was incredibly unsure of who he was and who he wanted to be. It was ironic

that she tended to think of herself in the same terms—
or did. But she had changed a lot in the last weeks.

"I'd rather not do that, Bobby Joe. In fact, I wish we
weren't having this conversation."

He shot her a sidelong look. "Me neither. But if talking can keep this engagement going, then let's talk."

Bobby Joe's reluctance was so obvious that Mary
Beth couldn't help her next question.

"Do you mind if I ask why you want to keep it going?"

He answered quickly and a little irritably. "Because
I want to marry you, Mary Beth. It's the logical next
step in my life. I want us to have a fine home and children and all the good things in life." He spoke as if
he'd rehearsed the words, wrapping up with what
seemed to be an afterthought. "And I love you, don't
forget that."

You almost did. Just in time she stopped herself from
blurting out the comment.

The conversation was going downhill. His sullen silence conveyed a very different message from his carefully delivered speech.

If only the Westons and Caines didn't know each
other and didn't live in the same town. If only the extended family hadn't reached out to her and made her
feel immediately as if she was one of them. If only
Parr, the wild card in this confusing game, hadn't
made advances that left her dizzy with desire . . .

Mary Beth forced her thoughts away from her
overwhelming memories of him: the sheer physical
power of his presence, the brooding darkness of his
eyes, the skilled lovemaking of an experienced man

who seemed to understand precisely what she craved most—and gave it to her.

No. That had to end. She would not and could not be so influenced by emotion, not when the happiness of others depended on her eventual decision.

"So? What now?" Bobby Joe asked.

She blurted out the first thing that came to her mind. "Maybe we should separate for a few weeks."

Bobby Joe clutched the steering wheel with a taut-knuckled grip while she waited anxiously for his reply. It wasn't long in coming.

"That won't solve a goddamn thing," he muttered. "Unless you've already made up your mind that you want out."

"No." Mary Beth stared out the window into the surrounding blackness. "I haven't."

Alma stood at the kitchen sink, rinsing the scrubbed dishes and handing them to Howard, who dried and polished them with a tea towel.

"It's kinda fun doing them the old-fashioned way," he said.

Alma hmphed. "That's because there were only two of us eatin' dinner."

Howard stacked the clean plates and put them in a cupboard. "Which was excellent. Thank you again."

"You can cook next time. Heard you know how."

"Did Mary Beth tell you that?"

"As a matter of fact, she did. She's proud of your housekeeping accomplishments."

Howard gave a slight sigh. "Learned the hard way. I was all she had, growing up."

Alma leaned back against the counter, smoothing her apron for a moment. "How come you never remarried, Howard?"

The older man took a few steps to stand right in front of her. He took her in a loose embrace and pressed a kiss to her forehead. "Because you weren't available."

That left a lot unsaid as to why. But he knew a fair amount about the scandal that had shattered the Weston family and still haunted her sons. He and Alma were fine with keeping the past in the past.

Alma lifted her rounded arms and draped them over his shoulders. "I am now," she said with a mischievous gleam in her eye.

Howard laughed and chucked her under the chin. "Aren't you supposed to be meeting Bobby Joe in a bit?"

She nodded. "Yes. He went out with Mary Beth. Sure hope they're getting along better than they were."

"What does he say?"

Alma mimicked her son's breezy tone. "Everything's fine."

"Is it?"

She leaned away from him. Howard rested his hands on the counter edge behind her, still keeping her within his arms.

"I do wonder, Howard," she said quietly. "But I won't pry. Young folks need to work things out on their own. They just don't seem to appreciate all our hard-earned wisdom." The joke fell a little flat. "Does Mary Beth confide in you?"

"Sometimes. Not recently. Maybe I shouldn't ask." He straightened, letting her step away from the sink area. "I do have an interest in the outcome. It's a tricky situation, with them being engaged and all, now that you and I have decided to keep company."

"Mm-hm. It sure is. But Bobby Joe doesn't seem inclined to confide in me." Alma moved to the table, wiping the already clean surface with a dish towel until it shone.

"That's his prerogative," Howard said. "And I hope that everything is, as he says, basically fine."

"Unless he's lying to me," Alma said with characteristic bluntness.

"Would he do that?"

"All children lie to their mothers." She took the trouble to neaten up the paper napkins in the holder until all the corners came to the same point.

Howard took one of the vinyl-upholstered seats around the dinette, resting his hand on the table. "He's not a child, Alma. Bobby Joe's a grown man. You have to let go."

Alma flicked the dish towel in his direction, which Howard dodged. "Did I ask for your advice?"

"No. But you know I meant well." He pulled her down into his lap.

"Oh, Howard." She ruffled his salt-and-pepper hair. "I don't worry about him lying to me. I wouldn't be much of a mom if I couldn't figure that out for myself in a hot minute."

"So what are you worried about?"

"That he's lying to himself. Pretending everything's fine when he knows it isn't."

The older couple stopped their gentle teasing and contemplated that possibility.

"I suppose Mary Beth might do the same thing," Howard said resignedly. "Wouldn't want her to spare me the knowledge out of respect for my feelings. But I'll know, same as you. Let's cross that bridge when we get to it."

"Deal. Shake on it."

Howard gave her a reassuring hug instead and Alma settled her head against his shoulder. He took hold of one of her apron ties and pulled out the bow, holding the apron up for a second before he gave it to her.

"Did this come from a yard sale?"

"Of course. My entire collection does."

"And how many do you have?"

She pondered the question as if the answer were extremely important. "Seventeen so far. If I spot a vintage apron with two pockets and lots of rickrack, I just have to have it."

"I guess I know what to get you for Christmas."

She poked him in the chest, her expression indignant. "Howard Caine, you can do better than that."

"Don't you know when I'm ribbing you?" He gave her another squeeze. "Now that's the last hug. You have to meet up with Bobby Joe. Is that him honking outside?"

Alma swore long and colorfully. "Better not be. I didn't raise him to be rude."

Howard eased her off his lap and got up to go to

the window. "Nope. Whoever it was kept on driving."
He closed the curtain. "Go get ready. I'll be right here
waiting for you when you come back."

The country road had no lights. Alma hung on to
the strap of her seat belt as if her life depended on it.
"Bobby Joe, please! You're going way too fast."

"Nobody else out here."

"Slow down. I mean it."

Frowning, knowing she couldn't see his expression,
he obeyed his mother nonetheless.

"That better?"

Alma let out the breath she'd been holding and
looked over at the speedometer. "Forty-five is still ten
miles over the speed limit."

He shrugged. "You wanted to get out of town."

"Bobby Joe, don't get carried away. All I said was
that I didn't want to be overheard at some local place.
Iminga isn't as small as it used to be, but plenty of
people know us both."

"I could pull over around here. We can talk in the
car."

"Keep going." They were definitely out in the
boonies. After passing the tiny gas station and its attached convenience market several miles back, Alma
hadn't seen a single house. Huge live oaks spread their
branches over the road, draped with moss that offered
only intermittent peeks of the full moon above.

He sped up again. Alma braced herself against the
dashboard with one hand.

"What's gotten into you?"

Bobby Joe didn't answer for another half mile. "Guess I'm just restless."

"Any particular reason?" Alma dreaded what he might say.

"Mary Beth and I aren't getting along."

She'd suspected as much. But now that he'd been unexpectedly honest, he slowed down even more, which was a blessing.

"Well, that's normal enough," she said firmly. "Being engaged isn't all hearts and flowers."

"Tell me about it," he muttered.

"I can't take sides, Bobby Joe. But I'm here. I'll listen."

"It's complicated. I don't want to discuss it while I'm driving." The road widened and a sign for an exit that would take them to the highway appeared on the right.

"Fair enough."

"There's an okay restaurant over the county line. All booths. They leave you alone."

If that was the restaurant's only claim to fame, that was good enough for Alma. She just wanted to get out of the car.

"All right. I ate with Howard but we didn't have dessert. I could have decaf coffee and pie. How about you?"

"Haven't decided." Bobby Joe got the car up to highway speed well before the merge, pressing his foot down on the accelerator so hard that his mother lurched forward in her seat before the seat belt caught and held her.

"Was that necessary?" Alma glanced worriedly over

at her son. The glaring illumination of the highway made his eyes glitter. Unless it wasn't the lights doing that. "Are you on something?"

"Nope."

"You drive like the devil's after you."

"I'm going as fast as everyone else," he defended himself.

"But—" A sixteen-wheeler rumbled by on the left, blasting a warning that made Alma jump. "Oh, sweet Jesus."

"What?"

"As if you didn't know. That damn horn scared me half to death."

"At least it wasn't my driving."

"If you get pulled over, don't say I didn't warn you," she said acidly. "Can we go a different way? Is there an access road or something?"

"Don't think so." Bobby Joe almost looked like he was enjoying himself.

A customized pickup appeared in the passenger-side mirror, catching up with them fast on huge, jacked-up tires, its front grille gleaming like monster teeth. "Bobby Joe! Someone's tryin' to pass on the right!"

He swerved into the left lane seconds before the pickup thundered past, belching exhaust from double mufflers.

"I hate those fancy trucks, driving like they own the road! But everybody's driving crazy tonight," Alma wailed. "What in hell is going on?"

"It's Friday and it's the start of a four-day weekend," her son pointed out. "Everyone's getting out of town.

Calm down." He turned to smile at her, his eyes not on the road, not seeing the beginning of a sharp curve ahead.

But Alma did. A little too late. "Look out!"

Metal screamed and tore open as the car slid into the guardrail and bounced off, spinning around, glass flying everywhere. Sparks shot out in jagged plumes, scorching the asphalt, melting it as the car slowed and crashed into the divider again, rocking on shredded tires. Other vehicles skidded to a stop just inches from the horrific crash. Black smoke rose and drifted, invisible against the night.

Parr left his car at the far side of the graveled area by the bridge, ignoring the other vehicles parked a little distance away. The occupants hadn't come out here to enjoy the soft air of early summer or catch the scent of honeysuckle on the breeze wafting over the country river. Back in the day, he'd done the same, romancing one girl after another behind the rolled-up windows of his first car, taking full advantage of the only privacy to be found in a small town.

Tonight all he wanted was to be alone.

The bridge was seldom used, intended mainly for farm vehicles, but it did have a pedestrian walkway. He'd figured that out on the long-ago night his date ditched him here, getting back into her own car and driving off in a huff about something he couldn't remember. Funny that he couldn't remember her face or name either.

But every now and again, he came back to the bridge just to think.

Brilliant moonlight shimmered on the dark, flowing water, beckoning him onward. Parr entered the walkway, continuing for several minutes until he stopped at the middle of the bridge where the river widened and deepened into deceptive calmness. There was still a powerful current below the surface. He leaned on the rail, looking out and up.

The full moon was enormous, hanging low in the sky, its unearthly glow revealing flat fields that stretched for miles. The silvery landscape was drained of color, except for dots of amber high atop the light poles of the highway in the near distance. The roar of traffic was barely audible. If not for the way sound carried over water, Parr wouldn't have been able to hear it at all.

Thoughts of Mary Beth preoccupied him, above all, the unspoken plea in her gaze—*take me, take me away*—that she never voiced. He'd forced himself to resist going further every time he gazed into her long-lashed eyes. Holding her close was sensual torture. Her every innocent move put him in mind of other, far more carnal temptations, although he doubted Mary Beth was doing that on purpose. She probably didn't realize just how gorgeous she really was. Those lips, luscious and tender as sweet berries, and the silken, fire gold hair that he'd run his fingers through, and that curving body, alive with barely touched sexuality—it all dazzled him. Under those prim blouses and neat buttons in a row, there was another Mary Beth. He sensed her desire, not only for physical release that his brother wouldn't or couldn't give her, but for freedom to escape.

Parr wanted to shower her with the love she deserved, awaken her to the erotic joys his deepest male instincts told him she was capable of.

That was a dream that would never come true.

She wasn't his. He couldn't claim her for his own, even if his brother abandoned her. Not without fracturing the family a second time, an unconscionable thought for Parr. The Westons—his mother, brother, and himself—had found a measure of peace, but it had taken years.

He'd forged himself a good enough life, succeeded in his business, and had more than his share of fine women. Parr had always made sure they enjoyed themselves to the max. Admittedly, on his terms: no commitments. No drama. Just mutual pleasure and affectionate farewells.

Until Mary Beth happened. If he couldn't get her out of his mind, he had to stay out of her life. He wouldn't remain in Iminga a minute longer than it would take to complete the renovations for his mother's house. That was how it had to be. And it wouldn't be wise to explain too much to Mary Beth.

But Lord, how he ached to have her near him again, secure in his arms. To kiss her angel face once more, for the last time. The words he could never say to her echoed in his thoughts. *I love you, Mary Beth.*

The faint thin shriek of a siren reached him. He could just see the flashing top lights of an ambulance making its way through invisible cars on the distant highway. Then there was another. And another. The three emergency vehicles stopped in the same spot. Their rotating lights were bright red against the dark sky. The sirens cut off.

The accident had to have been a bad one—he'd volunteered as a first responder himself in college—but he had no way to tell precisely how bad from where he was. He hoped there were survivors. Parr turned and walked back to his car.

Bobby Joe slumped over the steering wheel, not knowing that Alma was beside him, limp as a rag doll and covered in blood. They didn't see the people who were brave enough to run to the wreck, or the flares that were quickly set around it. They were injured, deafened, in shock and in pain. Mother and son floated in and out of consciousness, struggling to breathe.

"Ma'am? Ma'am?" A smoke-streaked face peered into the shattered window. Alma groaned faintly. "She's alive."

Urgent voices faded in and out. "For now."

"What about him?"

"Steering wheel's got him trapped."

"He can't feel it. Looks like he's out cold."

"Help on the way?"

"Called, yeah."

"Here they come."

"Jesus. Can they get through?"

"Hope so. That guy may not make it."

Chapter Ten

Parr bulldozed through the swinging doors marked NO ENTRY as soon as he figured out that Mary Beth was on the other side of them. He spotted her in an empty evaluation room, just sitting there, her head against the wall and her eyes closed.

The sheets on the bed had been dragged from the corners of the mattress and left bunched in the middle for removal. There were splotches of blood in the folds.

"Jesus. Where are they? I got here as soon as I could."

Tears coursed down her cheeks in a slow trickle. She seemed not to have heard him. He put his hands on her shoulders, rousing her. "Mary Beth."

"Huh?"

"Are they in surgery?"

She collected herself, looking dazed. "No. I don't think so. The trauma team had to stabilize them—it was crazy. They wouldn't let me see Bobby Joe. Your mother was in this room. I stayed with her until they took her away."

"Was she conscious?"

"Yes. And able to talk. She may have broken her spine. She couldn't feel her legs. But apparently she's better off than Bobby Joe. He was in the next room. I only know what I could hear through the walls."

The late hour and start of the weekend had filled the ER to capacity. Moans and drunken yells were audible. Some had to be suffering in silence. The others made up for it.

A brawny male nurse walked by fast and stopped in his tracks when he saw Parr. "My friend, I don't know who you are, but you can't just blow past the admitting desk and roam around this hospital."

"Gee whiz. I didn't sign the clipboard. Sorry about that."

Parr's sarcasm could be a prelude to a totally irrational fight. Mary Beth intervened.

"It's all right, Wayne. He was looking for me. He's Alma Weston's son and Bobby Joe's older brother."

The nurse sized up Parr. "Oh. I didn't know. Mr. Weston, until your mother and brother are admitted to their rooms and the attending doctors give the okay for visitors, this is as far as you go. Do you understand that?"

"Yes," Parr growled.

The brawny nurse ignored his belligerence, looking to Mary Beth as if he assumed she could control Parr.

"Miss Caine, I'll be back as soon as I know more about your fiancé. Mr. Weston, I can tell you right now that your mother is scheduled for a CAT scan immediately."

"Thank you. And hey. Next time I'll sign." Parr sucked it up and apologized to the nurse.

"Do that. The rules are for everyone's safety. We get a lot of crazy people in here, especially on Friday nights."

"I understand," he muttered. The man left them alone.

Parr sat down next to Mary Beth, enfolding her hand in his. He had to be devastated, but she could feel the same warm strength flowing from him that she'd sensed from the beginning. Her fear lessened, but it didn't go away entirely.

"Was Bobby Joe drunk?" Parr asked bluntly.

"Alma swore he wasn't."

"She's his mother. *Our* mother. If she got hurt because he was careless—"

"It's not like he made a statement. The cops were here but the doctors wouldn't let them get near him. He came in unconscious."

"Must have been chaos."

She nodded wearily. "It was. I did hear someone say his blood alcohol level was normal. That's not the issue, Parr. He has a head injury. A bad one. Apparently there's no telling at this point how bad it is."

Parr swore viciously and got up to pace, too upset to sit. She thought for a moment that he might punch the wall.

"Don't take it out on the hospital," she said quietly. "They're doing everything they can."

"Yeah? How do you know that?"

Still reeling inwardly from shock, Mary Beth thought to herself that for Parr Weston, fear equaled rage. Rage at the pain his loved ones had to suffer, rage at himself for being helpless to do anything, rage at the randomness of fate.

"Because I got here before you. I saw them being brought in from the ambulance. They let me stay with Alma."

"At least she had you. If I'd known sooner—why were you called instead of me?"

She dropped her aching head into her hands. "I don't know for sure. The paramedics checked the ICE contacts on Alma's phone and reached me first, I guess."

In case of emergency. He knew he was on his mother's list. Parr fumed. He needed someone to blame. He needed reasons why the accident had happened. He had nothing to go on.

"You have a Tennessee area code. Mine is local," she added.

"But—"

"Does it matter, Parr?" she snapped. "I called you right away."

"Christ. Sorry." He leaned against the wall and hung his head. "I know. I just wish—I should have been here."

"You are now."

"Yeah." He straightened. "And I'm not going anywhere." Parr looked at her, fear and pain and fury blazing in his eyes. "Neither are you."

"Is that an order? What's the matter with you?"

"Sorry again. What I meant was you don't know how to do anything but the right thing."

She shook her head, not meeting his gaze. The quarrel she'd had with Bobby Joe only hours ago preyed on her mind. Had the crash really been an accident? Or had he been so upset with her that he'd gone off the road?

"I'm not so sure about that," Mary Beth replied in a low voice.

"I am," Parr stated.

She waved away his reassurance. "Just drop it."

"Okay." He looked at her thoughtfully for a moment before he began to pace again. "What now?"

"My dad's on his way. I wish he had someone with him in the car. His night vision isn't great. What if—" She looked up at him, her eyes welling with shining tears.

"Mary Beth . . ." He closed the distance between them with one stride. She rose and let him hold her, giving in to his comforting embrace with a sigh from the depths of her soul. The kisses he pressed to her forehead and wet cheeks had nothing to do with passion. They stood there, wrapped in silence, sharing the grief and uncertainty that had brought them to this place and left them to weep in each other's arms.

Two weeks later . . .

The tumultuous first days after the accident had gone by in a blur. Mary Beth and Parr had settled into a routine of sorts. Taking turns with room visits on different floors, overnight stays, getting updates from doctors when either of them could catch one, and practical advice from the busy nurses—by now, Mary Beth was numb.

She had slept in chairs and relied on midnight meals of stale peanut-butter crackers from vending machines when she ate at all, and helped to fill out countless forms for both Bobby Joe and Alma, giving the same information over and over as they moved from one stage of care to another. And here we go again, she thought. One more form.

"So you are Mary Beth Caine, with an *e* on the end, correct?"

"Yes."

"And your relationship to the family is . . . ?" The hospital social worker paused and looked up, his pen still on the top sheet of paper on his clipboard.

"I'm Bobby Joe's—fiancée." Mary Beth stumbled over the word. But it was still a fact. "Not quite a relative."

Needing something to do, she'd asked his doctors if she could speak to someone who'd help plan home care for him and his mother when the time came, and they'd recommended Ned Quinton. Parr hadn't been able to make the hastily scheduled conference. Mary Beth knew why the social worker asked her the question: her name appeared in both files as a contact.

"But still part of the family." Quinton's kind smile eased her nervous tension.

"Someday, yes," she said in a voice that lacked confidence. "We announced our engagement several weeks ago."

"I see. I'm so sorry that this happened."

The sympathetic comment was sincere enough. Ned Quinton didn't know the family. The hospital was a big one, miles away from Iminga.

"Though Mr. Weston is improving, according to his doctors," he added.

"Yes." She swallowed hard, trying to compose herself.

Mary Beth didn't share the social worker's professional optimism, not after the time she'd spent at Bobby Joe's bedside. Just to be with him and take care of the little things, like making sure the blanket didn't slip off the frame over the cast on his shattered leg. She talked to him sometimes. The neurologist had told her that he could hear, even if he couldn't respond.

Bobby Joe's head injury had required round-the-clock care in the days right after the accident, and the trauma specialist had thought it best to put him under deep sedation for a while, administering medication that kept his concussed brain from swelling.

He was lucid at times. Now and again he managed to say he was in pain and where it hurt. He realized he was in a hospital. But not why.

Yesterday morning he had squeezed her hand and mumbled her name before he drifted off again.

She'd felt like crying but the tears wouldn't come. The prognosis was guarded and there had been reason to fear at first that he might never again be the man he had been. But the neurologist cautioned against jumping to conclusions, pointing out that Bobby Joe was young and healthy, and might very well recover completely.

"His mother's still in intensive care, as you probably know." Ned Quinton's voice broke into her thoughts.

"I stopped by to see her this morning."

Alma Weston had regained full consciousness almost immediately but was still unable to walk or get out of bed. She hadn't broken anything—a blood clot on the base of her spine had temporarily paralyzed her.

The risk of infection, and other, more minor complications from the crash, had kept her in the ICU, where Howard Caine rarely left her side. She'd greeted Mary Beth with bright eyes and a smile, as usual.

Today—and every other day she'd visited—Mary Beth summoned up every cheery reassurance she could think of, making small talk that never touched on the last quarrel she'd had with Bobby Joe. His mother didn't need to hear about Mary Beth asking for a trial separation while they were still engaged. Her dad didn't either. She'd avoided his gaze, sensing that he might have guessed there was trouble between her and Bobby Joe.

Ned Quinton didn't have to know that either.

"Family and friends mean a lot to patients," he said absently, looking through the papers on his clipboard. "Now, if and when Mrs. Weston is cleared to go home, she'll need a hospital bed and some other medical and mobility equipment and probably a home health aide. I can coordinate that in advance if you'd like."

"Thank you."

"Once it's in the database, one of her physicians will sign the orders for everything she needs before she's released."

He said nothing about Bobby Joe going home. Mr. Quinton wasn't a doctor, of course, but Mary Beth had hoped—irrationally—that he might know something she didn't. She hadn't visited Bobby Joe yet.

Driving back and forth between Iminga and the hospital ate up what was left of her time when she wasn't visiting. Sometimes she just dozed off where she was and didn't bother to go home at all. But nothing else mattered more to her than helping the Westons and her dad.

Her request for a leave of absence from the school system had been immediately granted. The recovery was expected to take a long while, and she'd explained her role in it to the satisfaction of her supervisor.

When the time came, she and Parr would coordinate the caregiving. They were learning fast, but the potent emotional connection between them had been subsumed by worry and exhaustion. Guilt nagged at her. She couldn't share that burden with Parr.

What they felt for each other had to be set aside and they'd managed to do so, by unspoken agreement. As if it was a protective talisman against more bad luck, she continued to wear the pendant he'd given her. He hadn't asked about it again. The ruby strawberry was never in plain sight.

In the hazy days after the accident, they ran into each other constantly at the hospital, where there was no such thing as privacy. In Iminga, Mary Beth steered clear of the Weston house. She had a good excuse: Parr's crew was renovating Alma's kitchen in the meantime. He would take care of everything else for his mother, now that he'd moved to town from Memphis for an indefinite stay.

She didn't want to run the risk of being alone with

him, ever. Too many emotional triggers—and, if she was honest with herself, too much temptation to seek comfort in his arms once more. She had other things to think about besides Parr, and she needed to think straight.

The slow passing of time in a hospital, especially a large and unfamiliar one like Delta General, was disorienting. Mary Beth knew down to the minute when the nurses' shifts changed, but she often didn't know what day of the week it was.

Looking ahead was about all that kept her going.

Ned Quinton continued to fill out forms, referring to Bobby Joe's and Alma's medical files often and glancing occasionally at his watch, an unobtrusive hint that he was pressed for time.

"Is there anything else I can help you with, Miss Caine?"

"No," Mary Beth said. "I guess that's all I can do for now. It helps to set goals."

"Of course." He took a business card from his shirt pocket and handed it to her. "Please call or e-mail if you have any other questions."

"I appreciate that."

Quinton rose and they shook hands, and he went on his way.

Mary Beth collected her purse and jacket, which she slung over her arm. She couldn't leave without seeing Bobby Joe, whether or not he was aware of her presence. Heartbreaking as it was to be with him, especially when he struggled to speak, her sense of obligation won out.

She had to help him. That was all there was to it.

Taking the elevator up to the ward and finding her

way through the maze of corridors leading toward his room was something she could have done in her sleep by now. She nodded to the staff at the nursing station, and returned a few quick smiles as some looked up from their monitors to greet her.

"How is he doing today?" Mary Beth asked an RN in blue scrubs, an older woman she recognized as one who often attended to Bobby Joe.

"Better. He's been talking more, sometimes in complete sentences," the nurse informed her, seeming pleased to share the news. "Occasionally he mixes up words, but he's definitely been making an effort to communicate."

"That's progress." It really was. But Mary Beth understood that Bobby Joe's recovery wasn't something that would occur in predictable stages and might even reverse itself at times. He could still get worse before he got better.

She glanced toward the open door of the room, not sure why she was stalling. "Okay if I go in?"

The RN checked the schedule of attending doctors. "Morning rounds are over. No one's with him."

"Thanks so much."

Mary Beth walked to Bobby Joe's semiprivate room, surprised by the daylight pouring in. Yesterday he'd been on the gloomy side of the dividing curtain, unaware of the irritating, constant noise of a busy hospital, something that even she had ceased to notice.

"Hello," she said. "They moved you. Looks like you got the sunny side."

He focused on her face for a few seconds, then grinned. "The other guy checked out."

She put her things over the back of the armchair

provided for visitors and leaned over the bed, giving him a kiss on the forehead, avoiding the stitches on his bruised cheek. The IV bag on the stand by the bed was still attached to the port in his arm. Maybe the level of medication had been decreased. It was amazing that Bobby Joe could talk at all, let alone this well, this fast, so suddenly.

"The nurse said you're doing much better."

His gaze wandered to the racing clouds in the mostly blue sky outside the window, then returned to her. "Yeah. Parr was here."

So that was why he'd missed the meeting. He split his time at the hospital evenly between his brother and his mother.

Bobby Joe paused, as if collecting his thoughts took a lot of effort. Tactfully, Mary Beth adjusted the blanket tent over his casted leg and tidied up. She moved the room phone on the nightstand to get at several mini pudding cups scraped clean with a plastic spoon. Parr must have brought those from the hospital cafeteria. She tossed the cups and spoon into the wastebasket.

"Ooh, pudding," she teased him. "Lucky you. How does it feel to eat real food?"

He'd been living on liquid calories until a few days ago. His vital signs displayed on a swing-arm screen above the bed that received data from the soft clip on his finger. Heart rate, blood pressure, and a few other things she had yet to figure out were constantly monitored. Readouts and graphs in different colors were displayed on the screen.

Bobby Joe grinned again, weakly. "Good. They gave me a sandwich. I traded it to Parr for the pudding."

The effort of saying so much at once seemed to tire him. Bobby Joe closed his eyes. At some point they'd all been briefed on what to expect going forward: confusion, fatigue, spells of moodiness and inattention. The marked improvement in his speech and thinking was still a very good sign.

When she turned, Bobby Joe was looking at her as if she were a stranger who had wandered into his room, his brow furrowed.

"What's the matter?" she asked in a gentle tone.

"Parr told me I crashed my car." He looked out the window again. "I mean, I asked him. We didn't get into details."

At last. There had been a mutual agreement between all of them to wait for Bobby Joe to ask that question. No one wanted to bring it up out of nowhere and stress him. "Yes," she said simply.

"I don't remember it."

"That's because your head hit the steering wheel. Did Parr say anything else?"

"No. The doc sent him out so she could test me. Said he was a distraction."

Mary Beth had her own take on that. She had experienced the Parr Effect personally. So a female doctor wasn't immune either. "And then what?"

"I had to count backward from ten, then twenty. Oh, and tell her who the president was, stuff like that."

"How'd you do?" she asked lightly.

"I guess I passed."

"I'm sure you did."

Gingerly, Bobby Joe rubbed his temples. "I wish my head would stop hurting. Were you with me in the car?" His brow furrowed again and he stared anxiously at Mary Beth.

"No."

"Someone was. Who?"

Evidently his memories were incomplete. She half wondered if she should call in someone from his medical team. Mary Beth told herself to calm down. It was best to be careful about how she replied. Thank God Alma had survived in relatively good shape and would most likely walk again.

"Your mother. I guess you don't know that she's here in the hospital."

"Parr didn't say. He had to go out. Said he was coming back."

"Well, she's not on this floor," Mary Beth added. "Long story short, she was injured but she's going to be okay."

Bobby Joe closed his eyes. There was a rawness in his voice when he spoke again. "Was I at fault?"

"Apparently not. The car hit the divider on a blind curve, according to witnesses. Some cars got banged up and a truck was totaled. But no one else was injured besides your mom."

"I want to see her."

"You will," Mary Beth reassured him. "Just as soon as we can figure out how to make it happen. Right now she can't walk and can't be in a wheelchair."

"Is she hurt that bad?"

"She's getting better, just like you are."

"Okay." His concern ebbed away. "Not like I can go

anywhere. This cast itches something fierce." He settled his head into his pillows, and that faraway look came into his eyes again. Mary Beth sat down. He'd managed a relatively complex conversation without zoning out, for the most part. Good enough. She didn't want to trigger a flood of recollections that he wasn't equipped to handle.

Even though she burned to know whether he remembered as far back as the quarrel right before the accident, she wouldn't dream of asking him that. If he eventually brought up the subject, she would . . . well, she didn't know what she would do.

Now that he'd turned a corner, that meant Bobby Joe needed her more than ever. She owed him her undivided attention and tender loving care. The embrace she'd shared with Parr in the emergency room seemed like a long time ago.

Mary Beth took Bobby Joe's hand in hers and held it, palm to palm. Bobby Joe's long fingers curled around her diamond engagement ring. "You're still my girl, right?"

"Yes. Of course." He didn't seem to notice the fractional hesitation in her reply. She was wearing both of the rings he'd given her, in fact. And—still hidden between her breasts—the ruby strawberry on its fine chain.

It was theoretically possible that someone could find it if she ever took it off and hid it somewhere at home. Against her skin, resting over her heart, the tiny gem was safe. Mary Beth knew exactly where it was at all times. It meant something to her still. She couldn't say exactly what, but then no one was asking.

There was a knock on the open door. Mary Beth looked up, startled. Parr stood on the threshold as if he'd been stopped there by an invisible force field.

Clearly, he'd heard Bobby Joe's affectionate question. And her automatic response. From the troubled look in his eyes, she could tell he didn't know it was automatic. Too bad.

She couldn't let go of his brother's hand just because Parr was looking at her. But Bobby Joe inadvertently helped with that particular problem. He pulled his hand free and waved to Parr. "Come on in, big bro."

Parr walked into the room, glancing around but not commenting on the move to the bed by the window. Mary Beth reminded herself that he'd been here already this morning. Maybe he'd even helped with the changeover.

Rather than stand apart from the injured man on the bed, he brought over another chair and set it beside Mary Beth.

"How's it going?" He sprawled slightly as he sat down, trying to get comfortable in the narrow confines of the chair, resting his hands on the curved armrests and extending his long legs under the hospital bed. He was wearing plaster-spattered work boots and heavy jeans. Mary Beth guessed that he had come directly from his mother's house, starting his day maybe even before sunrise, instructing the crew before he took off.

"Okay," Bobby Joe answered vaguely. "Everyone says I'm doing good. So I guess I am."

"And you?" Parr looked at her, his dark gaze steady and inescapable.

"Oh, about the same as yesterday." She did her best to keep her uneasiness out of her tone. "But I would say that Bobby Joe's more than okay. He's been talking and talking."

"That's great. Glad to hear it. Anything we can do for you today?" he asked his brother, who gave him a blank look.

"Yes." Mary Beth spoke for him. "He really wants to see Alma."

A ringing came from Parr's jacket pocket and he took out a smartphone. "That's why I'm here again, actually. Your dad suggested that they video chat." He tapped the screen and Mary Beth heard her father's deep hello.

"I'm in the room, Howard," Parr said. He glanced at his brother. "Bobby Joe, are you up for this?"

"All I have to do is lie here. So you could say I'm down for it. Not up." He smiled at his own joke. "Mom? You there?"

His mother's face filled the small screen as Parr held up the phone and pressed the icon for the video app. There was nothing for Mary Beth to do but listen. Bobby Joe took her hand again, rubbing the diamond ring absently.

"Bobby Joe. Oh Lord. It's true. You are better." Despite her condition, Alma was bubbling over with excitement. "I woulda called before this but Howard kept telling me to wait. Just so you know, a video chat was my idea, not his."

"Sorry. Guess I heard wrong." Parr chuckled. "You can take the credit, Mother. And if that app hadn't been invented, you would have invented it."

"Shut up. But you're right," she said proudly.

Bobby Joe let go of Mary Beth as he struggled to sit up. She propped an extra pillow behind his back and he caught her hand again, folding her fingers around his to show off the engagement ring. Parr angled the phone downward to capture that detail. Mary Beth was uncomfortable. He didn't have to make a movie out of the awkward situation.

Alma chattered away, then slowed down when she realized Bobby Joe wasn't following the stream of talk too well.

Mary Beth kept listening, unwilling to interrupt the extraordinary closeness that the Westons shared. Now and again her dad got a word in, but the conversation was somewhat one-sided otherwise: Alma talked and Bobby Joe was content to listen to her for once.

The sun brightened noticeably—it was getting close to noon—and he closed his eyes as if too much light caused him pain.

"Want me to close the blinds?" Mary Beth whispered.

Bobby Joe nodded, an action that obviously hurt him.

Mary Beth was able to reach the cord that controlled them from her chair. One pull and the window was covered.

"Mom. I need to rest." The blunt request took his mother aback, but then she seemed to remember the same facts they'd all been told concerning Bobby Joe's condition.

"Oh, of course. I don't know what possessed me to rattle on like that. I'm sorry, Bobby Joe."

"Don't be. It did me good to talk to you and see you."

After several maternal kisses and a promise to chat again soon, he handed the phone back to Parr, speaking in a low tone. "Thanks. Wasn't making excuses. I was starting to fall asleep. Didn't want her to think I was passing out."

"I understand." Parr let it go at that, looking at the phone again. "Howard, you still on?"

"Yes. Let me see my little girl, please."

Parr gave her the phone. The brief contact of his hand against hers was startlingly warm. Even warmer memories rushed through her mind until Mary Beth focused on her father's face.

"Hi, Daddy. Want to meet later for dinner?" It seemed like a long time since she'd been alone with him. Right now, Mary Beth truly needed his steadying presence.

"If it's okay with Alma, sure."

Alma laughed. "It most certainly is. I'm tired of you eating half of what's on my tray morning, noon, and night. Go out, by all means. But bring me back a piece of pie—I'd love some coconut pie. Cures all ills known to man and woman."

"Yes, dear."

Howard and Mary Beth set a time and said goodbye. She ended the call, giving the smartphone back to Parr.

He rose from the too small chair, discreetly stretching his long frame to get the kinks out, towering over both of them. Bobby Joe was drowsy. She guessed he would soon fall asleep and she stayed in her chair, close to him. It seemed safer.

Parr said good-bye, but his brother didn't answer.

"Don't worry," Mary Beth said. "I think the chat took a lot out of him."

"Guess so." There was concern in his dark eyes.

"All his doctors say it's normal for him to drop off like that. He still needs an incredible amount of sleep."

"I don't doubt it. He's not out of the woods yet."

She nodded.

Parr's intent gaze moved over his brother's face, studying the hollows under Bobby Joe's eyes and the deeply drawn lines of strain around his mouth. For a while he said nothing.

"I have to go," Parr said softly to him. "Mary Beth is still here."

Bobby Joe stirred in his sleep as if he was reacting to hearing her name.

His older brother heaved a sigh that could have come from the bottom of his soul. "All right. Call me if you need me, Mary Beth."

She was struck by how much meaning there was in his routine words. For her, anyway. Parr had no idea how much she needed him. But Bobby Joe was her priority now. That was how it had to be.

Parr paused for a moment, looking down at her. He was bold enough to bend over her chair, but the kiss he gave her was nothing special. A brief press of the lips against her hair, that was all.

She didn't look up. He strode out, saying nothing more, not even good-bye.

Mary Beth stayed for another half hour, until Bobby Joe's breathing was deep and regular. Only then did she tiptoe out.

"Hello," a different nurse, a new one, said. "Are you Mary Beth? I heard you're here a lot."

"Yes. But I come and go. I might take the rest of the afternoon off, actually. I should be back tonight."

"Oh. Well, I go off shift around five-thirty. I could leave a note for Mr. Weston to let him know you're out."

Mary Beth shook her head. "You don't have to. He knows he can count on me."

Parr wandered down the hall of a lower floor, not Alma's. The layout was about the same on each. No one knew him down here. He was looking for the meditation room and he found it.

The doors were open and no one was inside. Benches and chairs made of blond wood were placed a discreet distance apart to create privacy for visitors who wanted to be alone with their thoughts. The pale-toned walls created a soothing atmosphere.

Parr chose a chair and sat down. What a jolt. He'd seen Mary Beth by his brother's bed dozens of times. But Bobby Joe had been out of it, one way or another, until very recently. Today, he was speaking in coherent sentences at last, though slowly. And Mary Beth had told him, right in front of Parr, that she was his girl.

Only a heartless bastard could come between them now.

Parr couldn't do it. He wanted her desperately,

more than ever, but he couldn't satisfy a desire so purely selfish—and ultimately destructive.

He folded his arms over his chest and stared at the wall. He was unable to think of anything but Mary Beth. She was doing the right thing by his brother. Parr only hoped that it was right for her. But that wasn't his call.

He sat in the empty room for several more minutes. Then he left, no more at peace than he had been before.

A nurse assistant treated Alma to a sponge bath, with Howard on the other side of the curtain waiting patiently until the bath was over. He rose when the assistant trundled past him, pushing the bathing items on a small trolley.

"You decent?"

"More or less." Attired in a quilted bed jacket, her thick hair combed into a semblance of an updo, Alma called him in.

"Before you go," she said, "I want to talk about that video chat. Seemed to me that Mary Beth looked sad, awfully sad."

"I couldn't say, Alma," Howard replied. "I didn't talk to her until the very end."

"Something isn't right between her and Bobby Joe," Alma insisted. "They did quarrel, more than once, and I still don't know exactly why. And he seemed so upset the night of the crash. He came to get me right after he'd been with her."

Howard listened.

"When they were holding hands just now, showing off that ring, I got the feeling that she was doing it for us. Not for him."

"Parr took the video," Howard pointed out. "So whatever you saw was his doing. I don't think she was showing off. That's not like Mary Beth."

"I won't argue. You know her best."

"Yes, I do. And I think you're reading too much into it, Alma."

She pulled a folded tissue from the pocket of her bed jacket. "Maybe." Her voice was shaky. "But I'm worried. Bobby Joe looked half alive."

The frailness of the woman making the statement wasn't lost on Howard. Nothing could stop Alma from being a mother hen to her boys.

"Now, now. Don't make yourself crazy. He's doing better, everyone says so. You just think about taking care of yourself for once."

She wiped her eyes. "Not sure I know how. I still can't feel my toes or move my legs. And I hate being stuck in bed."

Howard patted her arm. "Quit fussing. Lie back. Your favorite show is coming on, I checked the TV guide. I have to confess that I saw this episode, but we can still watch it together."

"Don't you dare tell me how it turns out, Howard Caine. And don't doze off halfway through. You're having dinner with your daughter."

She took the remote from his hand and switched on the TV. He stretched out as best he could in the chair and held her other hand. Alma gave him a fond glance. "Look at us. Like old married folks."

"I was thinking the same thing."

He winked at her and squeezed her hand. She sighed with happiness.

"We can talk about that later," she said softly. "After the show."

Chapter Eleven

Mary Beth felt guilty for leaving Bobby Joe. She told herself that she had earned an afternoon off. The evening, when she would meet up with her dad, was hours away.

She could drive to Iminga and back in that stretch of time. But it seemed like a huge effort with little payoff; she wouldn't be able to get anything done around the Caine house and her dad had hired day help to come in anyway. She got in the elevator and pressed the button for the lobby. The gift shop was located there—she wanted to pick up something small for Alma, something pretty. It didn't much matter what.

The cafeteria was right next to the shop. A cup of coffee might snap her out of her own mental fog. She was still analyzing Parr's abrupt departure from Bobby Joe's room. Was he angry with her or just sad? She knew why he was upset. Nothing she could do about it.

It was impossible to make everyone happy. She felt like she was about to collapse from trying.

To distract herself, she read the notices on the elevator wall.

Caregivers need care too! Our support group meets every Wednesday at six in the conference room by the lobby. See you there so we can share.

No thanks. Mary Beth didn't want to share. Her troubles were trivial compared to what Alma and Bobby Joe had gone through so far. And it wasn't over.

The doors whooshed open and she walked out. A sign in the gift shop window said CLOSED. There was no indication of when they might reopen, and the lights were off inside. She browsed the window, making note of several items that Alma might like.

Then she moved on to the crowded cafeteria, getting her own coffee from an urn and adding a muffin to her order. With the cup and saucer balanced on a tray, she went looking for a quiet spot where she would be invisible, lucking out with a small table in a corner.

The hot, strong coffee did the trick. She felt better after the first few sips, but had to force herself to nibble at the muffin. She set it aside on the paper plate.

"Eat that."

The deep voice startled her. "Parr." She drew in a deep breath and let it out slowly, calming herself. When he'd exited Bobby Joe's room, she'd thought that he was leaving the hospital, done for the day.

And—she finally realized what had been bugging her—in some unspoken way, he'd seemed done with her. As if she'd planned for him to come in and see her holding hands with Bobby Joe.

Didn't Parr get that she had to maintain an illusion for the sake of his brother's recovery? She wanted Bobby Joe to believe she would be there for as long as he truly needed her, wearing the rings he'd given her, encouraging him and cheering him on.

Parr had better not give her a hard time about it here.

"Mind if I sit with you?" He loomed over her. Her eyes were about level with the steel buckle of the plain black leather belt threaded through the fraying denim loops of his jeans. She looked up and fixed her gaze on his unsmiling face.

"Um—no." She looked around. All the other tables were taken. She couldn't very well refuse. "I thought you'd left."

"I got as far as the parking lot and realized how hungry I was. Figured I might as well eat here first and then find someplace to get a little work done."

He set a battered canvas tool bag down on the floor. She caught a glimpse of a laptop and roughed-out construction plans inside it.

He pulled out the plastic chair and sat, putting a wrapped roast beef sandwich on the dinky tabletop. He seemed too big for the space he was in, as usual. She wasn't sure if the ravenous look in his eyes was just for the sandwich.

Now that they were alone, if she didn't define the word too precisely, the impact of his physical presence hit her all over again. Massive. Muscular. And in charge.

Parr pointed to the muffin. "Come on. Don't just pick at that. You need to eat."

She took another small bite and put the muffin back on the paper plate, crumbling it.

"I don't want it."

"Sorry."

Mary Beth noticed that he looked strictly at her face, never at her hands. She hadn't taken off either ring. He would just have to get over his jealousy or whatever it was that was bothering him. She wasn't going to talk about it. But she had to talk about something. "Are those plans for your mother's kitchen?"

"Yeah." He got the hint. "I still like to draw mine on paper. Then I do them a second time, with CAD software on my laptop. Hey, I meant to tell you. I got Bobby Joe a tablet." He lifted it halfway out of the bag to show her the box.

"Nice."

"It's a good one and the hospital has free Wi-Fi. He can go online, look at Facebook, pick up his e-mail— it'll keep him from going nuts."

She could think of lots of not-so-great things Bobby Joe might do with time to kill and Internet access. Mary Beth wouldn't have given him a tablet. But Parr meant well.

"When are you going to give it to him?"

"Tomorrow, I guess. It could be from both of us, Mary Beth."

She smiled thinly. "No. You bought it. I'll let you do the honors."

He shrugged and put the tablet back into the canvas bag.

"What are those other sketches? That doesn't look like a kitchen."

"It isn't. I decided I'd take on the renovations for Bobby Joe's office."

That was something she hadn't expected to hear.

"Seriously? That's a lot of work." She couldn't think of anything else to say. Evidently Parr was going to be around Iminga for even longer than she'd thought.

"Nothing my team can't handle. That old sign painter gave us all a tour this week. He's a character."

"Mr. Corlear works hard."

"He finished the gold lettering on the front windows and he's starting a roof sign. Nothing's too good for Bobby Joe." Parr's wry comment made her curious.

"And that's why he gets in over his head. Forgive me for being nosy, but is BJ paying for the renovation?"

"Nope. I am."

"But—"

"His bank account is cleaned out, Mary Beth. I guess I should say our account. Both of our names are on it."

"You two have a joint account?"

"Had it for years. Sometimes I fronted him money for houses he wanted to flip. He always paid me back, sooner or later."

"How?"

"That's between me and Bobby Joe."

The Weston brothers stuck together like glue, despite being diametrically opposite personalities. She shouldn't have asked. Something had happened to the family—some kind of tragedy, a story she still didn't know and that Alma had never told her—that made Parr protective to a fault.

"Okay. But being overextended is nothing new for him."

The remark wasn't meant to be unkind. It was more like a warning, though Parr had to know it. Maybe Parr was at a point in his life where he made so much money he didn't care if his brother wasted some.

He didn't dress like he had money. Still, in those worn jeans and the flannel shirt rolled up over his biceps, and those work boots, he got more side glances from the women in the cafeteria than any of the handsome young men sporting white jackets and stethoscopes. They stuck together and loudly talked shop, like they had something to prove. Parr didn't. He was his own man, and he dominated every setting she'd seen him in.

"That's beside the point," Parr said. "Here's how I see it. If it turns out that he can't manage on his own—I mean, if his recovery takes longer than expected or if he changes his mind and decides he doesn't want to run a bricks-and-mortar business—then the building can be put up for sale."

She had to hand it to Parr for taking action without calling a family conference on the subject. But he could have consulted her. She suspected that neither brother had wanted her opinion on the pending deal.

Noted.

She wouldn't have to feel quite so guilty when she ended the engagement. Could be months from now, though, when she could decently do so and prepare Alma in advance for the bad news.

If only she could resolve her feelings for Parr before

that. Like right now. She had no idea what he was thinking. His businesslike manner didn't match the brooding look in his dark eyes. He didn't stray from the subject he'd brought up.

"Bobby Joe could find a buyer quickly for a renovated property with that much space," Parr continued. "The neighborhood around the courthouse is coming back."

"So he said."

"He wasn't wrong and it's still true. Buying in before a boom is good strategy," Parr reminded her.

She matched his cool tone. "Do you really think he could recoup his investment?"

"Very likely, yes. I can't be absolutely sure—the real estate business is chancy."

"That's quite a commitment. It's your money, though."

Parr must have done extraordinarily well on the Memphis deal he'd mentioned. So be it. Someone had to help Bobby Joe financially. She didn't feel entitled to question Parr's motives.

"Look, if his plans don't work out, the resale profit will help fund his future."

Mary Beth knew what he meant. He wasn't that optimistic about Bobby Joe either. Parr ate some of the sandwich and put the rest of it back in the wrapper.

"I haven't heard anything from his doctors that we could take to the bank, put it that way." He brushed a few crumbs from the table. "Bobby Joe is 'doing much better.' Okay. But that isn't the same as 'completely recovered.' That may never happen. So it's up to us to see that he's set."

Basically, she agreed with what he was saying. But what he had just said gave her pause. *Up to us.* That part had her looking everywhere but at him for several seconds. There is no *us*, she wanted to tell him. That was just too complicated to even think about.

He must have thought she was about to quibble about something else, because he held up his hand to stop her. "By the way, he told me before the accident that you weren't exactly thrilled about him buying the old building instead of renting it."

Mary Beth ignored the reference to her. She didn't love the idea that Bobby Joe discussed what she said and did with his brother. "Don't tell me the offer was accepted."

To her surprise, he nodded. "I let the buyers know that I would guarantee his bid and the down payment on the loan."

"Really." Evidently Parr was getting things done behind the scenes. "Where do you find the time to do deals on top of everything else?"

"Helps to have help." At her questioning look, he explained. "My guys don't need me breathing down their necks to finish projects. And I can rely on Gail to run things for me in my absence. I've never been away from Memphis for this long, but so far, everything up there's going smoothly."

"I see." Mary Beth hadn't liked his assistant all that much, but it was a good thing that Parr was able to be here.

"Okay. Getting back to Bobby Joe's ill-advised business venture—"

"I didn't say it was ill-advised."

"No, but you're thinking it." His shrewd gaze made her uneasy. He'd damn well better not be able to read her mind all the time.

Parr continued. "The space will be finished exactly the way he wanted it. I hired a carpenter and a plasterer for interior finishing. They're real craftsmen and they work fast. If and when he's able to take over, it'll be ready."

"Great. Sounds like you have everything all figured out."

"This stuff, yeah. But then there's you." His voice was so low she could barely hear it. No one else in the cafeteria did. He wasn't making a scene, but she dreaded what he might say next. "Care to fill me in on whether you plan to stay engaged to my brother?"

She was astonished. But at least he'd gotten around to what was really on his mind. "I can't answer that."

"Don't marry him out of pity, Mary Beth. He won't be grateful."

His dark eyes held her gaze, but she still saw no clue as to his feelings in the black depths. "Did I ask you for advice on the subject?"

"No."

"Then don't give it," she snapped.

"I'm doing everything I can for him," Parr continued. "I'm grateful every day that I don't have to see his name on a wreath by the side of the highway. I'm sure you are too."

She stiffened. That almost sounded like a dig. But he didn't dwell on it.

"Anyway, he has to have something to look forward to," Parr added. He paused, looking into her eyes with unnerving directness. She met his gaze with an effort. "I guess he's got you, Mary Beth. That's something."

That was definitely a dig. She didn't deserve it.

"I don't want to talk about it, Parr." She set the empty cup down.

"Well, I do. Do you think pretending you're his girl is going to help him get better? I know you don't love him."

So that was it. Parr really was jealous of poor, banged-up Bobby Joe. Let him be jealous. It didn't mean she had to sit here and listen to him.

"Table's all yours. I have to leave," she said briskly, picking up her things.

He stayed in his chair. She was grateful for that.

"Where are you going?" he asked.

"Nowhere in particular."

His gaze held her there.

"Well, nowhere that would interest you. I was thinking of buying new curtains for the kitchen in our house." That was a lie. "There's a housewares store not too far from here." That was true. "They have a good selection. Ruffles, gingham, maybe plain shades—I haven't decided."

Surely he wouldn't invite himself along on a boring errand like that. She'd tell him nothing doing if he dared to.

"Have fun," he said.

Mary Beth gave a nod and made her exit. She could sense Parr's eyes on her back as she maneuvered through the tables.

She had to get away from him.

Mary Beth went through the cafeteria doors without looking back.

She scrabbled through her purse, looking for her car keys. The damn purse had a habit of eating them. Her fingers closed around them. Mary Beth lifted her head and looked for her car. The lot was nearly full. Visitors generally arrived in droves by late afternoon.

The doors clicked open when she pressed the remote to unlock them. Absentmindedly, she slung her purse over her shoulder, then took it off again, about to put it in the passenger seat when she got in. A woman walking hurriedly through the rows of cars caught her eye.

Luellen. Her high heels clicked and every step made her tight skirt stretch to accommodate her stride. It clung. She'd gained a few pounds.

That was what happened when you hung around in mall food courts, Mary Beth thought furiously. And only Luellen would squeeze into an outfit like that to visit a hospital.

She was mad enough to spit. Mary Beth wasn't going to let her supposed rival treat Bobby Joe like a wounded hero and chat up the nurses. Unless—it was nearly unthinkable—he had invited her.

That was impossible. He was in no shape to set up

a rendezvous. And Parr hadn't given him the tablet yet. This had to be Luellen's big idea.

The other woman stopped to take a call on her cell, turning by chance in Mary Beth's direction. Her red-lipsticked mouth gaped, and not because she was holding up her end of the unheard phone conversation. Even under her makeup, it was possible to see the color drain from her face.

"I'll get right back to you," Luellen said hastily, ending the call and slipping the phone into her tiny tote as Mary Beth approached. "Hello. This is a surprise."

"What are you doing here?" Mary Beth inquired.

"Probably the same thing as you," Luellen said airily. "I came to see Bobby Joe."

"You have some nerve."

Luellen stood her ground in sky-high heels, her long legs wobbling. "How is he?"

"Better. But the nurses would have told you that. You didn't have to show up."

"It's a free country. You can't stop me," Luellen retorted.

"No, but I can make you feel good and goddamn sorry you decided to do this."

Luellen cleared her throat and gave Mary Beth a cold stare from her superior height. "Why would you want to do that?"

Her rudeness only made Mary Beth more angry. "You know perfectly well why. There's no need for you to upset him, or his mother."

The mention of Alma seemed to put a dent in

Luellen's confidence. But not for long. "I'm not here to see Mrs. Weston. I doubt she even knows who I am."

"Oh, she knows, Luellen." Mary Beth fisted her hands on her hips and glared for all she was worth. "Trust me, she knows."

Luellen cleared her throat. "Well. That can't be helped. And there is nothing wrong with my visiting Bobby Joe. I did call in advance."

They stood there for a few moments in a standoff that neither would break.

"You spoke to him?" Luellen had to have called the room phone.

"No," Luellen replied.

Bobby Joe's cell had been destroyed in the crash. Mary Beth's memory flashed on how she'd snooped through it, looking for Luellen's number and not finding any calls to or from her after the engagement party fiasco.

Parr had it now. He'd been handed the box with Bobby Joe's and his mother's personal belongings—or what remained of them—when he'd arrived at the ER. Mary Beth thought fleetingly that could have been his reason for purchasing the tablet.

"I spoke to a nurse just a few minutes ago, who was very helpful. She informed me that Bobby Joe didn't have visitors at the moment," Luellen continued.

"Aha. So you went out of your way to confirm he was alone."

"Don't put words in my mouth, Mary Beth. Now, if you'll excuse me,"—Luellen tapped her foot impatiently—"I want to pick up a bouquet for him."

"The gift shop is closed."

"Is it? You seem to know a lot about this hospital."

"I'm here a lot. Every day, in fact. Nights too, sometimes."

Luellen was clearly losing patience. "How sweet. Everyone says you're a very sweet, conscientious type of girl. Pure as the driven snow too. You're practically a saint."

Mary Beth guessed where Luellen had probably picked that up: Bobby Joe. Had he ever regaled Luellen with tales of Mary Beth's sexual inadequacy? She flinched inwardly when she recalled her failed attempts to seduce him after the engagement party. The preening woman in front of her was a bitter reminder that Bobby Joe did as he pleased.

Mary Beth still didn't regret being with him every day since the accident. Out of loyalty, she told herself. Not love.

She wasn't a saint. Stupid was more like it.

Mary Beth glared at Luellen. "No, I'm not."

"Oh, yes, you are. Especially compared to me, the town tramp."

"Don't flatter yourself."

The other woman's finely arched eyebrows rose almost to her hairline. The symmetrical tops of her silicone-enhanced boobs put in an appearance as well when Luellen huffed out an indignant breath.

Mary Beth heard heavy footsteps and looked over her shoulder. A security guard was coming their way. Maybe it was a coincidence or maybe he'd picked up on the confrontational vibe.

Somehow, she controlled her anger—getting into a catfight in a parking lot might get her and Luellen on the front page of the local paper. That wouldn't go over too well with the county superintendent of schools.

She was going to have to let Luellen go.

What the nurses might think if another woman showed up at their station, mincing around, was none of Mary Beth's concern. She just hoped they would catch Luellen in the act of swiping a bouquet from someone else's room for Bobby Joe. Mary Beth wouldn't put it past her.

She stepped aside, spearing Luellen with a final look that made it clear how she felt.

"Thanks so much," Luellen chirped for the benefit of the guard lingering in the background. "It's good to see you again, Mary Beth."

The security guard stayed close by. It occurred to Mary Beth that he had nothing to do at the moment but check out attractive female visitors. Well, she could find something for him to do. When Luellen had sauntered away, she waved him over.

"Can you fix a flat?"

"I sure can. My name's Grady. Which car is yours?"

"That one." She indicated the spot where she'd parked. For a few seconds, she entertained a wild notion of puncturing one of Luellen's tires. But no. Where there were security guards, there were security cameras. However, she could sic creepy Grady on Luellen and let her deal with his lecherousness. Petty revenge was better than no revenge at all.

She hadn't been this angry after the accidental encounter, if it could be called that, at the mall. But Luellen making a sneaky visit to the hospital was planned and deliberate. As far as Mary Beth was concerned, it was the ultimate insult and Luellen didn't get a gold star for discretion because she'd called in advance to find out if Bobby Joe was alone.

When it came right down to it, the problem was still Bobby Joe. Mary Beth had to admit that she didn't trust him, even though she was willing to help him. Most likely there was always going to be a Luellen in his life. Her suggestion that they separate had only been a way to wriggle out of the engagement little by little, and dial down the hurt for his mother.

Grady cleared his throat to get her attention. "Them tires look all right to me."

"Yes. Sorry. I didn't explain myself. Nothing's flat yet." She pointed to Luellen's retreating form. "But she has a slow leak in both of her front tires."

Grady scratched his head. "Both? That's kinda weird. Did she go over a curb or something?"

No, Mary Beth thought. Men. Lined up in a row, flat on their backs, for her to make a stunt jump. One of them was mine.

"I don't know. If you could take a look when you get a chance, it's the white Mercedes coupe. She should be back before evening."

"So I should talk to her before she drives away. Okay."

"Thanks."

Luellen would pitch a fit if she happened to catch

this guy crawling all over her car. With a little luck, Grady might even scratch the flawless paint.

"If it's later, no problem. I'd see her coming in the dark," he said with a leer. "No doubt about that."

"Grady! Get over here, you jackass!" His fellow guard hollered for him from the parking attendant's booth.

Mary Beth found a ten and handed it over. "Let me know how it works out."

"You betcha." He looked as joyful as if he'd won the lottery. It wouldn't be a problem to find out exactly when Luellen left the parking lot or to keep tabs on her in the future.

"I have to be somewhere else right now," he said.

"Sure thing."

She got into her car as Grady tipped his cap to her and ran off. She just sat there and fumed until the heat made her start the engine and turn on the air-conditioning. It cooled her down in more ways than one. Damn it. She was sorry she'd reacted like she had. She wasn't going to stick it to Luellen or her tires. She didn't have anything sharp enough to do the deed.

Mary Beth shopped instead. She blew a hundred dollars on things she didn't need and would return within a week, still in the shopping bags with labels attached, just to have something to do.

Bobby Joe would be expecting her soon. Mary Beth, teeth gritted, would be there. His previous visitor ought to be long gone—Luellen was no ministering angel of mercy. To be on the safe side, however, Mary Beth would circle to make sure the white Mercedes wasn't hidden somewhere. Grady could help her with that.

Her phone rang. Mary Beth pulled over to the side of the parking lot for the shops and picked it up. "Hi, Dad."

"There you are. I called a few times."

"I was inside a store. I guess I didn't hear it ring."

"Did you forget about meeting me?"

She winced. "Yes. I did. Totally. Sorry."

"It's okay, honey. I know how much you have on your mind. I was thinking I'd head home, though. Alma practically kicked me out of her room."

"You know she loves you."

"Keep saying that. She hasn't."

She smiled at her dad's rueful comment. "Give it time, Daddy."

He laughed a little. "All right. But I'm not used to this. Women played the game differently back in my day."

"Alma does things in her own unique way. She's one of a kind."

"Don't remind me," he chided his daughter. "I might start missing her too much before I can get back to Iminga and see what needs doing around the house."

Mary Beth felt compelled to make up for her forgetfulness. "All right. But are you sure you don't want to have dinner? I'm not really hungry but I feel bad about standing you up."

"Some other time, honey. Believe me, I'm not mad at you one bit. So don't you worry."

"Okay. I won't."

They exchanged affectionate farewells and Mary Beth drove out of the lot. The looming bulk of Delta General Hospital glowed white on the horizon ahead. She'd be there in ten minutes or less.

On the dot, her car rolled over the spikes as they flattened into the asphalt.

Grady was in the attendant's booth with several other guys, a paper cup of coffee in his meaty hand. He nearly dropped the cup when he saw her car go by.

She saw him again in her rearview mirror, standing there and waving, and she slowed to let him catch up.

Grady huffed and puffed to the side of her car. She rolled down the window.

"She didn't stay too long, miss. But she was ticked off when she saw me checking out her tires, like I was gonna steal them or something. I started to explain but she just got in and drove off."

"When was that?"

"About half an hour after you left."

Factor in the pointless shopping Mary Beth had dawdled over and about three hours had passed, all told. But Luellen had stayed only long enough to reach Bobby Joe's room and return to the parking lot. So she hadn't had time to get up to her nasty brand of trouble. Maybe a nurse had chased her out. Mary Beth wondered what Bobby Joe would say, if anything. It really wasn't right for Luellen to show up unannounced.

Grady seemed to be thinking of something else.

"And just so you know, I didn't see nothing wrong with her tires either."

"Thanks, Grady. I appreciate your attention to detail." She pressed the button to roll up the windows and the security guard straightened quickly. He walked back to the booth, taking his time.

The guys started to rag on him the second he walked through the flimsy screen door.

"Back so soon? You're slipping, Grady."

"What are you talking about?"

"She's cute. If you like strawberry blondes," one man said.

"As it so happens, I do not," Grady said a little pompously. "But the lady with the Mercedes, now, *she* was definitely my type."

"What about the other one? The looker who came in right when Miss Mercedes left?"

Grady shook his head. "Nah. Too much makeup. Kinda stuck-up. A city girl, most likely."

"You talking about the tall gal? With sapphire blue eyes?" The attendant checked his receipts. "I got a credit card slip right here for her. She signed her name nice and clear. Gail Cash. Tennessee license, as I remember. Had to ask her for ID because of the credit card. And . . . there was a Memphis car dealer frame around the plates," he finished triumphantly.

"Nice going, Sherlock. Let's look her up online," another guy joked.

"Nothing doing. We're on the job." They tilted their chairs forward until the legs hit the floor. Then they stayed where they were, shooting the breeze.

* * *

A faint trace of perfume lingered in the air in Bobby Joe's room. It wasn't a scent that Mary Beth knew and it seemed a little sophisticated for Luellen.

He was in dreamland. He looked more rested than she'd seen him look since he'd been assigned to this room. The fluorescent light bar in back of the bed had been dimmed way down.

Besides the perfume, there was nothing that indicated an alien female presence. Still, Luellen could have—whoa, Mary Beth told herself. She needed to get a grip on her own jealousy. Bobby Joe hadn't done anything to trigger it this time. His former flame had simply seized what looked like a golden opportunity to get next to him and, for some unknown reason, hadn't stayed very long.

She heard the chime for an incoming text on her phone.

Parr.

She didn't have to exercise maximum self-control to respond, unlike actually talking to him. Either way, she wasn't going to mention Luellen. She didn't see any need to discuss her with Parr right now. Maybe ever.

Even though Bobby Joe was sound asleep, she stepped outside the room.

Mary Beth tapped the screen to pick up the message.

Hey. I'm in Iminga. You back at the hospital?

She thought about not replying. That wasn't an option. They were still a team.

Yes.

A few seconds passed.

I'm sorry. Truce?

She slid down in the chair that had been left unoccupied in the hall.

Okay.

Got good news about BJ.

Tap tap. **Tell me. Am with him now.** She waited.

Do we have to text? Is he sleeping?

She peeked into the room. Parr didn't have to know
she wasn't right by the bed.

Yes.

Talked to BJ's neuro. That was text-ese for neurologist.
Abbreviations helped with so many specialists involved
in Bobby Joe's and Alma's care. **He could be out in a
month.**

Mary Beth typed a response. **That's not much time.**

Much less than they would probably need, in fact.
His next text made that painfully clear.

My mother's doctor says with the right setup she
could be home in two weeks.

Mary Beth knew how much Alma wanted to get out of the hospital, but it would take a major effort to be ready in time.

Lots to do first.

He took a little while to reply. I know. But kitchen's almost done. New stair lift, grab bars, a recliner that will get her on her feet—I'm making a list.

On her feet—Mary Beth's eyes widened. Is she walking, Parr?

Took her first steps this afternoon between the balance bars. Physical therapist was impressed.

While Mary Beth had been gone. She regretted missing the great moment. The quarrel in the parking lot receded and seemed a lot less important.

Can't wait to tell Bobby Joe when he wakes up.

Wish I was there.

Mary Beth could practically hear Parr sigh. But she preferred not to be subject to the influence of his voice. He had an unfair advantage there.

Talk to u later.

Okay.

She went back into the room and sat beside Bobby Joe. He looked so peaceful; waking him up for any reason seemed like a crime. It was enough that she was there.

His head turned to one side on the pillow and his eyelashes fluttered almost invisibly, as if he were seeing something in his dreams.

Mary Beth murmured soothingly and he settled down again. The tent over his healing leg was taut. The covers were draped uniformly over each side of the bed. He didn't seem cold, but she draped a smaller, thin blanket over his shoulder, the one nearest to her, just in case. He stirred in his sleep.

She took a paperback book from her purse and settled down herself, resting her aching feet on the understructure of the hospital bed. The room chair was uncomfortable and reading wasn't happening. She couldn't pay much attention to the words on the page. Then he mumbled something.

Sounded like *sugar*. Then *yeah*.

Mary Beth wondered whom he called *sugar*. Not her, not ever. Which meant exactly nothing. There couldn't possibly have been any fooling around with Luellen. She squelched the ridiculous thought. This was a hospital, for God's sake. Bobby Joe had a long way to go toward recovery, despite the positive news Parr had shared.

It was seeing her so-called rival so unexpectedly that had her so rattled. Two little words mumbled under the influence of—she peered at his chart, noted the unpronounceable generic drug—okay, call it sleepy juice. And she imagined the worst.

The book in her lap fell to the floor. Mary Beth waited a few moments to pick it up, hoping she hadn't wakened him. But he had sunk into a deeper, motionless sleep. She tried to read again and gave up.

Not even the chime from her phone made him stir. Bobby Joe was really out, maybe for the night. Parr had sent another text. She tapped the screen.

Guess what?

She slid down in the chair. She could be too tired to play guessing games with Parr. Maybe not.

What?

Eve's in labor.

She'd been aware that his cousin, whom Mary Beth hadn't seen since her birthday party at Alma's house, was near term, but she had no idea of the due date. It didn't matter now. A new baby was on the way. More good news. Another text followed quickly.

AJ took her to the ob-gyn. Looks like it's time.

She texted back. That's great. Everything okay?

She's calm. They went back home. Suitcase packed last week. AJ's nervous. Second baby, could come quick.

Mary Beth shook her head, although she wasn't qualified to discuss the question from a medical stand-point. If she's lucky. Did you tell Alma?

Of course. First thing. Sorry. You were next.

Don't apologize. She's your mom. And the great-aunt.
She must be over the moon.

Desperately knitting is more like it.

Mary Beth looked at Bobby Joe. It almost seemed
worth it to wake him up for news like this. The nurse
came in before she could.

"Oh. Didn't know you were here," she whispered to
Mary Beth. "He had a few visitors today. I think he's
more tired than usual."

"I can take a hint," Mary Beth said with a soft smile.

"But I didn't mean you should go," the nurse began.

"Seriously, he's out," Mary Beth whispered back.
"We might as well switch off the light. I can come back
in the morning."

"I'll tell him you were here," the nurse said. She
studied the monitor on the swing arm over the bed.
"Everything looks fine. He might not have to have the
finger clip on if he keeps doing this well."

"Good to know."

Mary Beth got ready to go, elated by the thought of
a new life to be as she said good-bye and left the room.
She thought about who she was to the latest member of
the family and decided on honorary aunt. No matter
what was to come, she was connected to all of them.

She texted Parr again while she waited for the elevator.

I'm on my way.

He answered. Don't rush. Apparently Eve won't get off the sofa. AJ says she says she knows what she's doing.

The elevator beeped its arrival. Mary Beth got in. Another text followed.

Poor AJ. He's going crazy.

She snickered and typed a reply. Why do men do that when they're not the ones having the babies?

I don't know. What should I do?

Mary Beth typed a reply. Wait for me.

Chapter Twelve

"I never held a newborn before."

Mary Beth looked at the tiny infant swaddled in pink flannel. She seemed so small inside the hospital bassinet. Her round head sported a stretchy cap of fine knit, also pink. She seemed utterly content where she was.

The Rosses had paid for a private maternity suite, which was comfortably furnished and painted in soft pastels.

"Amanda won't mind." Eve smiled at her, standing on the other side of the bassinet and holding her four-year-old daughter's hand. "Is it okay with you, Carrie, if Mary Beth holds your new sister?"

"Tell her to put on a gown first," Carrie stage whispered. "Visitors are s'posed to wear 'em."

"You're right, honey. Mary Beth, you'll find several peachy-keen pup tents in that closet."

Mary Beth laughed but did as the junior nurse in training had requested. "Do these come in more than one size?" she asked Eve.

"Afraid not."

The voluminous gown was easy to slip on but not easy to move in. It hung down to her ankles and flapped at the sides.

"Peach is your color," Eve said mischievously.

"If you say so. Okay, I'm ready," Mary Beth said to Carrie. "But how about if I sit down in that stationary rocker first? Then your mother can bring me your new baby sister."

"That's a good idea," Carrie said seriously. "You better not drop her."

"Oh Lord. This is a huge responsibility." Mary Beth looked a little worried but she opened her arms to the sleeping bundle of baby girl when she was wheeled over and lifted out. Amanda yawned hugely once the transfer was complete, then scrunched up her face into a comical expression.

Mary Beth was awed. "She's perfect. Look at her little fingers. Oh my. And those teeny-tiny fingernails. What a beautiful baby. Hello, Amanda. Welcome to the world."

Carrie came over to make sure she was doing everything correctly. "She likes you. I can tell."

"That's wonderful. I like her. And you're doing a very good job as her big sister, Carrie." The baby gurgled as Mary Beth rocked her.

Eve looked pleased as she sat down gingerly on the edge of the bed. "Let me tell you, everything's different with the second one. You don't hover so much."

Carrie got busy with the splendid present Mary Beth had brought just for her: a Noah's Ark with baby animals, two of each. She'd saved Amanda's gift for Eve to unwrap once Carrie went home with her dad.

"How's AJ doing?"

"He's tired," Eve answered honestly. "But happy. And he's sure as heck not as tired as I am. The good thing is, he knows that. There's nothing he won't do for me and these kids."

"Amanda's not a kid yet. She's just a teeny-tiny precious little pumpkin," Mary Beth cooed.

The unabashed baby talk made Eve laugh. "Listen to you."

Mary Beth didn't care what she sounded like. "What a plump little rumpkin this pumpkin has." She patted the baby's bottom. "Is this all diaper?"

"Pretty much," Eve laughed. "She only weighs seven pounds."

"Seven pounds and three ouches," Carrie added without missing a beat.

"You mean ounces," her mother said. "But you're right again. Smart girl." She ruffled her daughter's hair and caught her fingers in a tangle. "Oops. I don't think Daddy's been combing your hair."

"I won't let him," Carrie informed her. "You have to come home."

"I will, honey. Very soon. The doctor is coming tomorrow to make sure I'm ready."

Parr stood outside in the hallway, the lavish bouquet he'd brought for Eve held behind his back, as if he'd forgotten all about it. He couldn't take his eyes off the serene vision of Mary Beth with a newborn infant

cuddled in her arms. Eve was talking to little Carrie—
he could hear them but he couldn't see them from
where he was.

Being invisible was a privilege. The moment was
magical. He could have looked at Mary Beth for hours,
until someone got around to noticing him. He had
never seen her this way.

The peach-colored material that concealed her
down to her ankles cast a glow on her pale complexion.
But that alone wasn't what made her so radiant.

She was purely happy.

He chided himself silently for not realizing how
hard the bedside vigils and constant attention to his
brother and mother at the other hospital had been
for her. Away from there, she blossomed again, her
cheeks rosy from the warmth of the room beyond the
open door.

Her strawberry blond hair had been pulled up in a
loose bun that didn't have enough hairpins to hold
every wayward curl. A few had escaped and lay against
her cheek. A longer tendril curled down her neck. He
could just see a few of the delicate freckles that he
liked so much.

He longed to kiss the soft skin of her shoulders
once more, but the giant gown thing had her covered.

Mary Beth, with her gorgeous curves completely
concealed and her arms full of someone else's baby,
was dazzling. It was all too easy to imagine her holding
his baby.

He had never had such a thought before in his life.
Fatherhood hadn't been on his five-year list of things

he wanted to do. Not even his ten-year list. Suddenly it seemed like an urgent priority.

The tenderness in her expression, the pretty smile when she laughed at something his cousin Eve said, and the joy in her green eyes made his heart race. He knew he was looking at the woman of his dreams.

The hell of it was that he couldn't have her.

He had to snap out of it. He couldn't walk into that room looking starry eyed and sentimental. His cousin Eve would instantly guess at his true feelings for his brother's fiancée.

Bobby Joe would get up and walk again if he could see Mary Beth like this.

Parr amended the thought after a moment of reflection. Maybe he would. And maybe not. Bobby Joe didn't talk much about Mary Beth when she wasn't there. He didn't seem all that grateful for her devotion when they got a chance to talk in private.

Parr hated to think that his brother was putting on a show for the family, especially their mother. But he wasn't sure of it. However, if that proved to be the case, the problem wasn't something he could resolve tonight.

He took one last, long look as if he wanted to remember what he'd just seen forever. Then he stepped forward and knocked lightly on the open door.

"May I come in?" He held out the bouquet.

"Parr! My goodness! Look at those beautiful flowers. I'm honored."

Eve took them from him, smiling like a beauty queen. Which she was, in a delightfully disheveled,

I-just-had-a-baby way. She wore a multicolored chenille bathrobe she'd brought from home and fake fur scuffs.

"They match my outfit," she said, holding them front and center.

"You look great," he said gallantly. "Hello, Mary Beth."

She nodded and murmured a greeting, completely absorbed in the baby.

"How'd you get past the dragon at the nurses' station?" Eve asked. "Visiting hours are almost over."

Carrie looked up. "I didn't see a dragon."

"Don't worry, little girl." Relieved of the bouquet, Parr scooped her up. "There isn't one. To answer your question, Eve, I turned on the charm. She gave me five minutes."

"You have charm?" Eve looked at him dubiously. "I'm not seeing it."

"That's because we grew up together. Carrie, can you show me that new toy? Who gave you that?"

"Mary Beth. Put me back on the bed."

He settled the little girl right in the middle and listened to her explanation of why Noah had to have two of everything. "I see. But there's only one ark," he said, opening and closing the stuffed door.

"Don't confuse the issue," Eve told him.

The baby began to fuss and Mary Beth looked up anxiously. "Did I do something wrong?"

"No. She's probably hungry." The experienced mother of two went over to the rocker and took Amanda back, putting her on her shoulder and patting her gently. It wasn't long before the baby was squalling good and loud. "I take that back. She's definitely hungry."

A nurse came in.with a bottle of formula warmed and ready "We could hear her down the hall. This is just for backup, if you need it," she said to Eve.

"Hope I don't," Eve chuckled. "I think I remember how to breastfeed. But thanks. I might not always say no to a supplementary bottle for her if I'm tired."

The nurse set the bottle on the nightstand and looked meaningfully at Parr. "Your five minutes are almost up."

He put a finger to his lips to hush Carrie, who seemed as if she was about to mention dragons. She sealed her lips tightly shut.

"I guess that applies to me too," Mary Beth said with a sigh. "Carrie, can you help me with the gown?"

"Okay." The four-year-old girl slid off the bed. She tugged at a sleeve and the whole thing slithered off. Mary Beth bunched up the peach-colored material and stuffed it into a tall basket for laundry.

"Daddy will be here soon," Eve reassured Carrie. "Maybe we'll let him burp the baby."

Carrie giggled. "Okay."

Her newborn daughter squalled briefly once again as Eve sat cautiously in the rocker and got her settled in the crook of her arm. Carrie watched with renewed interest.

"You know what they say. Three's company. Five's a crowd," the nurse reminded Parr, pleasantly enough.

"Mary Beth and I were just going."

Parr made good on that statement by slipping a hand under her elbow and escorting her to the door. Mary Beth cast a longing look backward at the room and sighed. "Bye, Eve. I'll come by when you get settled in at home. But I'll call first."

"No. Text only. If the phone rings and I have to talk, we'll wake up the baby. I keep mine on silent."

"She really does know what she's doing." Parr's grave voice was an echo of his own text to Mary Beth when he'd announced the imminent birth of the baby. "Let's go."

"Thanks for coming," Eve said quietly, about to unfasten the front of her gown underneath the robe. Enthralled by her new sister, Carrie stood by the rocker, her chubby hand on her mother's arm. "And thanks for the flowers. Give my love to Bobby Joe and Alma."

"We will."

A busy new nurse took a minute to look at Bobby Joe's page on Facebook.

"And that's me," he explained, pointing to a selfie taken before the accident.

Mary Beth thought with annoyance that the nurse undoubtedly could have figured that out but was obviously humoring him. Bobby Joe was getting up to flirting speed again.

Nothing Mary Beth could do anything about. Plus he loved his new toy. Parr's gift had been a huge hit.

"And that's me with my best buds at a bar having a hell of a time . . . and those are the fantastic spareribs I had at the barbecue joint only you can't see them because of the coleslaw . . . and that's my uncle's dog and—"

"Who is that darling little baby?"

Bobby Joe grinned. "Amanda Ross. She just joined the family. She's my cousin's kid."

"Couldn't be cuter," the nurse said. "Okay. I'm all done. See you tomorrow, Mr. Weston."

"Thanks for stopping by."

Mary Beth sighed inwardly. She ought not to care that he was acting like his old self again, but she sort of did. It hadn't been that long ago when she'd been thrilled that such a sought-after guy paid attention to her. And . . . a few others. Seemed like ancient history.

He had yet to mention Luellen. Mary Beth was willing to bide her time. It was a test. If he never mentioned that his former flame just happened to stop by, then he didn't want her to know. Mary Beth was damned if she'd humiliate herself by asking the nurses about who visited him. She did wonder if Bobby Joe had assumed they wouldn't tell her. Maybe former flames counted as confidential medical information.

"Mary Beth, want to look?"

He held out the tablet, but she didn't take it. "You already showed me those."

"Yeah, but I uploaded new ones. I took some of myself, and the nurses took a few just for fun."

She shot him a narrow-eyed look. "What for?"

"I want to remember my days at Delta General. Every golden hour means so much."

She had to smile. "All right."

There were many more than she'd thought, taken at odd angles in low light. She skipped his selfies and looked at the group shots. Mary Beth knew a picture of Luellen wouldn't be among them, taken on the day she ran into her. Parr hadn't given his brother the tablet yet.

But—what was that? She looked hard at a blurry image of a woman, standing with a couple of nurses in one shot. She was cut in half in another, but Mary Beth would swear that was Gail Cash.

"Is that Parr's assistant?"

"Huh?" He took the tablet from her outstretched hand. "Oh yeah. Out in the hall. I guess one of the nurses took those. She drove down the day before yesterday from Memphis. Parr asked her to."

"He didn't tell me that."

"I was going to. Don't get your feathers up, baby."

"I'm not. Just asking. You're really making the most of evening visiting hours, aren't you?"

He smirked. "Are you jealous? You don't know how good that makes me feel."

Not her. But she knew that her reaction had to do with Parr, not Bobby Joe.

And Parr had his own agenda, which he seemed to be trying to pass off as concern for his brother. She hadn't denied Parr's statement about her not loving his brother and she hadn't admitted to it either. His unsolicited advice to her not to marry Bobby Joe still rankled. He didn't have the right to tell her what to do or even make suggestions—talk about a conflict of interest. The decision was on hold.

She cared for Bobby Joe. She'd be by his side as long as he needed her. That was one definition of love. Just not everlasting love.

Mary Beth took a chair, feeling ignored by Bobby Joe as he stared into the tablet, half hypnotized, scrolling through comments, shooting off replies, having a grand old time reconnecting with the world.

The odd thing was that she didn't mind.

The spa hot tubs were designed for individual use, not sharing. Mary Beth half floated in one, looking over the edge at her friend in the tub next to hers. Jackie Bledsoe rested her turbaned head on a rolled towel and inhaled the fragrant steam drifting above the water's surface.

"You were right," Mary Beth murmured. "This is heaven. I'm not leaving. Ever."

Jackie's giggle was barely audible. "Told you."

"Don't know why I waited so long."

Jackie replied with a thoughtful sigh. "It doesn't matter. I finally got you here."

"Do you think we could have massages after this?"

"Already signed you up. My treat. Now go soak your head."

Mary Beth slid further down—and down some more—until her ears were underwater. She gazed up at the spa's domed ceiling, decorated with crystal stars and a blue moon. The hot water lapped soothingly around her cheeks and her strawberry blond hair floated free. She hummed blissfully. No one needed her here. No one could even find her here. She could float forever.

Instrumental music, vaguely exotic and relaxing, was pulsing softly through hidden speakers when she finally rose up and pressed the water out of her hair with both hands. Rivulets ran over her breasts and back. "I feel so much better."

"Bet Bobby Joe would love to see you like that."

"Maybe."

"What do you mean, maybe? Does he know how lucky he is to have you? You're at the hospital every day. Some folks were wondering if you'd moved out of Iminga."

"Really?"

"Yes."

Mary Beth sank back under the steaming water, not looking at Jackie. She heard noises from the other tub, like Jackie was adjusting her position or rewrapping her turban. Without looking over in her direction, she reached for a rolled towel and put it under her neck, then closed her eyes.

A minute later, a deluge of cold water over her head made her gasp. Jackie waved a long-handled dipper at her. "What possessed you to do that?" Mary Beth shrieked. Shivering, she grabbed a warmed towel and threw it over her shoulders.

"If you go from hot to cold, it blasts wrinkles."

"Are you trying to say that I have them? Because I don't. I'm twenty-five."

Jackie used the dipper to pour cold water over her flawless face. "Preventive maintenance is crucial to preserving your youthful freshness."

Mary Beth rubbed her face with another warmed towel, muffling her laughter. "Are you reading from that brochure?"

"No. I memorized it. I love this place. I intend to

preserve my youthful freshness until I'm a hundred and five."

"Good luck." Mary Beth sank back down. They had the hot tub room to themselves at two in the afternoon. Jackie worked nights as a hostess in an expensive restaurant and Mary Beth still hadn't gone back to her day job.

"You need to take better care of yourself, Mary Beth."

"If I had more energy, I would. But I'm just worn out," she admitted. "There's more to do every day. It's like I don't know where I am sometimes."

"You want my advice?" Jackie asked. "Be a little selfish sometimes."

"I can't." Mary Beth had used up all the warmth in the towel over her bare shoulders, and it was damp from her drenched hair. She dragged it off and set it aside, reaching for another one that was nice and dry, and snuggled up in it. "You ever been in a hospital for a long stay or had someone you love in one?"

"Can't say that I have. But I know Delta General is the best hospital for miles around."

"Yes. I'm glad Alma and Bobby Joe are there and they're getting the best care available. But they still need us to keep them company, fetch things, read to them. . . ." She trailed off.

"Us?"

"Me and Parr. Bobby Joe's older brother."

"Oh yeah. Heard of him."

Jackie's tone was neutral. Mary Beth hoped she would say more, but Jackie didn't. Stillwaters, the expensive restaurant where she was hostess, was the kind of place where men brought women they wanted to impress, not a family type eatery.

"Anyway, Mary Beth, you can't do everything. I doubt anyone's expecting so much of you. There are aides and volunteers around, right?"

"Sometimes. Not always right when you need them. I don't want Bobby Joe to have to wait for a pillow to prop his leg or to get left in some hallway when he's waiting for an X-ray. And there are things that the aides can't handle."

"Like what?"

Mary Beth was reluctant to get into it. But it was a relief to talk freely to someone who wasn't a family member.

"Like . . . well, when Bobby Joe was unconscious for so long, all I could think was what if he wakes up screaming? I felt like I had to be there all the time. If he had a nightmare or didn't know where he was, I didn't want him seeing a stranger's face when he came out of it."

Jackie considered that possibility. "Oh. Hadn't thought of that. But he isn't under sedation anymore, right?"

"No."

Jackie lifted herself out of the hot water and wrapped a giant towel around her entire body, knotting it at the top so it wouldn't slip. "Quit sloshing around. Let's go get a rubdown."

Mary Beth hoisted herself up and accepted the towel Jackie held out, covering herself. "Looking forward to that."

Jackie wasn't likely to ask pointed questions with

two masseuses there to listen in. She reached down to the small tray where Mary Beth had put both diamond rings and the necklace with the strawberry ruby. Jackie glanced at the jewelry and focused on the pendant. "That's a pretty little thing. Where'd you get that?"

"It was a gift."

She hoped Jackie would assume that Bobby Joe had given it to her. She was relieved when Jackie seemed to lose interest.

Mary Beth kept everything on the tray, which she held as her friend collected the personal items she'd brought into the hot tub room—among them, a smartphone. Jackie was never without it. "Give me a sec. I have to text the other hostess. Cherry and I were planning to swap shifts."

She tapped the screen, humming. "Cherry knows Parr from back in the day."

"Oh?"

"Yeah. She's older than me. I think they were in high school together. She happened to mention that he'd come in to Stillwaters."

"Really." Mary Beth hoped that sounded nonchalant. Her mind raced with questions. Who was with him? Did he come more than once? When?

"You never met Cherry, but she kinda knows who you are," Jackie added.

"Because of Parr?"

"Sort of. Bobby Joe too. He used to hang out at the Stillwaters bar before you two got engaged, you know. Sometimes he had dinner."

"You never told me that." Jackie was leaving out crucial details, like whether her philandering fiancé had played footsie under the damask tablecloths with Luellen or some other married female. How long that had been going on, she had yet to learn. Did it even matter at this point? She was just glad Bobby Joe had never taken her there. There was nothing worse than a knowing look from a waitress who got to meet all her favorite customer's dates. Just not at the same time.

"I'm not supposed to talk about the customers," Jackie said primly. "But of course we all do. The waitresses especially. Now that big brother Parr is back in town, the consensus is that both Westons are super hot, but Parr has the edge."

"How about that. Maybe I should stop by. How's the chicken salad?"

"Lethal. You have been warned." Jackie finished texting.

In more ways than one, Mary Beth thought. "Then I'll skip it. I see plenty of Parr as it is."

Jackie led the way down a short corridor to the beauty salon area.

"I was thinking about mani-pedis for both of us. And hot oil treatments to condition our hair and then a shampoo and blowout. What do you say?"

"Bring it on."

A few days later, Mary Beth felt like the spa day had been nothing more than a wonderful dream. The deep relaxation she'd experienced had ebbed away in mere hours. She was back to doing everything for everyone again, much as she tried to slow down.

She couldn't complain. Parr was doing even more,

especially on the home front. His crew had worked overtime under his direction, and he'd done more than supervise. She'd seen how he could swing a hammer and knew he'd worked as hard as his guys.

Mary Beth almost envied him the opportunity to tear down walls and pound nails. Sounded like a great way to get rid of tension. Now that official release dates had been set for both Alma and Bobby Joe, she felt more irritable than ever. She hadn't been sleeping well.

She was with Parr in the hospital cafeteria, which was relatively empty between breakfast and lunch, having coffee. She shouldn't. Too much made her jumpy and this was her third cup of the morning. She blamed it for the fight she seemed to be picking with him over nothing.

"Gail? She's gone." Parr's response was matter-of-fact. "And to answer your other question, I'd asked her to drive down because the contract amendments for the new project needed a real signature. I can't do everything via e-mail."

"FedEx would have been faster."

"What's it to you?" He seemed amused.

"I just think it's weird that neither Bobby Joe or you told me she was coming or when she was leaving."

Parr shrugged, rolling up plans, which were dog-eared by now, and gathering up paperwork, all of which went into the big canvas bag on the extra seat.

"So what? She's back in Memphis. And it wasn't only the contracts. The old carpenter who's doing the finishing work on my mother's kitchen left behind a whole case of woodworking tools and he had to have them. And I needed clothes."

The idea of Gail selecting he-man outfits and carefully packing them for her big bad boss irked her a lot. Mary Beth blurted out one last question. "Couldn't you just go to the mall?"

A smile flickered around the corners of his mouth. "I like the clothes I have. New jeans are stiff. I don't have the time to break them in."

"Oh. I see."

It was a good thing that there was no one close enough to eavesdrop on the tetchy conversation. Mary Beth couldn't seem to stop herself. The two paper coffee cups had been drained and stuffed with napkins. She pushed them to one side with her finger.

"You really don't have anything to worry about, Mary Beth."

His calm reply grated on her ears. She was too frazzled to be soothed. There was more to do than ever at the hospital and in Iminga.

Nothing was ready. Her dad was a nervous wreck trying to get their house fitted up so that Alma could stay with him until the renovations—which had gone over budget and past the completion date—were done. Besides not sleeping well, Mary Beth never got a chance to go to the gym. Yoga wouldn't cut it. Spinning on a stationary bike might do. Working herself into a mindless frenzy sounded pretty close to what she was doing here at the hospital, but without the loud music.

"So tell me about what you're up to." His tone was encouraging. "You mentioned bringing in some work yourself so you could stay caught up. That's a good idea."

"I finished it."

"Good for you." He was patronizing her, not encouraging her.

Mary Beth twisted the ring on her finger. The second one, the let's-kiss-and-make-up ring, which was beginning to itch.

Parr ignored her fidgeting. They hadn't discussed her plans or his or the engagement ever again. That was still on, as far as Bobby Joe knew. He went out of his way to be lovey-dovey to her, especially in front of the hospital staff and his mother, who now was able to visit him using a wheelchair. Bobby Joe himself was stumping around pretty well with a cast and a cane. He was a little different somehow: more impulsive and quick to get angry about small problems that had never bothered him before. At least he was just as quick to forget what troubled him.

"When does life get back to normal? For Alma and Bobby Joe. And for me. And you."

He snorted. "The docs keep saying this is the new normal. I'm not sure what they mean. I was okay with whatever was normal before."

Parr had had enough of the hospital too, evidently. When she thought about it, he was doing double the work she was.

Mary Beth changed the subject. "It's going to be a great day when we bring them home."

He drummed his fingers on the table. "Forward, march."

"You can lead the parade," she said tiredly.

"I can see it. Family and friends. Hope I have a few left. Haven't talked to any of them for too long. Except Gail."

An ex-lover didn't count as a friend, in Mary Beth's opinion, and that made her ask a question she knew damn well she ought to have kept to herself the second it was out of her mouth.

"That reminds me. Did you know that Gail stopped by Bobby Joe's room when she was here?"

When Mary Beth couldn't sleep, she obsessed about things like that. Exactly why she'd brought it up now, she couldn't say.

She still wasn't going to mention Luellen's brief appearance on the same day, partly because it was a while ago. Their visits could have overlapped, which raised an intriguing possibility that she also thought about in the wee hours of the morning: maybe Bobby Joe's former flame was put out by the sudden arrival of glamorous Gail.

"No." There was a tiny flicker of disapproval in his eyes, she was sure of it. Then Parr smiled and whatever she'd seen vanished. "When was that?"

"A while ago—I don't remember exactly. But I found out the next day."

"Found out? It's not a secret that Gail was here."

"Well, no." Mary Beth felt a little foolish. "Anyway, I spotted her in a group shot on Bobby Joe's tablet, with some of the nurses. He's addicted to that thing by now."

"Cut him some slack, Mary Beth. Can you imagine what it's like to be trapped in bed for weeks?"

She conceded the point with a tiny nod. "I just thought Gail would've told you."

"She didn't or I don't remember it," Parr said blandly.

It was clear that he minded the lapse on some level. He wouldn't say why.

"Bobby Joe didn't tell me either, actually."

"Not a biggie. They did meet before at your birthday party. So why wouldn't she stop by? Everyone's rooting for him."

"Yes. He has a twenty-four-hour fan club going by now. Night shift nurses. Day shift nurses. Visitors. And me, the faithful dog." The edge in her voice made Parr cock a dark eyebrow at her. Mary Beth tacked on an apology. "Sorry. That sounded sort of surly."

"You need to take a break."

Mary Beth waved the idea away. "I'm not stuck here, Parr. I have a car. I can leave anytime I want."

"Then why don't you just go and have fun? It'd do you a whole hell of a lot of good."

His blunt question made her scowl. "I don't know. I guess I don't feel like doing fun things alone."

"How about—" Before Parr could get another word out, she held up both hands to stop him.

"Rules of order. I'm not taking any more questions from the floor. Do not volunteer to be my Fun Coordinator. I don't think it's a good idea if you and I hang out together. He's bound to find out."

"Hmm. Maybe so. Of course, I could always take you out and tell him myself."

"Forget it." Mary Beth had been trying to persuade herself to face the fact that the Weston brothers were basically bad news. The recent intel from Jackie only confirmed it. They shared too many traits: both were way too cocky and much too good-looking and well over the legal limit when it came to attracting feminine attention. Just her luck to be engaged to one and fighting a pointless crush on the other.

Parr leaned forward and chucked her under the chin. "Don't be so prickly, girl. I'm just trying to help. If you think what we're doing for those two is hard now, just wait until they get home. But I get to go back to Memphis when all is said and done, though. You're staying right here."

His fingers moved lower and he found the chain that held the ruby strawberry.

"Don't, Parr."

He pulled on it gently, leaning even closer. In another second the fine links were draped across his palm and the pendant dangled from his fingers, glowing red. "Just checking."

"You're not the only one."

"Beg your pardon?" He let the shimmering gold chain fall from his fingers down into her blouse.

"Bobby Joe did too."

"What do you mean?"

"He went fishing for it like you just did and he asked where I got it."

Parr shifted in his seat. "When was that?"

"The night of the accident. A couple of hours before. We were in his car, in fact."

"Oh." His expression turned serious. "And what'd you say?"

"Just that it was a gift. He seemed suspicious for,

like, three whole seconds. Then he laughed it off."
Mary Beth tried to think how best to explain Bobby
Joe's theory that a virgin couldn't cheat, until Parr's
dubious look made her nervous. "As far as I know, he
doesn't remember it. Why should he? He didn't care."

"Mary Beth. I know you're not telling me something."

"That was the truth," she insisted.

"Not entirely." He straightened in his chair. "Come
on. Out with it."

"I don't know what you mean."

He folded his arms across his chest. "Bobby Joe's
remembering more and more. And no, he didn't say
anything to me about the necklace. But he told me
yesterday that you two had quarreled that night and
that you'd suggested a separation."

"Just my luck," Mary Beth said bitterly. "I guess now
you think I'm at least partly responsible for the accident."

He shook his head. "No. Not at all. But I do have
one question."

Parr's intense gaze made her want to get up and
go away. "Go ahead."

"Why do you keep wearing the pendant?"

"I don't know. I shouldn't." She reached up a hand,
but before she could touch the chain, Parr had captured her wrist.

"Don't take it off," he murmured. "If he doesn't
know where it came from, I'm not going to tell him.
Are you?"

She hesitated. "No."

Chapter Thirteen

"Come on. Let's get out of here," Parr said. He gathered up all his stuff in one hand and guided her out of the cafeteria with the other.

Mary Beth didn't protest.

He brought her to his pickup and opened the door for her, then went around and tossed the canvas bags and other things into a storage space behind the front seats.

"Nice rig." Mary Beth stepped up and swung herself into it as he did the same on the other side. "I assume you own this one."

He shrugged and put the key in the ignition. The engine started with the kind of quiet roar that said expensive. "That's right."

Her hand rested on the seat. The upholstery was new, with a luxury feel under her hand, and the cab was spacious, with a real backseat, unlike the classic Thunderbird he'd rented when he'd first been back in Iminga. Still and all, Parr had managed to turn her brief ride in it into mind-melting intimacy.

Anything else, the gearshift would have been in the way. And bucket seats definitely kept passenger and driver separated. So much for sexy sports cars. A top-of-the-line pickup had plenty of room to get in trouble.

Not a chance of that. The honking horn she heard was all too familiar. She fought the temptation to slide down in her seat like a caught-in-the-act teenager. Her dad had stopped in front of Parr's truck before it could move and was waving to them both.

Parr blew out a frustrated breath and put the truck in park. Then he rolled down his window to respond. "Hello there, Howard."

"Thought I might find you here. Alma said to track you down."

"What's up?" Parr asked.

Her dad acted as if he hadn't heard the question. "Mary Beth? Is that you?"

She sincerely hoped Parr hadn't been seen with females her father didn't know around the hospital or its parking lot. But she kept that thought to herself. "Yes, Daddy. Parr was just about to . . . take me home."

"Oh. Okay, well, we could all meet there if you like. Your mama has come up with a plan and we need to discuss it."

"Sure." Parr's amiable reply didn't match the set of his jaw. "Lead the way."

He followed Howard Caine's sedan out of the lot without grumbling, not looking at her or even talking.

Mary Beth saw to everything once the three of them were inside the Caine house, using her grandmother's best platter to carry sandwiches into the dining room, prewrapped and stone cold. Her father bought them at the megastore by the dozen and basically subsisted on them, still not having time to ever cook.

The two men sat down at the table, which gave off a faint, pleasant smell of lemon oil even though no one had used it for weeks. She went back into the kitchen for lemonade in a pitcher and fancy cookies still in the box, and the basket that was kept stocked with paper plates and napkins and plastic cups. Mary Beth figured that under the circumstances she'd more than met the sacred requirements of southern hospitality. If any of her great-great ancestors wanted to turn over in their graves at such an informal meal served in a real dining room, they were free to do so.

"Thanks, honey," her dad said. "Give a shout next time for some help."

"Everything was right where I needed it," she said, sitting down next to him. Cool and calm, she met Parr's eyes.

His big hands were clasped together on the highly polished table, which reflected his face above them. Even with the buffer of her father's presence in the room, Parr's gaze unsettled her.

Howard indicated the platter with a generous wave of his hand. "Help yourself, Parr. Have two. Have three. Mary Beth won't touch 'em and I'm sick of 'em."

She shot him a sideways look. "That's not very gracious of you, Daddy."

He chuckled. "No sense pretending, is there? It's not like any of us has had the time for all that."

Parr chose ham on a roll and Howard did too. She

selected a pimento-cheese that didn't look too lethal and nibbled cautiously on a corner once she'd gotten it unwrapped.

"All right. Here's the deal," Howard said when the box of cookies was passed around. "Parr, of course you know that Alma wants to stay here with me when she's released, which will be ahead of Bobby Joe."

Mary Beth spoke up quickly. "Which is fine with me." Surely her dad didn't think she'd be upset if Alma took up temporary residence in their house.

"I just wanted to be sure we all understand each other," Howard said, looking a trifle embarrassed.

Mary Beth smiled at him. It was true that in all the years of her upbringing, no woman had ever been invited to dinner, let alone stayed the night. Her father was nothing if not discreet.

"Thanks."

"And Parr—that means Bobby Joe would be back in your house fairly soon."

"I don't think of it as mine," Parr said. "It belongs to my mother."

"Well, I didn't quite know how to say it and I don't want to be giving orders here. I'm just conveying Alma's thoughts on the subject, Parr."

Mary Beth and Parr exchanged a look that expressed their mutual amusement. It was kind of funny that Alma and Howard felt obligated to be so cautious. The older couple's affection was obvious to all, and if they thought it was a secret—or ought to be one—

Parr interrupted her thoughts. "I appreciate that, sir. You've been her rock."

Howard Caine looked at his daughter. "Now, I'm

not kicking you out, Mary Beth. You, ah, have your bedroom here just like always. Unless . . . well, you and Bobby Joe won't have much privacy over there, what with the construction crew going night and day to finish up."

Her dad wasn't ever going to get used to the fact that she wasn't a little girl. And Mary Beth respected him too much to push the point. She patted his hand. "Don't worry. We'll figure it out." She didn't look across the table. It was easy enough to read Parr's expression in the polished surface.

He didn't seem overjoyed by the thought of her and his brother together at the Weston house, but since that was about the last thing she wanted, he didn't have to worry on that score. If Alma preferred to stay with her dad, that was fine with Mary Beth. Besides, fooling around would probably be out of the question for Bobby Joe.

The arrangement made sense. For now.

"What do you think?" Bobby Joe leaned on his cane and gestured expansively around the first floor of the old office building with his free hand. "Are we going to get rich people in here or what?"

Antique furniture, including a sideboard and a long settee, had been placed to good effect on newly refinished floors. The pieces were solid and simple, nothing ornate or overly fancy.

"Everything looks expensive." Mary Beth didn't bother to ask about the cost. If Parr was covering most of it, his younger brother didn't have to worry.

"That's the effect I want. Knock 'em dead, right?"

"I guess so. Once you revive them." The summer sun shone through the plate glass of the large front window and it was uncomfortably warm with the door closed. "How about the air-conditioning?"

"Parr recommended central air. When it's installed, Robert Joseph Weston and Associates will be the coolest place in town."

Mary Beth didn't ask who the associates were or would be. The extra word had probably just looked more impressive on the sign. She walked over to a framed display of properties for sale. "Are these exclusives?"

"No. I got them off the multiple listings," he said breezily.

He'd chosen big houses and estates. None were local. But she supposed that didn't matter to potential clients. Mary Beth didn't pretend to know anything about real estate.

Bobby Joe was heading toward the staircase but he stopped when a pretty woman paused in front of the window, shielding her eyes to peer through the reflection on the glass.

"Hello, honey. Come on in," he murmured. Then he winked at Mary Beth. "Don't worry. She won't."

"How do you know?"

"Because the door is locked. She's been by a couple of times."

The brunette gave him a dimpled smile, obviously not seeing Mary Beth standing in the shadowed interior. Since he'd gotten out of the hospital, Bobby Joe was magically more attractive to the opposite sex. The limp helped more than it hurt, apparently.

"I think she's just trying to figure out when we officially open," he added.

That date was several weeks away. Mary Beth had been charged with organizing the grand opening. However, in a town like Iminga, it wouldn't be all that grand. Homemade cookies and nonalcoholic punch was what she thought would do, with colorful balloons outside and a sign to let people know they were in business. Bobby Joe had other, more grandiose ideas. Parr had asked her to talk him out of it. So far he'd seemed willing to listen.

Alma had volunteered to bake cookies and that was all. And even Parr seemed to have his limits.

Bobby Joe acknowledged the brunette's curiosity with a nod just before she saw Mary Beth, who'd stepped forward. The woman's smile faded away and she moved on.

"Told you. Come on upstairs." Bobby Joe was taking them one at a time. Mary Beth followed slowly.

There were oak desks and swivel chairs, all vintage. Two brand-new computers were on the floor, still in sealed boxes. "Is it safe to leave those here?" she asked.

"The security system will be hooked up this afternoon," he said, sitting down in one of the swivel chairs. His leg would eventually heal completely, but he still needed to stay off it as much as possible.

Before the accident, he would have pulled her into his lap and had his hands all over her. Today, he was all business, in a scattershot, easily distracted way. It was clear to those who knew him that his mind functioned differently now. Whether the personality change was permanent was an open question.

For that reason, she had avoided the subject of a separation. Bobby Joe had yet to bring it up since he'd left the hospital, where he'd mentioned it to Parr that one time in private and then apparently forgotten all about it.

He used the cane to spin the chair around, smiling with satisfaction, master of his little domain. Did Bobby Joe even know how much Parr had done to jump-start the business in his absence? She sort of doubted it. At least Parr wasn't around to confirm or deny anything—he'd gone to Atlanta for some reason he hadn't chosen to reveal.

Mary Beth took the other chair. There was something else they needed to discuss: exactly how he planned to run the office by himself. She didn't want to be enlisted for that, not when the two months she had off every year—a major benefit of being a school social worker—had started. The long leave she'd taken to help care for Bobby Joe and Alma had flowed into the beginning of summer almost before she'd been aware of it.

"Which desk is yours?" she asked.

"The big one."

She pressed her lips together for a couple of seconds, not wanting to say something tactless that might tick him off. Besides being impulsive, Bobby Joe was quick to take offense. "Have you given any thought to hiring office help?"

"Sure have."

Okay. Maybe he was more on it than she'd thought.

"That's wise. I know it's possible to go it alone in real estate, but why would you want to?"

"Parr recommended looking for someone with Gail's qualifications. I could use an assistant with that level of experience."

Mary Beth gave a reluctant nod. "I don't doubt it. Maybe she knows a likely candidate."

"Not around here. But I'll give her a call, ask for some tips."

Gail on the phone was not as troubling as Gail in real life. It was true that Mary Beth had only met her once in person, but something about the way she moved had reminded her of a snake in a garden. Coiled up but watchful, with her gaze fixed on Parr—and at a family party too. Even in the random photos Mary Beth had seen by chance, Gail had been half hidden.

Mary Beth didn't suppose that Gail had any particular interest in Bobby Joe, only that perhaps the woman wanted Parr to think that might be the case.

Her uneasiness grew as Bobby Joe sat idly listening to the unanswered ringing. "Guess she's not there." He spun away from Mary Beth when Gail finally picked up.

"Hello," he intoned. "This is Robert Weston speaking, from Robert Joseph Weston and Associates." He broke into laughter. "Don't I sound like a big shot? How are you, Gail? How's the weather in Memphis?"

A response that was too soft for anyone besides Bobby Joe to make out actual words reached Mary Beth. Did Gail have a sixth sense for the presence of someone listening in? Could be.

"Lucky you. Seventy-two degrees sounds like heaven," Bobby Joe said into the phone. "It's hotter than Hades down here. Now, I know you're working hard and I don't want to keep you, but I was wondering . . ."

He explained what he needed in terms of information and ignored what Mary Beth surmised was a promise to call him back later—or a brush-off.

"Gail, you can take five minutes to talk to me. My brother won't mind. He's the one who said I should call you." He lowered his voice to a seductive pitch. "And he's not there, now is he?"

His endless flirting was nothing new, but it bordered on compulsive now. His behavior disturbed Mary Beth. The conversation could be entirely practical on Gail's side, but Bobby Joe made it sound intimate.

Mary Beth left the room, preferring to wander through the small building rather than listen in. She went up to the third floor, a smaller, garretlike space that seemed larger than it was because of the white walls. The skylight in the ceiling had been propped open a few inches to air out the smell of fresh paint. A stepladder stood in the open position, but the inevitable mess of tarps and buckets and brushes and rollers had been cleared away.

She touched a fingertip to the wall just to make sure it was dry, then looked up when a shadow passed over the skylight. Mary Beth relaxed when she remembered that Mr. Corlear was on the roof, repairing the support for the big sign that had been snapped by a gust of wind during a recent thunderstorm. His heavy footsteps moved to the side of the building and down the metal ladder that was fixed to the exterior wall.

Parr hadn't been able to get Bobby Joe to see reason when it came to things like big signs. But that was Parr's problem. Mary Beth was concerned about other things. She took a seat at a small desk, brooding as Bobby Joe went on talking one flight below.

Her own phone rang and she took it out of her pocket and looked at a text reminder that her bill was due. After all that time in the hospital, she'd undoubtedly gone way over on minutes and messaging. Mary Beth didn't want to review the total.

She tapped the screen and smiled at the wallpaper photo of baby Amanda sleeping like an angel, her plump cheeks flushed a delicate pink, a tiny bow attached somehow to her wispy hair. Mary Beth thought about calling Eve and decided not to. Amanda could squall good and loud when so inclined, and Mary Beth didn't want to be the one who set her off.

"You there?" Bobby Joe called to her, his voice echoing up the stairwell.

She sighed and called back. "Yes. Where else would I be?"

"Smarty-pants. I just didn't know if you were up or down."

She could say the same thing about herself but for different reasons. "Want me to—"

"Just stay there." He came slowly up the stairs and appeared in the door frame. "Are you mad at me?"

"No."

The curt reply didn't seem to make much of a dent

in his self-satisfaction. Even with the limp, there was a swagger to his step as he came into the room.

"Sorry. Gail and I lost track of time," he offered.

It wasn't much of an explanation, but Mary Beth didn't want to argue.

"So how do you like it up here?"

Mary Beth ran a hand over the fine veneer of the small desk, deciding to humor him. "It might be my favorite of all the rooms. I like the skylight."

Bobby Joe leaned against the stepladder the painter had left in the room. "I had you in mind when I picked out the doll house furniture. It's your size, baby."

Mary Beth managed a smile.

"Want to know what I had in mind?" He quickly answered his own question. "That you might want to use this for a work space someday."

"Oh? But I like my job. I'm not quitting."

"You could double your income as a consultant," he said.

Like he knew anything about the school bureaucracy.

"I don't think so. Education budgets are getting trimmed right and left."

Bobby Joe shook his head. "Negative thinking won't get you anywhere."

"That's practical. Not negative." She was wary about where this conversation was going. Lately, he latched on to improbable ideas and let go of them in the next minute, during mood swings that rarely made sense. Humoring him only seemed easy. They'd been on the verge of quarreling more than once, but Mary Beth had stopped herself in time.

"Well, I had a key made for you," he said, taking various items out of his pockets and setting them on the fold-out section of the ladder. Business cards. A pen. His smartphone. "Shoot. Maybe I left it downstairs."

A distant knock reached them.

"Now, who could that be?" Bobby Joe asked her.

Mary Beth figured it wasn't the brunette. "I heard Mr. Corlear on the roof and then on the outside ladder. Must be him."

Bobby Joe nodded. "Of course. He did ask if I could give him a check."

"Where is it?"

"I didn't make it out yet. Besides, there's a couple of things I wanted to discuss with him," Bobby Joe said. He went out to the staircase, leaving her there.

Mary Beth was in no great hurry to join him. She looked around the sunny room, and then up when a breeze whispered through the skylight. She ought to close it.

She pushed the ladder directly underneath and lifted the heavy glass by the metal frame, releasing the latch that also served to prop it open. The skylight settled into place and she stepped down, collecting Bobby Joe's personal items.

His smartphone buzzed in her hand. She didn't look at the screen and she wasn't going to answer it. She wasn't even tempted to snoop. What would she find out that she didn't already know? It was a sure thing that Luellen had called, probably several times. And maybe others. The hell with it. She was so drained she didn't have the energy to be angry. Jealousy hardly seemed justified, under the circumstances.

Mary Beth left the room and went downstairs.

"There you go, Pete." Bobby Joe clapped Mr. Corlear on the back. "Thanks so much for the quick fix on the sign." He handed over the signed check just as she reached his side.

Mary Beth couldn't help noticing that Parr had countersigned it first. Bobby Joe moved a few steps over to one of the desks to enter the amount in a ledger that hadn't been out when she'd looked around before. The ledger was the old-fashioned kind that had perforated stubs to the left of the checks. Her side glance at the top page—six checks with one gone—told her that there was only one check left with Parr's bold signature. The other four were completely blank.

So he was staying in control of what his younger brother spent and tracking it. That was a relief, if only for Bobby Joe's sake.

"The weld should hold," Mr. Corlear said, folding the check and tucking it in the pocket of his work shirt. "If not, call me right away."

"You bet."

Affably, Bobby Joe showed him to the door and the two men said their good-byes as Mary Beth looked on.

"Where were we?" he asked her absently as he turned back into the main room.

"Talking about a key that you had made for me. Here's your things." She handed them over, taking a chance on him not recollecting what he'd said about her becoming a consultant.

"Oh, right. And I thought I had it in my pockets."
He set the phone and other items on top of a desk and
opened its drawers to rummage through them. There
seemed to be only a few office necessities rattling
around inside—rolls of tape, sticky notes, pencils.
Bobby Joe pulled out the wide, flat drawer in the
middle of the desk. There were several keys with paper
tags, lying there in no particular order.

"Bingo." He chose a key, seemingly at random.

"How do you know that's the right one?"

Bobby Joe winked at her. "They're all the same."

Which begged the question of who the other four
or five keys were for. Mary Beth told herself to just not
think about it.

He presented it to her with a flourish.

"Thanks. But I don't know if I'm ever going to use
it." She slipped the key into her purse.

Bobby Joe lifted her chin so he could look into her
eyes. "Listen. You and I need to talk."

"Maybe some other time. I'm tired. It's been a long
day."

"Was it? You're on vacation." His fingers tightened.

Mary Beth jerked her head and stepped back.
"Stop it."

He seemed momentarily disconcerted. She reminded herself of what they'd been told to expect.
Erratic social interactions, for one thing. Grandiose
moods followed by consuming self-doubt was another.
And diminished awareness for other people's boundaries.

"That means he's going to get on your nerves a fair

amount," one therapist had said in plain English. "Try not to take it personally."

Bobby Joe thrust his hands in his pockets and walked away from her. "Ever since I got out of the hospital, it's been different between you and me."

"How so?" Her voice sounded thin and reedy, even to herself.

"But then you'd changed before that." He turned to face her squarely. "And that's what I want to talk about. I finally remembered what happened before the accident. You came right out and said we should separate for a while. I've been waiting for you to bring it up again."

"I—I never found the right moment." She prayed for patience. Explaining her reasons why could set him off somehow.

Bobby Joe frowned as he studied her. "Am I wrong? Didn't you say that? I told Parr you did."

Mary Beth quailed under his steady gaze. Confessing she'd known that since the day she'd met Parr in the hospital cafeteria could be the spark that would ignite a major fight. But she had never asked Parr about his response.

"And what did he say?"

She hadn't planned to ask that question. As soon as it was out of her mouth, she regretted it. Especially when Bobby Joe answered.

"He told me I shouldn't give up."

Mary Beth swallowed hard. "Really."

"And I'm not going to. That wasn't all I remembered," he added. "When that car hit the guardrail, it was you I thought of. And what we had."

A pretend engagement, she wanted to say. She'd been absurdly naive and he'd gotten away with outrageous behavior that hadn't improved. If anything, it was worse. He seemed to have entirely lost the ability to see himself as others saw him, and he'd never been good at it to begin with. Even Alma would admit by now that her darling second son felt too entitled to everything he wanted. Mary Beth couldn't fathom why Bobby Joe wanted to keep on pretending. "We can't go back to who we were then."

"It wasn't that long ago, baby." His tone was pleading. "Don't give up on us."

The repeated words rocked her to the core. Why would Parr give his brother advice like that? She couldn't begin to guess.

"I can't say one way or another. Maybe this isn't the best time to discuss it," she hedged. "You have a lot of things to take care of and right now—"

Bobby Joe frowned again, darkly. "I wish I knew why everyone's treating me like I can't think straight. I'm sick of it."

He moved over to the main switch plate by the door and started switching off lights one by one with vicious snaps.

She opened the door, alarmed by the suddenness of his ugly mood, and unwilling to be trapped inside with him. The air outside was steamy, enfolding her in summer heat rising from the sidewalks. The breeze that had blown through the old building's uppermost floor couldn't be felt down here.

Bobby Joe pulled the wood-framed glass door shut with a bang that rattled the panes. Then he locked it from the outside and stalked away without a word. She saw him reach Alma's car, which she'd given him to drive now that he could. He opened the door and got inside. The roof light illuminated his face for several seconds until he put the car in gear and drove past her without looking at her.

There was nowhere for her to go but home. Her own.

Mary Beth tiptoed past the arched doorway to the living room, grateful that her dad and Alma were watching baseball with the volume up high. Alma was settled into a huge armchair and her dad had the recliner and the remote. Engrossed in the game, neither saw her.

She made it all the way up the stairs to her bedroom and tossed her purse onto the bed. Her smartphone skidded across the comforter and Mary Beth retrieved it.

Bobby Joe hadn't called to apologize and that was just as well. She needed a reason to not be with him. Parr hadn't called either, but she hadn't been expecting him to. She tucked the phone into her purse and set it aside on the night table.

She changed out of her clothes into jersey-knit pajama bottoms and her softest T-shirt, then flopped onto the bed, staring at the ceiling. Out of recently acquired habit, her fingers traced the fine chain that held the hidden gem Parr had given her.

It was the only reminder she had of his passionate tenderness toward her and the seductive words he'd whispered in her ear the very first time he'd held her. *"I want to kiss you. But you want more, don't you?"*

He had known instinctively that she did. Parr Weston's experience more than made up for her burdensome innocence.

Afraid, she'd pulled back, deeply unsettled by what she felt for him, fearing what other people might think of her, retreating into the role she'd always played: a good girl. She'd tried to believe in Bobby Joe's promises and done her best to not upset his devoted mother.

Her fingers tightened on the chain and the clasp suddenly opened. She could feel the fine links slide down over her collarbone. Mary Beth rolled on her side, pulling carefully on the chain until it was draped over her fingers and the ruby strawberry was resting in her palm, warm from her body heat.

She peered at the clasp. It hadn't opened—it had broken apart from the chain at one end. A tiny ring that held them together had cracked. She looked closer. The chain itself had snapped in a different place. An infinitesimal link dangled free. It wasn't something she could fix. She would have to take the necklace to a jeweler for repair. Until then, she couldn't wear it.

Mary Beth sat up, curling her fingers around the precious memento. The box it had come in was stashed in the back of a dresser drawer, along with the wrapping paper, which she'd kept too.

She found the box and put the necklace into it, replacing the lid and rewrapping it, using a bit of the original tape. Not exactly sealed but safe enough.

The tilted mirror over her dresser reflected her hands as she worked on the box. She set it inside her jewelry chest and shut the lid, tipping the mirror straight to look at herself.

Her face was pale and drawn. She was inclined to think of the doubly broken chain as a sign of some sort—and not a good one. Mary Beth picked up a brush and dragged it through her tangled hair. Parr's gift had brought nothing but bad luck.

Chapter Fourteen

"I do know that Bobby Joe's been a handful lately, Mary Beth. I just want you to know how much I appreciate your patience with him."

Alma moved around the kitchen of the Caine house, using the counters and the dinette chairs for something to hang on to. The renovations at her house were almost done, but the dust from the sanding and fine finishing bothered Alma, who'd decided to stay on.

Mary Beth didn't mind having her around at all. In fact, she found Alma's presence a comforting buffer. Bobby Joe was less inclined to pitch fits in front of his mother.

Still, she wasn't quite sure how to reply to Alma's remark. "Did Parr tell you that?"

"Yes. We had a little talk before he left for Atlanta."

Her dad, by coincidence, was there too. A long-planned trip to see his beloved Braves in action. But as far as Mary Beth knew, Howard and Parr had no plans to meet up.

"Seems like you and Bobby Joe could use a little

time away from each other," Alma continued in a matter-of-fact voice. "Was it him or you that came up with the idea of a fishing trip?"

Bobby Joe had left yesterday to drive down to the Gulf with friends. Their parting had been cool, though courteous. Mary Beth knew it would be only a matter of time before they officially broke up. Telling Alma was still the sticking point for both of them.

"One of his buddies, actually. I didn't mind a bit."

Alma chuckled. "I never did myself. I don't like worms or sitting in a boat in the broiling sun. Whew. Just thinking about it makes me tireder than I already am."

It had been about all Mary Beth could do to not jump up and take over the job of tidying up the already clean kitchen. Alma had insisted on helping out. There wasn't a speck of grease or a crumb in sight, and all the dishes had been put away.

"I hope he gets whatever's bugging him out of his system. Sometimes I think I indulged Bobby Joe too much when I was raising those boys," Alma said thoughtfully. "Even before the accident, he didn't seem to be as grown up as Parr was at the same age."

Mary Beth nodded politely. She didn't want to get into it, not on such a scorching day. The air conditioners were set on maximum but the house still felt a little too warm. At least she could wear a scoop neck tank without having to worry about the ruby necklace being remarked on. Though she missed it, now that the chain was broken.

She was still going to have it fixed. Just not at the jeweler's in Iminga.

Alma finished wiping imaginary spots and eased herself into a chair, heaving a sigh of satisfaction.

"There. Nice to be able to sit down in something that isn't a wheelchair." She smiled. "I like being able to walk on my own. Slow and sure, that's me."

The blood clot at the base of her spine had diminished and then vanished. Most of the time Alma didn't need her cane.

"Please don't overdo it."

Alma winked at Mary Beth. "That's not likely with you around watchin' and worryin'. But I like to make myself useful."

"You don't have to do a thing in our house," Mary Beth reminded her. "But if you insist . . ."

"It's good for me." Alma looked out the window as if her mind was elsewhere for a few moments. "Now, Mary Beth, you can say no, but I did want to ask you a favor."

"Go right ahead."

Alma folded her arms and leaned on the table. "I had a mind to go out to Brickell, the town where the boys and I used to live."

"Oh." Mary Beth was startled by the idea.

"Would you like to go? I've been meaning to get my affairs in order—" She broke into laughter at the expression on Mary Beth's face. "Don't worry. I plan to be around to annoy everyone for years to come. I'm not dying."

"I didn't mean to suggest that."

Alma shook her head, still smiling. "I'll tell you what started it. I got all fired up when I thought about my birthday coming up. I'm going to be seventy. Seemed like high time for me to deal with a lot of things I've been putting off for too long."

"I understand."

"So anyway, Sheila Palmer, an old friend of mine from Brickell, called last night. She wants to sell her house this year and she was going through the shelves in her garage. Lo and behold, she found boxes of photos and knickknacks I stashed there years ago. I'd forgotten all about them."

That must have been when the Westons left, never to return. Mary Beth stuck to practical considerations. "How many boxes? My car isn't that big."

"Sheila said there were about five or six. As I remember, they were on the small side and none of them were heavy. It's just that she doesn't know what I want and what I don't want. So I have to go look, at least."

Alma lifted the pitcher of sweet tea nestled in a bowl of ice on the table, looking at Mary Beth first. "Wet your whistle?"

"No thanks."

The older woman poured herself a small glass, drinking it with a thoughtful expression. "Do you know the town?"

"No. I don't think I've ever driven out that way."

"It's real country. Brickell is about fifty miles west of Iminga. It's much smaller, though, and it's so pretty. There's lots of trees—giant old tupelos and loblolly pines. And bald cypress down by the water. It's a whole lot cooler than here, that's for damn sure."

Mary Beth's automatic thought was for Bobby Joe. If he came back while she was gone, he could manage without her, now that he had been cleared to drive again, at least on local streets. She wanted to avoid him and this was an easy way out, just like the fishing trip. He hadn't wasted any time hitting the road. Mary Beth figured she might as well.

"Sounds nice. I could really use a mini vacation."

Her answer must not have sounded nonchalant enough. Alma's forehead furrowed with concern. "You mean that, Mary Beth? How bad has it been?"

"Not that bad. I don't want to complain."

"Oh, go ahead. Better let off some steam." The older woman clasped her hands on the table. "I know Bobby Joe has had his ups and downs since he got out of the hospital. Seems to me he's not himself yet. But I believe he'll recover fully."

Mary Beth gave a slight nod. When and if that happened was anyone's guess.

Alma's gaze seemed troubled. "But that's not all I'm worried about. You're not the same either."

"What do you mean?"

Mary Beth had tried hard to always act like nothing much was the matter.

"We've all changed," Alma insisted. "Just because you weren't in that car doesn't mean the crash didn't affect you."

Mary Beth silently conceded the point.

"You've got to be honest with yourself about whether you want to go on, Mary Beth."

Mary Beth had no answer to that. "Bobby Joe and I are going to talk when he comes back."

Alma heaved a sigh. "Sometimes that can help. But even before the hospital and all that, we—Howard and

I—could see that things weren't going well. Him going right back into business doesn't help."

Did his mother know how much Parr had poured into Robert Joseph Weston and Associates? Mary Beth doubted it. It would be a while before there was actual income. There had been some interest in the properties posted on the office walls. But nothing Bobby Joe could take to the bank.

"I just hope he succeeds at it, and that it's what he really wants to do," Mary Beth said.

Whatever happened, Mary Beth knew by now that Bobby Joe would put himself first. Her career wasn't something he'd ever paid much attention to.

"I suppose it will work out one way or another. Should I be optimistic?"

Alma looked to Mary Beth as if expecting an answer. Mary Beth gave an infinitesimal shrug that was neither a yes or a no. Alma waited for several moments before she spoke again.

"Maybe the accident just postponed the inevitable. I wish it wasn't that way, but I'm prepared to accept what has to be."

Mary Beth leaned across the table and patted Alma's hands, aware of the tension in the older woman's tightly clenched fingers.

"Bobby Joe and I haven't made any decision one way or another," Mary Beth said gently. "But you're right. Things are rocky at the moment. Maybe I should have confided in you."

Alma shook her head. "I understand why you wouldn't. It's not necessary, Mary Beth."

"I feel so bad about you worrying."

Alma unclasped her hands and spread her fingers on the table, fiddling with a sterling silver band set with turquoise that she'd had forever. She still wasn't wearing an engagement ring, Mary Beth thought absently. Her dad must be waiting for the right moment.

"Now, now. Just thought I'd say my piece, that was all."

Mary Beth put her hands in her lap. The diamond rings Bobby Joe had given her felt heavier every day.

"I understand." She was beginning to, anyway. It occurred to Mary Beth that her own mother, had she lived, would have had similar concerns. "I appreciate it, Alma. But I think we should change the subject."

The older woman seemed relieved. "You bet."

"About Brickell—I didn't make any plans for the summer." Mary Beth kept her tone neutral. "How long were you thinking of staying?"

"A few days. Maybe more if you like it there." The hopeful expression in Alma's eyes and her beaming smile got to Mary Beth. "You don't have to run back and care for my son, you know. It'd do him good to not take you for granted."

Mary Beth managed a semi-smile in return. Alma was right about that.

"Then let's go," Mary Beth said.

"Right now?"

"How about as soon as we pack?"

Alma rose stiffly. "Yes. Oh, I do love running away. And it serves Howard right for ditching me for another darn Braves game."

"We can leave a note for him and call Bobby Joe from the road."

The prospect of getting away quickened Alma's careful steps. She was almost out of the room when she turned to Mary Beth and winked. "They'll survive."

The drive from Iminga was uneventful. Mary Beth rolled down her window, enjoying the sultry breeze that floated over endless fields to reach them, bringing the green scent of growing crops. It sure was a change from Iminga.

Alma had talked a blue streak for the first half of the trip and not just to Mary Beth. She'd video-chatted with her niece Eve Ross and cooed at the sleeping baby girl in her arms.

Mary Beth kept her eyes on the road but she'd been happy to listen in and say hello to the Rosses. Alma had wrapped it up when the baby fell asleep, and then she worked her way through her contacts list, chatting briefly with pals who were glad to hear that she was well enough to undertake a short journey.

The last ten miles had been phone free. The reception wasn't too great this far out in the country.

Mary Beth glanced over at Alma, whose eyes were closed.

"You might want to wake up. I think we're almost there."

"If you insist." Alma yawned and looked out the window.

"Am I right?" Mary Beth asked.

"I do believe you are, according to that road marker. It just looks different, that's all."

"How long has it been since you went back?"

"Mercy. Let me think. I don't know exactly. Quite a while. Slow down. That's the driveway."

Mary Beth slowed almost to a stop to take the right turn into it, following its meanders and bumping gently over the unpaved parts.

"Yikes. These ruts are deep. How's your back?"

"Doesn't hurt a bit," Alma said. "But I wouldn't want to do this in the dark. You'd end up in the trees."

As Alma had promised, Sheila's house was really in the country, though technically within the township of Brickell.

Mary Beth took a deep breath. Leafy trees on either side of the driveway made dappled sunlight, punctuated by birds that flitted from branch to branch above. One zoomed in front of the windshield and Mary Beth braked.

"Sorry. How's your back now?"

"Don't ask," Alma said. "All I'm thinking about is how good it is to be here."

Mary Beth saw white up ahead. "Is that the house?"

"Sure is."

The driveway widened and then Mary Beth saw all of it. Sheila Palmer's house was a fine old place, covered in white clapboard and trimmed with delicate gingerbread.

There was even a wraparound porch that overlooked a small, round pond from one side. Mary Beth looked more closely at it. It wasn't a pond but a pool, designed to look like a natural part of the landscaping. Nice.

The tall, wavy-glass windows reflected the car as they

drove up. "Now, what is that van doing here?" Alma wondered aloud.

A large van with a rental company logo had been pulled up at the other side of the house. The open rear doors afforded a glimpse of taped boxes stacked inside, shoved all the way to the back of the cargo space.

Alma didn't have to wait more than a few seconds for an answer. Sheila, a reed-thin woman with pure white hair, ran down the stairs to greet them.

"Hello there," she said, leaning into the open window. "They must be done tearin' up the county roads like they always do in summer. You got here awful fast."

Alma waved away the comment. "Mary Beth did the driving. She never once went over the speed limit."

"Nice work," Sheila said. "And hello, Mary Beth."

"Hi, Sheila. Thanks so much for inviting us."

"Oh, don't thank me. I plan to put you two to work immediately."

"Not me. Where's the hammock?" Alma joked back.

"Under the sweet gum tree, where it always was. You two come on in and have some lemonade and pie first."

She opened the passenger door and helped Alma out, taking the cane that Mary Beth handed to her.

"What's the van doing here?" Alma asked her friend.

Mary Beth listened to the conversation as she got their overnight bags out of the trunk and slung them over her shoulders.

"I rented it and hired a fellow, Bud, to help pack. My

real-estate broker told me to cut down on the clutter and there's a giant flea market this weekend. A friend of mine has a table. He said to come on out. He'll sell stuff for me. Thinks I could make a mint."

"Then there's hope for us all," Alma laughed. "Bet you're the only person who has more trinkets than I do."

"Maybe so. Careful now." Sheila kept a watchful eye on Alma as she mounted the wide front steps.

Mary Beth brought up the rear.

"Would you mind setting those bags outside for just a bit?" Sheila asked her, pointing to a wicker sofa and matching chairs. "Right there would be fine. I don't want Shep and Beau knocking you over when you're carrying all that."

Mary Beth thought for a second that Alma hadn't mentioned Sheila having sons. Then the screen door blew open and a couple of big brown dogs burst out, bypassing Sheila and Alma and heading straight for Mary Beth. She tossed the bags into the nearest chair just in time.

Miraculously, they sat and stayed at Sheila's command. Except for their thick tails, which brushed the porch floor like they were sweeping it.

"Good dogs." Mary Beth patted each canine head in turn. Shep, true to his name, had the black muzzle and thick ruff of his breed, while Beau looked like more of a mix. They were powerful animals, about the same size.

Alma looked at the well-behaved animals a little nervously. "Do they always obey?"

"Of course." Sheila took a couple of dog treats from

a covered flowerpot. "I trained them myself. They're awful friendly, but they do make a lot of noise sometimes. Bark first, ask questions later. Isn't that right?"

Shep and Beau trotted back to Sheila, then sat again, panting, awaiting their reward.

"Mind your manners. And roll up those tongues," Sheila instructed them.

Done.

She balanced the treats on their noses.

Mary Beth laughed at the dogs' cross-eyed patience. Sheila snapped her fingers and they gulped the treats. "Go play," she instructed them. "They'll be back soon enough," she told Alma and Mary Beth.

Sheila assisted Alma over the threshold. Mary Beth picked up the bags again and stepped inside, letting her eyes adjust to the dimness after the strong sunshine. The interior was half hidden by a number of boxes placed haphazardly about, but Mary Beth could see that it was handsomely furnished with good antiques.

"Are you going to the flea market?" Alma wanted to know.

"Not today. Bud is still packing stuff upstairs. I tagged everything for him so I don't have to breathe down his neck. I'll introduce you later, but for right now, you all come into my parlor." Sheila led the way. "Take the settee, Alma. Mary Beth can have the armchair. I can't wait to hear all the news. It's been too long."

The two friends settled in, trading tales of old times for hours until Mary Beth took a surreptitious peek at her watch. She'd been entertained by their reminiscing but it looked to her like they were going to stay up half the night talking. Mary Beth decided to leave them to it as it was almost eleven o'clock. Alma seemed content to be there, even happy, as if she'd turned the clock back to her younger days.

"I'm afraid I'm going to have to call it a night," she said, rising from the armchair. She collected the glasses and snack plates on her way out. "Can I get you something from the kitchen?"

"No, but thank you, Mary Beth," Sheila said. "Us old biddies will manage. Hope we didn't bore you."

"Not at all," she answered truthfully.

"Go to bed, then. We're not done yet," Alma laughed. "But don't you dare wash up those dishes."

"Yes, ma'am." Mary Beth set the dishes and glasses in the kitchen, and took the rear staircase to reach her bedroom. It had an attached bath, a wonderful luxury. During the course of the conversation, she'd picked up the basics of Sheila's life story. She'd been the young widow of an older husband who'd left her plenty of money to keep up and renovate this fine old house. They'd had no children and Sheila didn't seem to have any regrets on that score.

Shep and Beau were recent acquisitions in a long line of beloved dogs.

The guest bedroom was blessedly free of cardboard boxes, which was good, because Mary Beth knew she would have stumbled into them if she had to get up at night. She'd reached the point of exhaustion where sleep would enfold her for hours.

But her dreams were troubled by a nameless feeling

of anxiety that only the streaming sunshine dispelled. Mary Beth opened her eyes, not quite remembering where she was for a few disconcerting seconds.

Scores of birds chirping and tweeting and carrying on in the trees that rustled right outside her window brought her back to her present reality.

Mary Beth pushed back the covers and got up, finding a short robe to put on over her pajamas. The welcome smell of coffee wafted through the air.

"Alma?" She asked the question quietly once she'd stepped out into the hall. The door to the other guest bedroom was ajar, revealing a messily unpacked suitcase on the unmade bed. The room was otherwise empty. Alma must have risen with the sun, for all that she'd gone to bed late.

Moving on, Mary Beth peeked discreetly into the master bedroom, which was also unoccupied, its canopy bed neatly made up and huge lace-trimmed pillows plumped.

She went downstairs and into the kitchen using the rear staircase again.

"There you are."

"Good morning," Alma said cheerfully. "I got coffee going. Ready in five."

"Thanks. I could use some. You're up early."

"I wanted to fix my hair." Alma patted the arrangement on her head. There was no other word for it. Her bouffant hairdo was being restored to its majestic height by jumbo curlers held in place by pins and a scarf tied with a jaunty bow over her forehead.

"So I see."

Alma patted the tower of curlers on her head. "How scary do I look?"

"Not at all."

"At my age, I have to work at being beautiful. Unlike you." Her tone was gently teasing. "My, how your hair shines in the morning light, Mary Beth. That natural red blond is just so pretty."

"Yours too," Mary Beth said loyally.

"Maybe it was something like your color back in the day," Alma laughed. "I honestly don't remember the exact shade."

She tightened the sash of her ankle-length robe, a chenille wrap that looked super comfortable. There was a distant sound of happy woofing.

"Should I let them in?" Mary Beth asked.

"Hell no. I just let them out," Alma said. "I prefer to have my coffee and muffin without being stared at by hungry eyes. And yes, I fed them." She walked over to a double set of windows and pulled the cord to open the curtains. "There's the porch. It's a beautiful day. Did the sun wake you up?"

"Pretty much. But I slept well."

"That's good. I'll tell Sheila. She likes people to be comfortable."

"I can tell her myself."

"She's not here." Alma poured two cups of coffee and brought them to the table. "Last night she decided to drive out early and give Bud a hand with unpacking and whatnot. She invited us, of course, but I just wasn't up for wandering around a big flea market. You could still go."

Left unsaid was that Alma preferred not to be alone

if she could help it. Mary Beth didn't press the point.
She was grateful to stay right here. Besides, she was
curious about the town of Brickell, which she still
hadn't seen.

"Aren't you going to give me the grand tour?"

Alma put a level teaspoon of sugar into her coffee
and stirred it slowly, adding a dash of half-and-half. "I
guess I could do that," she said in a measured voice.

There wasn't much to see in Brickell, but Mary Beth
and Alma were enjoying themselves. They drove down
the main street, looking at retail establishments.

The town was too small to have been taken over by
chain stores. Mary Beth guessed that the shops were
locally owned. Everything seemed to be lovingly main-
tained and there were wrought-iron benches along
the sidewalk, set between planters filled with flowers.
Brickell had kept its charm.

"There's the gift shop," Alma said. "I want to pick
up something for Sheila but we can do that later. And
there's the tea parlor. Hasn't changed a bit."

Mary Beth could see white chairs and tables through
the window. A collection of china teapots adorned the
low inside sill.

"It's pretty."

"Yes. And—oh, I remember that restaurant," Alma
said, turning her head. "It used to be called something
else. But it always had those rambler roses. Aren't they
glorious?"

Mary Beth slowed the car even more, leaning over a

little to admire the cascade of pink blooms trellised over the restaurant's big front window. It was impossible to see inside.

"Bet that's a nice place for dinner."

"It was back then. Parr and Bobby Joe's dad used to take me there once in a while."

"Want to go in?"

"No." There was something wistful in Alma's expression. "I'm still full from breakfast."

A nibbled mini-muffin and a cup of coffee didn't support that statement.

"Okay. Maybe later. We could go to a diner. How about that one?"

Trucks and cars were pulled up in front of a bustling eatery. Mary Beth read the sign aloud. "Visit Red Vinyl Diner for red velvet cake. Our burgers are the best and our shakes are simply super!"

Alma nodded. "That was true. And everyone used to go there too. But I expect it's under new ownership."

"Could be even better," Mary Beth said, realizing that Alma's energy had faded noticeably. "Want to go in?"

"I don't think so, honey. Tell you what. Let's pick up cold cuts and rolls at the convenience store and we can have ourselves a picnic somewhere pretty."

"All right. Whatever works for you."

Alma reclined her seat a little. "My back is hurting. I don't want to limp in with a cane and have people make a fuss. What if I see someone I used to know?

Then I have to explain the accident and . . . well, I'm just not up for any of that."

Mary Beth didn't argue with the rambling explanation. And she was fine with whatever Alma preferred. The convenience store was just down the street and she went in to get the food.

She'd left the key in the ignition and the windows rolled up so the air-conditioning would stay on for Alma's comfort. When Mary Beth exited the store, she saw that the passenger side visor was down, even though the car was parked on the shady side of the street. It was almost like Alma was hiding.

Mary Beth wasn't going to ask why. Maybe coming back here made Alma feel suddenly older than her years. But, Mary Beth guessed, more likely it had to do with whatever had happened that had caused the Westons to leave Brickell.

Mary Beth opened her door and slid in, handing a bulging plastic bag of sandwich makings and soda to Alma. "Sliced ham. Fresh rolls. Mayonnaise. Plus two bananas and a couple of moon pies," she said.

Alma chuckled. "Good Lord. I shouldn't eat all that. But I'm going to try." She settled the bag in her lap. "The road out of town is that way."

By then Mary Beth was looking over her shoulder and backing up. She didn't see which way Alma pointed and went in the opposite direction, distracted by what she was doing and the ringing of Alma's phone.

The older woman reached for the purse at her feet and peered at the screen. "Your dad," Alma said happily. "My goodness. Howard sent me a text. I do believe that's a first for him."

"I think you're right." Mary Beth smiled. "You're a bad influence."

Alma was all about communication. Howard did his best to keep up with modern life and he liked gadgets as much as the next guy. But he'd stayed away from texting, insisting that he liked to talk to people.

Evidently Alma had persuaded him to change his mind.

"I'm gonna answer it right now. If I don't, he'll think he did it wrong."

Alma fumbled for her reading glasses and slipped them on her nose, tapping at the on-screen keyboard.

"Tell him I said hello," Mary Beth instructed.

"I will." Alma and Howard exchanged messages for several minutes.

Mary Beth kept her eyes on the road and left Alma to it. She sensed the older woman's mood brightening with each incoming and outgoing beep.

Eventually Alma looked up. "Where are we?"

"I don't know." Mary Beth glanced down at the odometer. "About five miles outside Brickell."

"You went the wrong way." Alma's low voice sounded serious.

Mary Beth glanced at her. "I can turn around up ahead. Looks like there's a place to pull off."

Alma put the phone back in her purse, along with her reading glasses, as Mary Beth pulled into the weed-choked driveway of a boarded-up motel. The room doors were sprayed with graffiti and a couple stood open, offering glimpses of empty rooms with scarred walls where fixtures and pipes had been stolen for scrap.

There had to be more than one resident snake somewhere in the overgrown grounds, which Mary Beth had no intention of exploring.

The front office windows had been smashed in long ago. Shards of glass lay on the walkway that led to the rooms. A rat scurried into one of the rooms. Mary Beth shuddered. She hoped Alma hadn't seen that. The other woman said nothing.

The tires bumped over potholes as Mary Beth drove slowly in a half circle, pointing the car out toward the road before she rolled to a stop. The one-story structure was crumbling in places, held together by thick foliage that almost swallowed the old sign. But not quite.

Below the cracked neon tubing that spelled out VACANCY/NO VACANCY were faded letters in paint. ROOMS BY THE HOUR.

Mary Beth wasn't going to read that sign aloud. "Looks like the kudzu is winning," was all she said. "It always does."

"I'm surprised they haven't torn this damn place down."

Chapter Fifteen

Mary Beth turned her head, surprised by Alma's obvious anger. She waited for the other woman to say something, but Alma didn't. Her lips thinned and she stared straight ahead.

Without comment, Mary Beth pulled back onto the road and pressed down on the accelerator.

"Sorry about that. Not exactly a picnic spot, was it?"

Alma relaxed fractionally once the motel was behind them. Mary Beth could no longer see it in her rearview mirror, which meant Alma couldn't see it in the side mirror either.

"Keep going. We can avoid Brickell if you take a left on the road just ahead. There's a campground by the river about a mile out with tables and a comfort station."

"Sounds perfect."

Mary Beth slowed to make the turn, not inquiring why it was that Alma wanted to avoid Brickell. If she wanted to explain, she would, in her own good time.

* * *

Sheila had returned from the flea market by the time they pulled into her driveway, sated and a little sleepy from their outdoor meal. But Alma perked up again the second she saw her old friend on the porch, waving a welcome. The dogs were at her side, doing the same thing with their tails.

"I bought a peach pie," Sheila trilled. "How about we have some with fresh coffee?"

"Save me a slice," Alma said, getting out of the car and walking to her with the aid of her cane. "We ate too much as it is."

"Where'd y'all go?"

"Down by the river. We had ourselves a picnic. But I would love a cup of coffee."

"How about you, Mary Beth?"

She helped Alma up the stairs and went back, calling to Sheila. "None for me, thanks. I'm just going to take a minute and clean out the car."

"You bet."

The two older women went inside and Mary Beth slipped into the passenger seat. What she wanted to do was call Bobby Joe. He'd know the story behind the deserted motel. She located her phone in her purse but held it for a moment before she dialed his number.

He might not tell her. Maybe she should ask Parr.

Mary Beth paused to scroll through her messages. There was nothing new. She checked her missed calls, just in case he hadn't left a voice mail. She didn't see Bobby Joe's number.

Oh well. It wasn't like she had called him to see how he was doing. Alma was right about the two of them needing time apart. But she hadn't guessed just how frustrated and fed-up Mary Beth was.

At this point, Bobby Joe was probably happiest without her around. She felt the same way.

Mary Beth imagined him with his friends somewhere, baiting a hook and drifting around in a boat. It was harder to imagine him climbing into it with a broken leg, even though it had pretty much healed and he was sporting a soft cast he could take on and off.

She looked out the window for a few moments, the silent phone in her hands. Then she put it away and got out, picking up a few crumpled napkins and wrappers from the interior.

With a little luck, she could head for the kitchen and dispose of the handful of trash, then sneak up the rear stairs again. Mary Beth needed to put up her feet for a while more than she needed a gabfest.

She made it to the guest bedroom without being seen, heading for the divan, an overstuffed pink confection that she'd been meaning to try out.

Mary Beth kicked off her shoes.

Lulled by the soft chirping of the ever-present birds and the faint hum of insects, she dozed off. When she awoke refreshed, it was late afternoon. The sound of muted conversation reached her through the window she'd opened.

Alma and Sheila were still at it.

She ought to put in an appearance.

Mary Beth rose and walked to the dresser, running

a brush through her hair. She pulled it into a snug ponytail that was presentable enough, then went into the bathroom and splashed a little cold water on her face.

She went downstairs, not bothering to be quiet about it, just in case she had become a topic of conversation. The old stairs creaked helpfully. Sheila was laughing about something, but she stopped.

"That you, Mary Beth?"

"Yes it is." She reached the first floor and went directly into the living room. Since the flea market sale, there were far fewer boxes to negotiate around. Shep and Beau were snoozing in front of the fireplace, their muzzles resting on the cool flagstones.

"You look refreshed," Alma said.

"It's so peaceful out here," Mary Beth said, smiling. "I don't know how long it's been since I felt this relaxed."

"Glad to hear it." Sheila beamed at her. "Now, I think I just persuaded Alma to come to the flea market with me tomorrow."

"She says there's a party tent over the stall with her stuff to keep off the sun," Alma added. "And I can have my pick of the armchairs for sale if I get tired. Give me a feather duster and I'll do the trinkets before the customers come."

"Absolutely not," Sheila said imperiously. "There's no need to make yourself useful. Want to come, Mary Beth?"

Mary Beth hesitated. "Would it be very rude of me to say no?"

"Not at all." Sheila's sunny graciousness put Mary Beth at ease. "What would you like to do here?"

"I don't know," Mary Beth answered honestly.

"Well, then, just be a country girl and be happy. There's baskets on the garden fence, for starters. Pick whatever you want before the birds get everything."

"That sounds good."

"And I don't think you've enjoyed the pool yet. Take a dip, do laps, get some sun."

Mary Beth hadn't brought a swimsuit but she could make do with short shorts and a tank. No one would be looking.

"And of course there's the hammock for doing absolutely nothing at all."

"Sounds heavenly." Mary Beth was grateful to not have to be a third wheel. Alma seemed to have recovered her customary cheerfulness in the presence of her old friend. It could be a while before she was able to come out to Brickell again.

"That's settled, then," Sheila declared. "Alma and I will leave in the morning and you get a whole day alone. But first you have to tell me more about yourself. Alma thinks the world of you, Mary Beth. I want to know what you do and what you like." She pointed to the empty side of the settee. "Make yourself comfortable."

Alma scooched over to make room. "Don't worry. I won't let her interrogate you for too long, Mary Beth. I hear that peach pie calling."

"What the hell," Sheila said. "Let's have it for dinner with whipped cream. I don't feel like cooking."

* * *

Sheila had retired for the night, and Beau had followed her up the stairs. That left Shep to guard the household. The big dog was doing that in his twitchy dreams.

What with her nap, Mary Beth was wide awake. Alma was yawning. She'd set out two of the boxes that she intended to take home to Iminga and had finished going through the first one. Several piles of photos surrounded her.

"I'd rather paint a whole house top to bottom than sort through old snapshots," Alma said.

"There aren't that many." Mary Beth was burning with curiosity. Bobby Joe had only a handful of family snapshots, mostly of him at various ages.

She very much wanted to know what Parr had looked like in college and in high school. As a kid. Even as a baby. Why exactly, she didn't understand. Maybe to see certain character traits appear at different stages. He'd probably been a serious baby and then a stubborn kid. By his teen years, there would have been hints of his smoldering sexiness, once he'd fought his way out of the gawky stage. In college, well—he would be an earlier version of the Parr he was now, perhaps with longer hair in a trendy-at-the-time cut.

Mary Beth couldn't very well ask his mother to make a Parr pile so she could concentrate on him. There didn't seem to be a particular method to Alma's organizing, besides size. The square Polaroids were in one stack, the eight-by-ten school shots in another.

Older photographs, somewhat faded, were jumbled together.

"I never was much on making albums," Alma said with a shake of her head. "Maybe it's worse today, when everyone has a million digital ones. At least those stay in a computer."

She picked up a pile and riffled through it, keeping the backs of the photos to Mary Beth. "If you want my opinion, sometimes the past is best forgotten. But maybe someday my grandchildren will want to know who their kinfolk are. These right here are the cousins and second cousins."

She slid the photos into a manila envelope and wrote *Cousins* on the top. Then she tucked in the flap and set the envelope aside.

Mary Beth decided she was going to have to be a little less discreet. "Would you mind if I looked through some of these, Alma?"

The older woman didn't seem inclined to say yes to that suggestion.

"Not just yet. I don't want to get 'em mixed up."

"I understand."

"Would you hand me another manila envelope?"

Mary Beth obliged, sneaking a peek at the remaining piles on the table when Alma lifted her hand to take the envelope from her. There was Parr, in a football team sweatshirt. She'd been right about the awful college haircut. His youthful smile more than made up for it. But there was the same wary look in his dark eyes. Like he didn't trust anyone, even when he was smiling.

"I should have done this years ago. I hadn't realized

that so many of the photos were here—God knows there's hundreds more in my closet."

"You had two kids. So there's twice the number of photos." Mary Beth meant to reassure Alma. She did think there were nowhere near that many from her own childhood. Still, her father hadn't let them languish in boxes.

"Maybe so. But my sons might never get around to sorting it all out. Men don't understand what's important and what's not."

"My dad does. He did our photo albums." Howard had learned traditionally female tasks without complaint.

"Your father is a very good man. There's nothing he didn't do for you." Alma was thoughtful. "I wonder if being a single dad is easier than being a single mom." She sighed before she answered her own question. "It's a struggle no matter what. But worth it."

Mary Beth reached for another manila envelope. "Should I put the ones of Parr in here?"

Alma picked up a pen. "Let me write his name on it first."

Mary Beth seized the opportunity to fan out the photos and quickly look them over, recognizing the stamp of his strong personality from his very first days. By comparison to Eve's sweet newborn girl, Parr as an infant had been ready to take on the world. The thought made her wistful.

She realized that she missed him. Especially that natural strength and take-charge attitude. Couldn't be helped. He had a life elsewhere that had nothing whatsoever to do with her.

She quickly gathered up the photos when Alma held open the envelope. Mary Beth slid them in.

The next pile seemed to give Alma pause. Her voice was a little ragged when she spoke. "Well, there he is."

Mary Beth had already guessed the identity of the man in the black-and-white photograph that Alma held.

"Kenneth Parr Weston. My late husband. That was before we were married."

"He was a handsome man."

Alma didn't agree or disagree with that. She seemed oddly indifferent. "Parr was named for him, of course, but he goes by just the middle name. He always wanted to distinguish himself from his father."

Mary Beth knew better than to ask why. She was beginning to imagine what might have happened, and it must have had something to do with the derelict motel. There was no way it could ever have been a respectable place, not that far out of town and renting rooms by the hour.

"Maybe Bobby Joe told you about him."

"No."

"I loved Kenneth. But I never should have married him."

Mary Beth listened and let her talk.

"Unfortunately, he had an eye for the ladies and vice versa. I was so young and in love—and a fool for him. Took me years to figure it out," Alma said wearily. "When Bobby Joe promised he'd change his ways if you gave him a second chance, it meant so much to me. Kenneth never said anything of the kind. He just kept on doing what he wanted to do."

What happened? Mary Beth wondered. She hadn't spoken, but Alma could read the question in her eyes well enough.

"One night I just stopped believing in his lies." She pushed the creased photo away from her. "And then all hell broke loose. But I don't want to talk about it now."

Mary Beth wanted to put her arms around Alma and hug away the painful memories. But she knew from her own experience that it wouldn't work. The deep wounds of betrayal struck at the soul.

She looked down at the photo Alma had pushed away. Kenneth Weston had been a handsome man indeed, but there was the same weakness in his face that Mary Beth had come to see in Bobby Joe. Parr's fundamental strength came from his mother.

Yet both sons resembled their father more than Alma. Mary Beth scarcely knew what to think.

Hurriedly, as if she were sick of the task, Alma filled the remaining envelopes and peeled off the self-stick tape to seal them. Then she stacked them upright in the empty box, and set it on top of the second one.

"That's it for now. I can finish the sorting at home. Thanks, Mary Beth. I didn't mean to unload all that on you." She leaned back in her chair and rubbed her temples. "Gave me a headache. I'm going to take two aspirin and go up to bed."

Mary Beth got up to find Alma's cane. "There's a box of herb tea in the cupboards. I could make you a cup."

"No. But thank you." Alma grasped the cane and

rose from her chair. "See you in the morning. But maybe not. Sheila wanted to get an early start."

Mary Beth thought it was likely that Alma just wanted to put physical distance between herself and sad memories. Sheila had probably known Kenneth, and Alma could talk to her in a way she couldn't to Mary Beth.

"Sleep well," Mary Beth said softly. "And have a good time tomorrow."

Mary Beth stayed up for another hour, sensing a change in the weather outside. The living room was warmer and humid. She didn't know where the air-conditioning control was.

The sultry atmosphere made her restless. A thunder-storm seemed likely, but there was no distant rumble. There wasn't a sound from upstairs. Both Alma and Sheila had to be asleep.

Shep stayed flopped on the floor where it was cooler. But something made the dog lift his head and look around, as if he had heard a noise she hadn't.

Mary Beth couldn't shake the uneasy feeling that had begun to grow, though she thought closing the curtains might help. It took her several seconds to find the pull cord behind the heavy drapes. As she looked out the window one last time, she would have sworn she saw a flash of movement in the near distance. Something white or gray. But Shep was quiet. She was grateful for the company of the big dog and went into the kitchen to get a biscuit treat for him from the jar Sheila kept there.

"Come on, boy," she said softly. "Come with me."

The dog scrambled up and accepted the treat, letting her lead him out the front door to the porch. A motion sensor triggered the outside light as she stepped out onto the porch, her hand on Shep's collar.

At night the surrounding trees seemed taller and closer, impenetrable to the light from the porch. Shep's presence was a welcome reassurance.

She felt the big dog's hackles rise against her hand and the warning vibration of a growl from deep in his chest. They both looked around. There were plenty of places for someone to hide, but she saw no one. He must have smelled an animal. Something skittered through the undergrowth and she saw the same flash of white.

Mary Beth shook her head at her foolishness. It was a possum, that was all.

If anything, it was hotter out here. She finally saw a distant flash of lightning but heard no thunder. The storm might be as far away as Tennessee. Maybe it would pass them by.

Mary Beth would rather it didn't. A drenching rain and cool gusts would feel good right now and serve to dispel the odd tension that besieged her.

She heard her phone ring a few times inside the house, and then stop. Okay. She didn't have to run to get it. But she wanted to know who it was. Probably Bobby Joe, she thought, taking a deep breath and summoning up her patience in advance.

"Okay, boy. Back in." Shep obeyed, his paws clicking on the polished wood floor as he returned to his favored spot on the floor. Mary Beth locked the front door behind her and checked the kitchen door that led outside. It was already locked. Good enough.

She knew the dog would raise a ruckus if there was a reason to. Mary Beth looked around for her purse, spotting it on the hall table. She dug in it for her phone, which rang just as her hand closed around it.

Bobby Joe's number flashed on the screen. Mary Beth moved quickly into the living room, so the sound of her voice wouldn't disturb the women upstairs.

"Hello."

She heard only noise at first, incoherent chatter punctuated by a bar band warming up. Then Bobby Joe came on.

"Hey, baby."

Even just those two little words sounded slurred. Mary Beth suppressed the good advice she knew he wouldn't take: *You ought not to drink yet, Bobby Joe. Your meds don't mix with beer or booze.*

Once he'd had the first drink, there was always a second. And a third. She'd known that about Bobby Joe even before he'd gotten sloshed at their engagement party, and look what it made him do.

"Where are you?"

He laughed. "Lemme ask. Fred, what's the name of this podunk town again?"

Mary Beth couldn't make out his friend's reply.

"It's right on the Gulf," Bobby Joe added as further explanation. "We just went night fishing. Didn't catch a damn thing."

She heard hoots of raucous laughter. No doubt they were all drunk. Given the accident, she hoped they weren't getting behind the wheel after they were done boozing.

A sharp sound of crumpling metal made her hold the phone away from her ear. Bobby Joe liked to flatten his beer cans with one hand.

"Crushed it," Bobby Joe said to her with manly pride.

She'd guessed right. "I hope you aren't driving anyplace when you stumble out of there."

"Nah. They rent rooms out back. Or so the sign says."

Her whole body tensed. Maybe the Weston males had a genetic attraction to hot-sheet motels. Just her luck. "Better than nothing," she snapped.

"We can sleep it off. Get back on the road by dawn."

Of course. Tanked up on black coffee and still intoxicated. She shuddered. But what could she do? Wake up Alma and have her give Bobby Joe a talking-to? Like that would even work.

"Wh—when you coming back to Iminga, Mary Beth?"

She sighed inwardly. "I don't know. Your mother is happy here." Except for the unscheduled stop at the abandoned motel, that was true enough.

"Huh. Brickell blows, if you ask me."

"Actually, I didn't, Bobby Joe. It seems like a pretty little town. Sheila lives way outside it anyway."

"Oh yeah. Forgot about that. Hey, is Mom listening in?"

Mary Beth began to pace the living room. "No. She's asleep. So is Sheila."

"Tell her I'm all right."

Mary Beth couldn't keep the vinegar out of her voice. "Good to know."

"I don't want her to worry 'bout me."

The background noise got louder and more boisterous suddenly. It occurred to Mary Beth that there might be female entertainment at the bar.

"Parr didn't show, did he?"

His question surprised her. "No. Why would he? Did you talk to him?"

Bobby Joe let out a whoop. There were catcalls in the background as a bass guitar thumped a beat to strip to. Then more whoops.

Gross. Mary Beth didn't have to wonder why she didn't even feel jealous.

"Uh, yeah." He came back to the call. "Just now. Guess I didn't hear him right. He musta stayed in Atlanta."

He seemed to have lost interest in the stripper, because she heard a screen door squeak open and slam, then footsteps on a wooden walkway. The background racket softened considerably. "Okay. Now we can talk. I would've thought he wouldn't let Mother go back to Brickell."

There was one advantage to him being inebriated. She might be able to extract information from him. "Why is that?"

"Hang on. I need a smoke."

Mary Beth waited. A lighter flicked close to the phone and then there was the sucking sound of a deep drag on a cigarette.

"You could say we, uh, left under a cloud." He

coughed, like he was waving away smoke. "The three of us."

Not his father. She knew that much.

"Long time ago," he added, like that was a satisfactory explanation.

"Something happened," she said bluntly. She didn't care to reveal that Alma hadn't wanted to tell her either. "I suppose I don't have to know exactly what."

"Probably better that way." The cigarette he was smoking seemed to have made him more thoughtful. "Anyway, listen—if you're not coming home, then I might as well stay down here another day or two."

"Okay."

"Sheila's place was pretty in summer," Bobby Joe offered.

"It still is."

"I remember the yard. All those trees. You could get lost in them just a few steps away from the porch." The odd comment reminded her of how uneasy she'd felt just moments ago. The thunderstorm had been an omen—or maybe more like a sign, telling her to think twice.

"That's still the case," she said, not wanting to go down memory lane any more—or at least not with him. "Well, I guess I should get to bed."

"Imagine me tucking you in." The cigarette roughened his voice to something like intimacy, which made her even more uneasy. "Good night, Mary Beth."

"'Night." She ended the call just as one of his fishing buddies hollered at him to come back inside.

Mary Beth climbed the stairs, taking care to make as little noise as possible. Her bedtime routine never took long. She undressed and slipped into lightweight pajamas, then brushed her hair.

She pinned it up carelessly before she went through her things, looking for her toothbrush. Even though she had her own bathroom, the immaculate shelves and surfaces made her feel funny about leaving personal items around. Mary Beth kept all that in her toiletries case, which she unzipped.

A small white box occupied the clear vinyl pouch—she'd tucked it there, hoping there would be a jeweler in Brickell who could repair the chain without her having to leave the necklace there and come back.

She hadn't seen one today and they'd been pretty much all over the town. Besides that, Alma had been with her. Maybe she could venture into town solo if they stayed on.

She took out the box and opened it. The ruby pendant caught the light and sparkled in its nest of white velvet. Parr's wildly inappropriate gift would always be precious to her.

Mary Beth replaced the lid and put the box back. She could think more clearly when he wasn't around. Two states away seemed to be the right distance.

Despite the drama of the engagement party and the life-threatening accident, life was going to go on.

This would all blow over but, inevitably, she and Bobby Joe would break up. For all his passionate attention, Parr wasn't likely to keep on seeing her if it was no longer an exciting secret between the two of them.

She suspected it was the thrill of doing what he shouldn't that got him revved up. Maybe he was just accustomed to being the oldest, able to take away his brother's toys when he felt like it.

Mary Beth thought it over. It was true that Bobby Joe had been toying with her. But Parr had seemed utterly serious.

It didn't matter. The Weston brothers were all wrong for her, for totally different reasons.

There was every chance in the world, she told herself, that she'd find the right man, now that she knew who the wrong one was.

She went into the bathroom and studied herself in the mirror. The problem was that she didn't know who *she* was. Or who she wanted.

She did know how she felt. Frustrated and lonely.

Mary Beth snapped off the light after she'd brushed her teeth and flung herself into the huge bed, face down.

Chapter Sixteen

The clock read ten-fifteen by the time Mary Beth opened her eyes. Sunlight poured through the upstairs windows. It looked like another beautiful day but it was already very warm. With the curtains pulled open, she could see shimmering waves of heat rising from the fields beyond the trees. She stood on tiptoe, looking at the view of the surrounding country for the first time. The road into Brickell was visible but there wasn't a car in sight.

With the blazing sun and blue sky above, her uneasiness about being out in the sticks was forgotten. The extra hours of sleep had improved her mood considerably. She showered and changed into the shortest shorts she had, and a crop top.

Mary Beth went downstairs barefoot. She entered the kitchen, where there was a cross breeze from the two open windows. A note had been left on the counter next to a pair of red-handled clippers. A vase stuffed with multicolored summer flowers, fresh as the morning, kept the note from flying away.

Long day for us. Flea market first. Then into town.
See you tonight.

Alma and Sheila had both signed it. They'd left her a pot of coffee that was still hot. She poured a cup and took it out onto the porch, where Shep and Beau had commandeered the wicker sofa. They didn't even open their eyes when she stood in front of them, so she took one of the matching armchairs. Mary Beth sipped her coffee slowly, deciding to take Sheila's advice and be a country girl for today. When she'd finished it, she walked to the other end of the porch, trying to figure out where the garden was.

There was a path through the trees. It had to lead to the garden. Yellow plastic clogs had been set atop a stump where the path began.

Mary Beth felt a surge of happiness. Being alone, exploring a new place, not having a schedule was exactly what she needed right now.

She went back inside and made herself a quick breakfast of eggs and toast. Before she sat down to eat it, she turned on the kitchen radio and tuned in to a country station. There was Faith Hill singing about being a Mississippi girl.

"You and me both," Mary Beth said.

She ate in contented solitude, mentally planning her day. The garden first, before it got too hot. Then a hose-off, followed by a jump in the pool. Then she would change and saunter out to the hammock like a queen, a bug swatter for a scepter.

She deliberately didn't look at her phone.

There were only coffee cups and saucers in the sink, besides the single plate and cutlery that she added when she was done. Mary Beth pulled off her rings before she did the washing up. When she dried her hands, she didn't put the rings back on.

Garden dirt didn't go with diamonds. She was fed up with Bobby Joe, but that didn't mean she wanted to insult him, even *in absentia.*

Mary Beth went out and down the path, stopping at the stump. There was also a can of bug spray, which she hadn't seen from the porch. The cool spray tickled her bare legs and midriff, but it was worth it not to be eaten alive. She slipped the yellow clogs onto her bare feet.

The garden was only twenty feet from the house but the trees hid it well. It was enormous and rather unkempt. A profusion of tangled vines climbed one fence and made it sag. Small green and yellow squash hung under the sprawling leaves, and the bigger ones lay in the dirt, next to staked tomatoes that looked ripe enough to burst. The lettuce was a mess, mostly brown and withered from the heat. The tall, dark green leaves of collards could take it. A narrow brick walkway separated the vegetables from a cutting garden in riotous bloom. She recognized the flowers from the vase.

Mary Beth took a basket from the fence and opened the gate. She waded in, picking whatever looked good and ripe, from vegetables to berries, hoping she wouldn't have to fight that possum for the garden's bounty. But they were nocturnal, she reminded herself. That furry feeling by her ankle was only a thick-stemmed vine of some sort, reaching out to grab her and eat her alive.

The basket was brimming with goodies in only minutes. Mary Beth went out the way she'd come in, pausing at the fence to look behind her. She could swear there was no trace of her footsteps, as if the luxuriant garden had closed ranks against the intruder. Nature had a way of running rampant in the Mississippi climate.

She closed the gate and went down the path, stopping at the coiled hose by the side of the house to rinse off her haul. Then she turned the spray on herself to get rid of the dirt and bits of leaves that clung to her bare legs and arms, gasping at the water's coldness, but with pleasure.

The yellow clogs she slipped off by the back door to the kitchen, opening it just enough to set the dripping basket on the nearest counter, out of the heat. Then she headed for the pool. The radio was still playing but she couldn't really hear it and it sure didn't seem to bother the dogs. Both were still sacked out on the porch.

The close-cut grass beneath her bare feet was pleasantly warm and dry. The dark flagstones surrounding the pool area were another matter. They were really too hot to walk on, so Mary Beth ran.

She made a shallow dive into the deep end of the pool and came up swiftly, slicking her hair back over her neck with both hands. The water was as cold as the spray from the hose. The strong sun hadn't had a chance to warm it up yet. She didn't care. It felt great.

Once in the water, she saw a feature that had been invisible from the house: a mirror wall that reflected the entire pool and the artful landscaping around it.

In front of the mirror were a pair of wooden sun chairs, long enough to stretch out on completely when their backs were lowered flat.

For a while, she just floated on her back, gazing up at the trees rustling faintly overhead.

Then she swam. Back and forth. Over and over. As fast as she could. Working off the tension that had been part of her for weeks now, so embedded in her body and mind that she'd barely realized it was there until now. The cool, sparkling water seemed to dissolve it.

She should have done something like this during the incredibly stressful weeks at the hospital. Taking care of herself had been last on the list, a big mistake.

Mary Beth floated again, resting. Then she ducked underwater and swam there as long as she could. Breathless, she surfaced in a rush of bubbles, shaking her head to get the water out of her eyes as she reached for the tiled rim of the pool.

She blinked.

The scuffed toes of well-made work boots were directly in her line of sight.

"Parr?"

Mary Beth looked up at the tall column of man clad in blue jeans. Frayed white streaks defined his muscular thighs and a black leather belt did the same for his low, lean waist. Above that, a white T-shirt showed more of his incredible chest than she'd seen yet.

He needed a haircut. His thick black hair was getting in his dark eyes. Just your classic American stud, southern variety. She wished that she didn't react to him as strongly and instinctively as she did.

"Hello, Strawberry."

"What are you doing here?"

"Is that any way to say hello?" He folded his heavily muscled arms across that damn chest.

"What I meant was—oh, never mind. How did you get past the dogs?"

"They seemed to think I was a friend."

"Oh."

How long had he been watching her? Mary Beth kicked away from the side of the pool and sank under the water again. She swam to the far end of the pool and surfaced, hanging on to the rim with her back to him, as if she was catching her breath.

She didn't know why she wasn't that happy to see him. Maybe because he'd startled her. Maybe because—she had to admit it—he'd been away too long and she'd missed him more than she'd been willing to admit to herself. Mary Beth turned around. He was still there. She swam back.

"Looks like you're having fun."

"I was, yes."

"And now that I'm here, you're not?"

She paddled a little closer. "I didn't say that."

"Mind if I sit down?"

"It's not my house. But go ahead." She kept most of her body under water, paddling around. At some point, she would have to get out. Parr didn't look like he was going to go away.

Her day of blissful solitude, happy puttering around, and uninterrupted time to think or not think, was over.

"I guess I should apologize for intruding," he said.

"But mother said you weren't doing anything special today. I talked to her about an hour ago and I left you a message."

Mary Beth had been traipsing around in the garden then. Without her phone. That still didn't explain why he was here.

Parr pulled a wooden sun chair closer to the pool and stretched out on it, his arms crossed behind his head. She continued to swim, pausing only when her wet hair got in her mouth and she had to pull it out. She stood once and dipped her head, then flung her hair back over it in an arc that sent a shower of droplets in his direction.

"Enjoying the show?" she asked tartly.

Parr grinned. "So far, yeah."

His intense gaze moved over her soaked shorts and crop top. Somehow he could do that without seeming to leer or gawk. Then his eyes met hers. The hot fire in them made her sink down to her shoulders again.

She let her arms float on the surface, feeling somewhat less miffed. It was clear that he'd missed her too.

"How was Atlanta?" she asked. Small talk might keep her from jumping in his lap. Besides, she actually wanted to know what he'd been doing up there.

"I'm lining up another new project. Nothing's final yet. I thought I might as well come back. Gail can manage without me."

How very nice to know that, Mary Beth thought.

She moved to the shallow end and sat on a low step, still mostly in the water. "Bobby Joe said he talked to you last night."

A cloud came over Parr's face, as if the memory was distasteful for some reason. "Yes. He was having way too good a time and not making a whole hell of a lot of sense. Off the chain, as they say."

Mary Beth couldn't read his expression one way or another. "I hope you don't blame me for that. Coming to Brickell was Alma's idea. We all needed time off."

"That's so," Parr acknowledged. "And by the way, I would never blame you for what he does or says. Just keeping you posted. I assume he called you too. He said he was going to."

Bobby Joe again. Always around, even when he wasn't. "Yes, he did. When he was somewhat more sober."

"Good enough."

The awkwardness of the situation compelled her to be direct. "Parr, you didn't have to drive all the way up to Brickell to report on your brother."

"I suppose not," Parr said levelly.

"But here you are. Why?" She stopped talking, surprised by the intensity of the emotions Parr triggered in her when there was no one else around. Last time that had happened—in the mostly empty hospital cafeteria—he'd promised to keep his feelings for her a secret from his brother.

It wasn't really possible for them to have a casual conversation. Being alone with him was dangerous.

"Mary Beth." Parr's voice deepened and his dark gaze captured hers again. "I came up here to see you because I knew you were alone." He drew in a breath and let it out slowly. "Want to finish what we started?"

Something snapped in Mary Beth. The dutiful

daughter and faithful fiancée stopped wanting to be both, just like that. The one man who'd made her feel like a woman—who'd made her feel desired and cherished—was here. She could take full advantage of that or not. It was up to her.

They didn't have to go all the way. But if they did, that would be her decision too. Bobby Joe didn't own her. Parr didn't either. She just wanted to own this moment.

"When are they coming back?"

She knew he meant his mother and her friend.

"Not for hours." The reply was tantamount to saying yes. Yes to anything.

Mary Beth let her hands trail through the water as she walked through it to the pool ladder, going up step by slow step. Teasing him.

Parr sat forward to take in the sight of her as she rose.

She caught a glimpse of what she looked like in the mirror wall behind him. Her wet eyelashes were dewy and dark. Her drenched hair ended in rivulets that soaked the tiny, clinging top even more, and her exposed midriff sparkled with drops of water. The skimpy, dripping shorts covered only a few inches of her bare, rounded thighs.

The look in his eyes was worshipful. He could have been adoring a goddess. She wasn't one, but if he wanted to think so, Mary Beth was fine with that.

Her hands wrapped around the curved top of the ladder as she stepped up and out. Parr just about kicked the chair over as he rose and strode to meet her, resting his hands briefly over hers.

For a fraction of a second she remembered the rings she'd left in the kitchen . . . until his mouth came down over hers and her wet lips opened to him.

Parr brought her close to him, the warmth of his body erasing the cool sensation of her drenched clothes as he caressed her, pressing his full length against her as best he could, given his superior height.

His amorous attentions were the prelude to a kiss. His lips brushed the top of her head, her cheek, and then her lips.

She arched her back, wanting to feel all of him so intensely that it was almost painful. Parr cupped her head with one hand, not letting her escape his mouth. His tongue touched hers, sliding deeper, probing and sensual. She moaned softly, the low vibration adding to the exquisite pleasure of the kiss.

And if, she thought wildly, if he could do this to her with only a kiss, what would he be like in bed? Every forbidden thought she'd ever had spun in her mind. But this fantasy was real.

His head lowered to her neck and he found the sensitive pulse that he had never had time to kiss before. He nipped at it with practiced skill. A sensation like hot lightning shot through her body. Mary Beth cried out softly and clung to him, writhing.

Those strong hands moved down and slid up inside the back of the shorts. With the same sensual skill, intuiting the rhythm that aroused her most, he squeezed her behind while pulling her even closer, lifting her off her feet.

To be helpless in his hands for a few delicious moments was powerfully arousing. Mary Beth gave in to it, moving her hips tentatively, then wantonly, getting him rock hard inside those frayed jeans.

She wanted to rip them off. She ran a hand over one of his thighs, digging her nails in until he caught her wrist and set her down, all at once.

"Not yet, angel. I'm not done."

Her bare feet stretched as she stood on tiptoe. His hands cupped her breasts. Then he took her by the nipples, right through her top, watching her face as he teased them, making each nipple harder than she could have imagined with gentle tugs. His mouth lowered over hers again.

The double stimulation continued. Then he opened his hands and cupped each breast again, slowly rubbing, melting her with pleasure that went right to her core.

Let him take her. All of her. The continuing kiss kept Mary Beth from begging him to do just that.

After a while he stopped and simply held her, letting her rest her head on his chest. He stroked her damp hair.

"We need to take this inside."

"Yes," she breathed.

He bent and swept her off her feet, carrying her close to him. Mary Beth buried her face in his strong neck, inhaling his intoxicating scent, a mix of clean T-shirt and hot man. She clung to him as he got the screen door open and took her up the stairs with ease, as if she weighed next to nothing.

"Which room is yours?"

"Next one," she murmured.

Parr went in. She let go of his neck and slid down.

The bed was behind them. He got back to kissing her, taking his sweet time, exciting her in ways she hadn't known existed. His touch, his body, his lips—she craved it all.

"Close the door," she told him.

Reluctantly, Parr let go of her and moved across the room. Mary Beth didn't know whether to fling herself onto the bed or stand there.

She stayed where she was, digging her bare toes into the soft carpet. His gaze narrowed when he turned away from the door and looked over her head.

"What kind of car does Sheila drive?"

Her heart sank. "A silver SUV."

"I know that's the road to Brickell. You tell me if that's them coming toward us."

Mary Beth stood on tiptoe, looking over the top of the curtain cautiously. "Oh no."

Parr swore under his breath. "Get in the shower. You need a reason to look all rosy and glowing when they see you. I'll go downstairs and—hell—fix myself a snack or something."

He propelled her toward the bathroom. Mary Beth made no protest. She could cry in the shower if she had to, say something about the soap getting in her eyes.

"There's tomatoes in the basket on the kitchen counter. I was out in the garden before you got here."

"Okay. That's your alibi." He got her as far as the bath mat and didn't even kiss her.

"Then don't eat it," she muttered. She peeled off her wet clothes, kicking them into a corner. Parr was just going to have to wing it without her. At least his mother knew that he was here.

"I'm going to wait outside in my truck, like I just got here. They won't know. Got that? Act surprised when you see me."

"Yes." She turned on the shower full blast.

Chapter Seventeen

Mary Beth put on a demure blouse and buttoned it up, then slipped into jeans and flat sandals. She'd blasted her hair dry to buy herself additional minutes in which to compose herself, letting it tumble over her shoulders.

Skip the makeup, she told herself. Innocence was what she wanted to convey.

Conversation downstairs drifted up without her being able to hear the words. It was time to put in an appearance and act surprised, but not too surprised. She didn't want either of the women to suspect anything.

She went downstairs, following the conversation into the kitchen. Parr was seated at the table, a tomato sandwich on a paper plate in front of him.

"There you are," Sheila said. "Look who's paying us a call." She beamed at Parr, who got up as Mary Beth entered. "He was always such a gentleman," Sheila stage-whispered to his mother.

"Hello, Mary Beth," he said politely, as if he hadn't

just been wrapped around her yearning body, lost in mutual lust.

"Hi." Nonchalant tone. Wide eyes. No one seemed suspicious. "When did you get here?"

Alma got her two cents in. "He said he'd call you. I did too but your phone was off or the battery died."

Mary Beth feigned dismay. "Oh gosh. Could be either. Sorry about that."

"It happens," Parr said. "Anyway, I heard the shower running, so I didn't come in. Then these two came up the driveway."

"We had to rescue him from Shep and Beau. They believe in sharing the love, as you know." Sheila's comment was addressed to Mary Beth, who smiled in return. "And hey, thanks for filling up the basket," Sheila added.

"Oh, it was fun. The garden is amazing."

"It's out of control. Alma, are there more tomatoes?"

"Two," Alma said, looking into the basket. "No, three. Mary Beth, would you like a sandwich? We had lunch in town."

"Sure."

In five minutes, she was seated across from Parr, not meeting his gaze as they both ate. The two other women did most of the talking. Parr finished ahead of Mary Beth and took his paper plate to the trash can.

What a good boy. If they only knew. Mary Beth turned her head to chat with Alma instead of looking at Parr. "How was the flea market?"

"All my stuff sold fast," Sheila announced. She was making ice tea from a powdered mix in a pitcher filled with ice cubes and water. She moved to the sink to rinse the long spoon. "Mary Beth, are these your rings?"

"Ah—yes." Mary Beth looked at Alma, forcing down a flash of guilt before she spoke. "I took them off before I went into the garden."

Sheila picked up the glittering rings and held them out in her palm. "Here you go. You don't want to lose those."

Mary Beth slipped them on, avoiding Parr's gaze as long as she could. The conversation turned to other things and she joined in. When she looked at him again, his expression was serious.

He looked into her eyes, then down. Mary Beth reached up a hand and touched her neck. He had to be thinking of the ruby pendant. She hadn't gotten a chance to tell him it was broken. He hadn't noticed at the pool, but maybe he'd assumed she wouldn't wear it in the water.

If he had given it a thought at all. The searing sensuality of that encounter came back in a rush.

Mary Beth got up, confused and too warm to stay in the kitchen. She'd finished her sandwich anyway and did the same as Parr, taking her paper plate to the trash can.

"That was delicious," she said to Alma. "And now I'd better find my phone. Will you all excuse me for a bit?"

"Of course, honey. We'll be out on the porch." Sheila set several glasses on a tray and added the pitcher of tea. "Come on, Parr. It's your turn to get me caught up on your life. Alma says you're involved in a bunch of new business ventures. Are you rich yet?"

"Working on it."

After dinner was served and the dishes done, Alma and Sheila stayed inside to watch a tearjerker movie as Parr and Mary Beth wandered out to the porch. They took either end of the wicker sofa.

"You stay on your side," Mary Beth murmured. "And I'll stay on mine. I don't want to tempt fate."

"Do we have a choice?"

"No."

"Enough said. Nice night."

Lightning bugs drifted against the dark backdrop of trees, flashing to each other.

"They're so pretty. We don't get too many in Iminga." Mary Beth remembered that he hadn't lived there as long as her. And that he'd left town instead of sticking around the way she had.

"Bobby Joe and I used to collect them in jars around here," he said. "Then mother made us let them all go. She didn't want bugs in her house, not for a minute."

"I can imagine."

Some of the movie dialogue drifted out through the open window. Parr shook his head. "Sounds like unrequited love to me. Don't you always want to tell the people in a movie to wise up?"

"Sometimes."

Mary Beth leaned her head against the back of the

wicker sofa, wishing they didn't have to sit apart. But that was how it had to be.

He turned and glanced through the open window behind them, making sure that no one would over-hear. Then he turned toward her. "What happened to the necklace?"

She thought about telling him that she couldn't wear it all the time and decided on the truth instead. "The chain broke."

His dark eyebrows drew together in a frown. "Sorry to hear that. Mind if I ask how?"

"It just broke. I don't know how. I hoped to take it to a jeweler in Brickell but there isn't one."

"Give it to me. I'll have it fixed for you."

"It's upstairs. Shhh." She held a finger to her lips as a woman's footsteps filled the silence. Someone went into the kitchen and came out with some kind of snack.

"She's gone. Which one was it?"

"I couldn't see," Mary Beth said. "Anyway, I think our little ruse worked. That was quite a kiss. I wouldn't mind another."

"Not here. Not now."

Would it be whiny of her to ask when? Or just pathetic? Even in the dark, Mary Beth was well aware of the sexual heat under his cool exterior. He wanted her just as much as she wanted him. Bold as she'd been, playing the role of temptress felt awkward now. Of course, his mother was on the other side of an open window. At least they could talk, if they kept their voices down.

"You do something to me," she began. "I never got that far with Bobby Joe."

He seemed to go on the alert. "What do you mean?"

"We tried sometimes. I mean, I did. He wasn't that interested."

"That's not what I was asking. Were you talking about yourself?"

"Well, yes."

"So when you say you never got that far, you mean that you are . . ." His heavy eyebrows went up, questioning.

"A virgin. So what? That shouldn't change anything."

He didn't seem upset by the news—or her somewhat defensive tone. Just surprised. And curious.

"If you don't mind my saying so, Mary Beth, you sure don't act like one."

"It's not a life sentence. Just not that usual these days."

He gave a thoughtful sigh and studied her for a long moment. "I'm not criticizing you for it. But it does mean that whatever happens between us can't be just a fling. Not for me, anyway."

"I don't see why not."

Parr narrowed his eyes. "You sure about that?"

"Look, being a virgin is just not a big deal to me, Parr. It kind of was to Bobby Joe and maybe that's why—I'm beginning to think it's why he cheated on me."

The conversation from hell was underway. But it had to happen. Mary Beth wasn't going to quit now.

"Yeah. He wanted someone else, someone he could use and throw away."

The cynical words stung. She dropped the attitude

of an experienced woman and spoke from her hurting heart. "And who's to say you won't do the same thing? You're the brother who goes from woman to woman."

"Correction. One at a time, every time. And I never lied to any of them about what they were getting into."

"Thoughtful of you."

"You can skip the sarcasm. Those relationships weren't necessarily exactly what I wanted. But I would say I got what I needed and so did my women."

Mary Beth swore under her breath, than said, "You know something? You and Bobby Joe are so different I almost don't see how you can be brothers. You're honest but won't commit. He lies again and again, but he's not afraid of making a promise."

Parr stretched out his long legs and crossed them at the ankle. Then he folded his arms over his chest. "You sound like that old game, What's Wrong With This Picture? Repeat what you just said about Bobby Joe and see if you can figure it out."

"Don't be a smart ass."

"I'm a realist."

Mary Beth stopped talking, not wanting to get ensnared in an argument she couldn't win. Disappointment washed over her. She wasn't going to let him know that.

"Let's change the subject."

"That's probably a good idea."

"It meant a lot to your mother to come out here. And to me. It's been interesting to see where you and Bobby Joe come from."

"Oh?" Parr picked up on what was left out of that information. "Did she ask to drive by our old house?"

"No, as a matter of fact." That actually hadn't occurred to Mary Beth on the day they'd toured the town. "But we toured the main street of Brickell."

"I doubt it's changed much. I've never been back."

"She knew where everything was." Mary Beth hesitated. "Including that old motel. I went the wrong way and we ended up there by accident. She totally changed—the place freaked her out. What was that all about?"

Parr looked at her intently. "She didn't say?"

"I figured it had something to do with your father." She didn't want to confirm that Kenneth Weston had cheated on Alma when she wasn't sure if his sons knew that he had.

"Good guess. It did." He sighed. "Bobby Joe never told you about it, I suppose."

"No. Not a thing."

"Then I won't either. Some other time, Mary Beth." He got up, as if making it clear that the conversation was decidedly over.

She regretted the odd turn it had taken. But there was nothing she could do about it now.

His back was to her as he walked through the door from the porch into the house, his broad-shouldered silhouette barely fitting through the frame. He walked away from her without a backward glance.

Chapter Eighteen

"I do like a table set for four," Sheila chirped the next morning. She added cutlery next to the cheery yellow plates and rolled napkins adorned with daisy napkin rings. "Now where's Parr?"

Mary Beth had gone out early with the dogs, who'd ambled around and sniffed the property. She'd been sort of surprised to see his truck still parked there.

Sheila had offered him the finished room in the basement, which allowed him to move about without being heard by the women on the second floor. Parr had agreed. Mary Beth had thought that he might seize the opportunity to leave before any of them awoke.

Okay. He was here. She hadn't blown it with her inquisitive questions and boldness otherwise, unusual for her.

"Did you sleep well, Mary Beth?" Alma was in robe and curlers again, standing at the stove with a spatula in her hand, keeping an eye on a frying pan full of scrambled eggs.

The toast popped up, startling Mary Beth. "Yes," she fibbed. "Just fine."

"Would you go down and rouse Parr?" Sheila asked. "We're about ready to eat."

"Sure."

Mary Beth left the kitchen and went a few steps down the basement stairs, no further. "Rise and shine," she called.

"I'm up," Parr said.

She retreated.

Breakfast was over with quickly, and Mary Beth volunteered for the dishes. There weren't enough of them to run the dishwasher and she needed something to do.

Parr excused himself. The other two women disappeared to their respective haunts: Sheila to her first-floor study and Alma upstairs to fix her hair.

Mary Beth prepared a dishpan of sudsy water and did the juice glasses first, setting them in the second sink to be rinsed. The plates went in next. Actually, she dropped them, making a splash that soaked the front of her apron.

"Don't," she whispered.

Parr's hands had taken her by the waist. He let go but only to slip his arms around her instead. "No one's looking."

"That doesn't matter." She fumbled in the dishwater for the scrubber.

He bent his head, putting his lips right next to her ear. Just his breath was arousing. "I wanted to apologize for last night."

"Nothing happened," she answered, grabbing for a slippery plate.

Sad but true in more ways than one. Was he going to apologize for that? Undoubtedly not.

"You caught me off guard," he said. He nuzzled her neck.

"Stop that."

Parr sighed and lifted his head. "Can I get a do-over?"

"I'm not sure how you define the word, Parr."

"That's not an answer."

"It'll have to do." She put three scrubbed plates into the rinsing sink. "Now let go of me."

The sound of soft footsteps made him do it. He was standing on the other side of the kitchen by the time Sheila came in.

"Thanks so much, Mary Beth. Looks like you're almost done. My, you work fast. Is your mother done with her hair?" she asked Parr.

"I don't know. Just thought I'd hang out with Mary Beth here," he said, giving Sheila a great big good ol' boy grin. Mary Beth had turned away from the sink in time to see it.

"I just wanted to tell her that I got an e-mail from the town supervisor." Sheila went to the back staircase and called up. "Alma! It's going to happen!"

"Be right down," was the distant reply, over the roar of a hair dryer.

"What's going to happen?" Mary Beth asked, untying the damp apron.

"Your mother and I paid a call on the town supervisor. Seems that he was waiting for someone to complain and that's exactly what we did."

"Complain about what?"

"That old motel. It's an eyesore. He's going to ask the Brickell council for permission to demolish it."

The hair dryer was switched off and Sheila mounted the stairs.

Parr exchanged a look with Mary Beth.

"You don't owe me any explanations," she said in a low voice.

"I think I do," he said. "First of all, Sheila moved to Brickell after what happened at the motel. Right after, but I'm not sure she knows why my mother hates the place so."

"Alma can tell me herself if she wants to."

"I think it's better if I do."

She hung up the apron.

"Come on. Let's go for a drive. I'm not going to do it here."

He parked his truck by a lake covered in water lilies. A tall white bird stalked through the reeds, the only sign of life besides the two of them. He rolled down his window and gestured to her to do the same. "Unless you want me to turn on the air-conditioning."

"No. It's nice out. I take it this is going to be a long explanation."

"That's about right."

Mary Beth waited. Parr leaned forward, his hands clasped together over the steering wheel. For a moment his eyes closed and he almost looked like he was praying.

Then he sat back.

"It's not something I like to talk about," he said.

"But here goes. That motel was where my father was shot dead."

"What?" Her startled question was threaded with shock. Mary Beth had known nothing of that.

"He was having an affair with a married woman," Parr said simply. "And her husband showed up. There was an argument and it got ugly fast. Long story short, he got shot. Then the other man shot himself."

Mary Beth was stunned. It seemed impossible that she'd never heard about a tragedy of that magnitude. Were the people who knew about it trying to protect her—or themselves?

"They both died. The woman wasn't hurt. She hid in the room while the men argued outside. Then there was the fight. The deputies dragged her out—she was shrieking and clawing at them, like she thought they'd hurt her."

Mary Beth was horrified. "How did you know that?" It wasn't the kind of detail that would appear in the newspaper.

"I was there."

A profound silence enveloped them. The white bird stalked away out of sight but Mary Beth didn't see it go.

"How old were you, Parr?"

"Twelve."

Mary Beth chose her next words carefully. "And how did you happen to be at the motel?"

"I have to backtrack. I knew how to drive at that age."

That was no big deal. A lot of country kids did, especially boys.

"I was tall for twelve, never got pulled over. I didn't

drive crazy or show off, ever. So this older boy we knew would let me borrow one of the beater cars he fixed up now and then."

"But why—"

He held up a hand. "I'm getting to that. Have patience, Mary Beth."

The clear, reflected light filling the truck's cab showed the lines on his face. The memories he was reliving made him seem suddenly older than his years.

"I knew my dad was fooling around with someone," he went on. "Just not who. Mother didn't have a clue. She thought he could do no wrong." A bitter edge crept into his voice. "So that night, when he told her he was going out to play poker, I happened to have the car parked down by the corner. He didn't see me come out the alley when he was backing out. I caught up with him but he didn't notice. I followed him all the way out to that goddamned motel."

Mary Beth listened. She wasn't sure if Parr would finish the story.

"I parked my car a couple spaces down from his. It was pretty quiet. I wasn't sure which room he was in, either. I was about to turn around and go home when this other car came roaring in and a man got out.

"I ducked down when I saw the gun in his hand. He was yelling and pounding on doors—sweet Jesus, I was scared to death. But I looked up when he went past me. Then my dad opened the door right in front of my car. He ran out and got the guy in a hammerlock, tried to get the gun away from him." He stopped. "Guess he was trying to protect her or something."

Mary Beth felt sick inside. The passing of years

hadn't lessened the pain for the boy who'd witnessed the worst that adults could do.

"Then I heard shots. And my dad went down. There must have been a sheriff's cruiser close by because they got there quick. The other man put the gun to his head. The deputies tried to help them both but it was too late. One went in and got the woman. She was fighting him hard, screaming like a wildcat.

"But it wasn't just her. I heard someone screaming right behind me. In the car."

"What? Who?"

"Bobby Joe was in the backseat. He hung out there sometimes, climbed over and pretended it was his car, acted like he could drive. He told me later he'd fallen asleep there. He woke up when I was on the road out of town and he stayed down until after I got to the motel."

"Oh my God."

"He heard the woman's husband yelling, but he didn't know why and he couldn't see anything crouched down in the backseat. He didn't show his face until the sirens scared him. What he heard and saw was the woman and she was half crazy by then. 'You did it. You killed him. You did it.' She was pointing at this one and that one and finally she pointed at me.

"When it was all over Bobby Joe got the idea that I'd led the other man to the motel. He knew Daddy and I fought sometimes. He just didn't know why. Never over the usual teenage stuff. It didn't seem right to tell him that our old man was a lying, cheating bastard."

Parr paused. There was a coldness in his last words that Mary Beth had never heard in his voice.

"Even when he was older and knew the whole story—at least what the newspapers printed, because he could look that up at the library—he didn't want to believe my version."

"Two witnesses. And both of them kids. Jesus."

"I saw the shooting and the suicide," he said curtly. "Bobby Joe didn't. So he wasn't a witness to anything."

"Did you have to testify?"

Parr nodded. "In a manner of speaking, yes. With the murderer and victim both dead, it wasn't like a trial. The woman was cleared of any involvement. I don't know what happened to her.

"But I had to live with what I saw—and what I didn't do—for years after. I can still see it like it happened yesterday."

Almost two decades had passed.

"You can't still think you should have saved your father, Parr."

"I did then. And if Bobby Joe hadn't popped up from the backseat, I might have tried to interfere. Didn't matter, did it? We lost our dad and my kid brother ended up hating me. He told the story his way. Some folks believed him."

Mary Beth could imagine Bobby Joe doing just that, with a few embellishments thrown in for effect.

"For a while, I thought my mother did too." He clenched his clasped hands until his knuckles turned white. "But she swears not. Let's just say there were several versions of the truth. It all depended on who people wanted to believe."

A cloud drifted over the lake, then another. The

shadows were fleeting. Mary Beth looked up first. Parr didn't seem to have noticed.

They were utterly alone. No one could possibly overhear. But it wasn't like Parr was giving away secrets. He was telling the truth as he'd understood it, even if no one beside the authorities ever wanted to hear it or remember it.

As the only living witness to a murderous crime of passion, he bore a dual burden. Of remembering, because he had to in order to understand as he grew to manhood. And of forgetting, because he had to forget in order to keep going.

Mary Beth moved next to him on the truck's bench seat. He let her lean against him. She lay a hand over his. He didn't pull away. But he didn't embrace her.

His dark eyes stared out at the serene lake and the motionless lilies.

"Mary Beth, what you said last night about me and Bobby Joe—how different we are—that was more truthful than you knew. But there's more to it. We're different for the same reason. And now you know what that reason is."

"I—I appreciate you telling me."

He drummed on the steering wheel. "But you can't keep on with him."

She swallowed hard. "That's my decision to make."

Parr frowned and his jaw set in a hard line. "You don't have to allow him to ruin your life with his philandering and his lies. That's not going to change and you can't change him."

"Well." She blew out a breath. "If you've been doing so much thinking about what I should do with my life, then tell me what I should do."

"Just let me love you."

The simple words had a devastating effect. Tears welled in Mary Beth's eyes. She brushed them away before Parr could see her crying.

"It hit me like a sledgehammer the first time I ever saw you. Standing there crying like a lost angel. And when I found out who'd made you cry, I could hardly control myself."

"But you did. Really well." She still didn't understand how or why he'd done that, if what he was saying now was true.

"Mother made me promise to keep my distance, if it would help Bobby Joe win you back. So I did my best. I didn't think I was that convincing."

"No. You weren't. But I couldn't figure you out."

He pressed his lips together. "Sorry. You don't know how sorry I am."

"That's not enough. You and I hardly know each other, even now."

"Then we can start over."

She shook her head. "Not without good reason. I want someone who isn't going to run away."

He took her hand and held it. "That will be me. Forever. I never said that word before."

"Why not?" She edged away, expecting him to take her in his arms and melt her resistance.

His smile was heartbreakingly tender when he finally turned to face her. "Because I was waiting for you my whole life long. I never knew it until I saw your sweet face."

"But—"

"Here you are. Be mine, Mary Beth. All mine."

"I can't say yes, Parr. I just can't."

The intensity of his dark gaze got stronger. "You have, though. Just not in so many words."

"What are you talking about?" She tried to move away but found she couldn't. Not without jumping out of the truck. She couldn't walk back to Sheila's from the lake.

"You're not faking anything when I hold you. What we feel for each other is real, Mary Beth."

The truth of that statement unsettled Mary Beth. But she felt compelled to argue against it. "Wanting someone isn't the same as loving someone."

"It's a start," he said dryly. "I know for a fact that Bobby Joe never made you feel like a woman."

"Oh?" She barely suppressed her rising anger.

"Simmer down. He didn't say a word on the subject. I'm talking about the fire in your beautiful green eyes. You look at me like a woman in love for the first time."

She didn't know what to say.

"I doubt my brother would even know what I mean," Parr added. "But I can tell you right now that he's not man enough for you. And he's sure as hell not good enough."

"That doesn't mean—"

Parr silenced her with a kiss that left no doubt as to his intentions. Mary Beth yielded to it, craving the sensation, desiring him only, so aware of how much she needed him and he needed her that it hurt.

When she couldn't stand it another second, she pushed him away.

"No. We shouldn't."

Parr withdrew and sat for some moments in silence, not looking at her. His arousal was plain to see and she blamed herself. But someone had to stop this and it had to be her.

Breaking up was hard to do. The old song got it right. It was going to be even harder with two brothers in the mix.

The Weston family had been shattered once before and the fault lines had never mended. No matter how good it felt to be held by him, to kiss and be kissed by him, to indulge in foreplay that nearly crossed the line of consummated sex, she could not keep on, especially if it meant pretending to others that she was entirely innocent.

He was right about her saying yes without being brave enough to say it out loud.

That couldn't continue.

"Take me back, Parr. Right now."

Chapter Nineteen

Mary Beth was back in Iminga. Judging by the way she behaved after the return from Brickell, no one suspected anything out of the ordinary had happened.

Hello. Yes, we had a lovely time. Thanks so much for asking. But there's no place like home.

Which was exactly the same. The unchanging rhythm of a southern summer enfolded her. As far as their friends and acquaintances knew, she'd been her usual saintly self by agreeing to take her future mother-in-law upstate to see an old friend for a few days. Bobby Joe had gone fishing downstate. Parr had stopped by, not for long. Alma looked rested. That was about it for raging gossip.

And now, she had to plan Alma's birthday party. It was going to be a surprise and that meant Howard wasn't in on it.

Bobby Joe was showing a few houses today. She had the key to the office building that he'd given her. There was that little room at the top that she'd liked. She settled the strap of the huge tote bag over her shoulder to make it more comfortable. It was stuffed with art supplies and notebooks. She was going to get good and crafty where no one would bother her.

She entered, grateful that Bobby Joe had remembered to turn on the air-conditioning. The interior was cool as a cave but still sunny. She locked the door behind her and went upstairs.

First she took her purse out of the tote and set it aside on the little desk under the skylight. The small white box inside looked even whiter. She hadn't given the necklace to Parr to have repaired. He hadn't asked for it, either, just taken an abrupt departure from Sheila's house that hurt his mother's feelings more than a little.

Mary Beth got out the poster board. What she planned to do—splashy stencil art with rah-rah best wishes in marker—wasn't exactly mindless but it was close. Doing something with her hands was easier than thinking about everything she and Parr had discussed. Besides, she wanted Alma's birthday to be special after she'd been through so much.

Everyone who'd been at Mary Beth's birthday party in the spring would be there, plus Sheila, who'd promised to drive down. Life went on. Events and milestones needed celebrating.

Mary Beth glanced at the guest list. There was Eve and AJ Ross, and their little girl, Carrie, and new baby, Amanda, plus an assortment of second and third cousins. And every friend in the Westons' old address book, a metal-top thing that flipped open for snooping convenience. Mary Beth hadn't had to scroll through Alma's phone memory.

Absorbed in the task of adding all their names to one poster, she didn't notice that two hours had gone by. She felt a little faint. A new eatery had just opened on the other side of the square and she'd glanced at the menu. Lots of fresh salads and fried chicken too—her secret vice. She had to have some.

Mary Beth took just her wallet and the keys, leaving everything the way it was. She hoped and prayed there would be no drop-in visitors to Robert Joseph Weston and Associates today. Bobby Joe had told her that summer was slow, with a sales surge in mid-August before school started.

Whatever. So long as he had something to look forward to.

She had arrived at one half of the decision she faced. Mary Beth was going to break it off with Bobby Joe. After his mother's birthday.

She tried not to even think about Parr.

She reentered the office, looking up and down the street first before she pulled out the key, then locked the door behind her again. Still no customers, apparently.

Mary Beth stayed on the first floor to eat her bagged lunch. The small portion of fried chicken was made right, good and greasy. She made up for it with a large salad, eating that almost as fast, then stuffing the wrappings into the paper bag and leaving it by the front door. She'd take it all with her when she left shortly.

Fueled, she went back upstairs to finish the birthday project.

Something was different and it didn't take her long to figure out what.

Her bag had been moved. The little white box was gone. Mary Beth looked up at the skylight. It was closed. It locked on the inside anyway. She climbed up on the desk and examined it. Not only was it still locked, there was a tiny cobweb on it. No one had come in that way.

Had she imagined taking the white box with her?

She jumped down, stressed and creeped out. Nothing else had been disturbed. Okay, she told herself. The art stuff could stay. But she didn't have to.

She took her purse and left the tote, quickly exiting with the lunch bag, which went right into a trash can. Her car was close by. She could call someone from there.

Not Bobby Joe, that was for damn sure. And not the cops.

She would have to talk to Parr. Mary Beth ran down the sidewalk to her car.

A ladder slid down the side of the office building. Up on the roof Pete Corlear held on to the ropes that allowed him to lower it safely. He didn't see her go.

Parr asked her a lot of pertinent questions. But it all came down to the same thing. "They didn't take your phone? Just the necklace box was gone?"

"Nothing else. I'm sure of it."

"And you were alone?"

"Yes. I went out for lunch, but that only took me, oh, fifteen or twenty minutes."

"And you're sure you didn't leave it at home."

"Yes," she said exasperatedly. "I wouldn't, for about a thousand reasons, which I shouldn't have to explain to you."

"Got it." His matter-of-fact tone was infinitely annoying. The ruby strawberry still had sentimental meaning to her, even though he'd avoided her since she hadn't said yes. For all she knew, he'd gone back to Memphis on the first available flight.

But, oh God, did she miss having him near. More than ever. The feeling got stronger every day. She couldn't wait for summer to be over so she could go back to work and have something else to think about. Like . . . a future with no one to love. She snapped out of it when he asked another matter-of-fact question.

"Where are you?"

"Down the street from the building. In my car. I didn't want to stick around."

"That was smart. Don't go back in until I can find out more. You might as well head home."

She thought about ignoring that order—it wasn't a recommendation or a request—then decided to let Parr check out the situation without her. He was the only one who had a reason to keep his mouth shut about a minor theft that might have major consequences for both of them, in terms of what the family would think.

There wasn't anyone else she could call. The cops would ask her if she had a receipt, and she didn't. Her dad would want to know where the necklace had come from and he would be sure to ask questions. Bobby Joe was out showing houses and she wasn't going to interrupt him. The thought of the extra keys bothered her. He had the master key and she had a copy, and there had been those others in the desk drawer.

"I'll be right there."

So Parr *was* back in Iminga. He could have called or come by her father's house. Where he was staying was something she didn't want to know and wouldn't ask. Alma was safely ensconced in her newly renovated home and hadn't said a thing about Parr, though Mary Beth had only been by to see her once since the return trip from Brickell.

There was that Weston clannishness. There always would be.

"Maybe I'll see you later," she said tentatively. "Call me, okay?"

"If I can."

She tossed the phone into her purse.

He'd changed. But hadn't they all? Mary Beth had changed so much this summer, she wasn't at all sure where she fit in. But she did her dutiful best to be nice while she muddled through as usual. Her strong sense of family, of propriety, kept her within bounds.

It helped when dealing with Bobby Joe, whose behavior was still erratic. He did try to be affectionate, in a way she perceived as somewhat artificial. Mary Beth scolded herself for feeling guilty for not telling him immediately about the theft. But she did *not* want his mother or her father or him to find out about the pretty little necklace that Parr had given her.

She turned the key in the ignition and drove away. If it got around that the stolen necklace had been a gift from Parr, that wasn't the end of the world. She'd live it down somehow.

Parr parked on a side street and got out of his truck. The courthouse square was quiet, with only a few people on the sidewalks and none at all near Robert Joseph Weston and Associates.

But there was a ladder leaning against the office building.

Surely the thief wouldn't have used it in broad daylight. The thought was ridiculous. As Parr approached the building, an older man in overalls swung a leg over the roof and set his foot down on an upper rung. He went down it with slow confidence. Parr recognized the man on the ladder as Pete Corlear, who'd done the window lettering and roof sign for Bobby Joe.

"Hey there." Parr stopped.

Corlear, looking sun-dazzled, squinted at him once he'd reached the sidewalk. "Parr. Been a while."

"Yes, it has."

"I'd shake hands but there's fresh paint on mine. Just did some touch-ups. Whew. Hot as blue blazes up on that roof. I can't wait to get home."

"Is Bobby here?"

"Don't think so. But his lady friend—Mary Beth—was in for a while. Go on and knock. She could still be up in that little attic room."

"Probably not. I just talked to her."

"Don't you have a key, Parr?"

"Ah—I forgot to bring it."

"Well, I'd let you in but I don't have one myself."

"Not a problem. I can call Bobby Joe. Good work on the signs, by the way."

Corlear pulled out a bandanna and mopped his forehead. "Thank you. Feel free to mention my name. One job leads to the next. Bobby Joe said something about you two being more or less in the same business."

"That's right. Just not in the same town."

"Oh well. Have a good one." Corlear hoisted the lightweight ladder and walked away with it.

Parr crossed the street and went into the new eatery. He ordered a tall sweet tea to go but he sipped it inside, making sure that Mr. Corlear was gone before he left the shop.

Parr walked around the back and through the alley of the building. Then he took the key he'd kept from when he'd speeded up the renovations, in the name of helping Bobby Joe.

Who generally found a way to screw things up all the same. And had probably just done it again.

Parr let himself in and left the street door unlocked.

He went upstairs to the room under the skylight and satisfied himself that nothing was amiss. The bits and pieces of Mary Beth's artwork lay around and a half-completed poster took up most of the small desk.

Then Parr called Bobby Joe.

Parr's brother came up the stairs next, whistling. He stopped as he entered the room. "Didn't take you long to figure out who done it."

"You made it easy."

"Well, here's what I took." Bobby Joe removed a small white box from his pocket, but he didn't hand it over.

"How'd you even know it was here?"

"I can't take all the credit. There was an element of luck. But I did know what I was looking for and that Mary Beth was likely to keep it with her even if she didn't wear it."

"How so?"

"Mercy me, Mother Alma might find it!" he said in a falsetto voice. "Or golly gosh, Bobby Joe could look in my drawers! Dresser drawers, I mean."

"Knock it off," Parr growled.

Bobby Joe dropped back down to his normal tone. "A friend of yours gave me a few good clues." He smirked. "You two are no longer an item and she doesn't care if you know."

"Gail."

"That's right. She's an interesting girl in her own icy kind of way."

Parr thought that was an accurate description of Gail Cash.

"So why'd you have her wrap up this little box for Mary Beth's birthday? It wasn't nice of you to rub salt in the wound."

Parr shrugged, folding his arms across his chest. He refused to react to his brother's needling. "I know for a fact Gail wasn't wounded when I ended our affair. We weren't in love and there was another guy waiting in the wings."

"Yeah." Bobby Joe gave him a crooked smile. "Not me, though. I mean, not back then."

"Spare me the details, Bobby Joe. I just don't care."

"Okay. Then I won't brag. There were just a few times, anyway, before I ended up in the hospital. Well, once in the hospital. She stopped by to cheer me up."

"I heard."

"Don't get self-righteous, Parr." His brother's voice had a thin edge. "Not when you were trying so hard to get my girl. Didn't you ever consider waiting to see if I died? Nobody would've much minded if you'd consoled Mary Beth and then done what you'd wanted to do all along."

"Shut up. You didn't die. And she's not your girl."

Bobby Joe rattled the box. "Everyone thinks so. Here's the proof that she's not. I even know when you bought it."

Gail must have found the receipt. She did have access to most of his papers and bills.

"But . . ." Bobby Joe put the little box on the desk as if daring Parr to pick it up. "I didn't know you'd given Mary Beth that little ruby strawberry when I saw it around her neck. She acted like it was nothing."

"Well, it belongs to her. I'd like her to have it."

"Sure. When she hands over those two diamond rings to me. I think I can get a refund. So what's going on with you and my not-so-true love?"

"Absolutely nothing," Parr said in a low voice.

"Come on," Bobby Joe sneered. "You don't expect me to believe that."

"I'm not going to dignify that with a response. We're brothers. You know when I'm lying. And vice versa."

Parr's contemptuous comments forced Bobby Joe to abandon his position. "That's so," he muttered.

And Parr's reply had been completely truthful. Since leaving Brickell after Mary Beth's rejection, he'd stayed strictly away from her. He wouldn't have gotten involved in this current situation if not for the possibility of his mother finding out about what was, for all intents and purposes, a love triangle.

But Alma had survived something like that. In some ways, she couldn't be shocked anymore.

However, the thought of Howard Caine's reaction to such a tawdry scenario did concern Parr. Mary Beth's father was an upright man who'd lost a beloved wife too young and who loved his only daughter more than his own life. When he found out that both Weston brothers had some sort of claim on her, he would be fighting mad.

"Just give the necklace to me and I'll talk to her. You'll get the rings back, if that's what she wants to do, and I suspect she does. She's not like Gail."

Without a word, Bobby Joe handed him the box.

"Mother doesn't need to know about this," Parr warned him.

"I won't tell her," he muttered.

At least his brother still had some sense of filial obligation, Parr thought grimly. That was good. If not, Parr would have to knock it into him.

Bobby Joe made his way to the chair Mary Beth had used. "I guess you're not going to bankroll the business from here on."

Parr straightened. "You're my brother. I made a promise. But my commitment will end in six months."

Bobby Joe looked up in surprise. "Good enough. But don't you want me to promise something in return?"

"Yes. Leave Mary Beth alone. I know she doesn't want you, but I'm not so sure she wants me."

Parr got the last seat on the last flight of the day to Memphis. Darkness had fallen by the time the plane landed. He went straight into town and to his office.

There was no one there, but Gail seldom worked late. She was efficient in all that she did.

He rolled a chair over to one of the file cabinets and starting going through the paid bills. He preferred to retain hard copies of everything and had never signed up for online billing.

It was time he did. A few months were missing.

He got online and signed up for paperless, checking back a few months, looking for a date in spring.

Bingo.

He found one line of user data, one particular number, called only once, that told him everything he needed to know.

Parr heard the door of the office open very quietly and then shut.

Gail strolled in, her long legs covering the distance into the file room, and perched on a chair. Butter wouldn't melt under her butt, Parr thought.

"Hello. You wanted to see me and here I am." Her voice was throaty and low, like she was expecting this to be fun and games.

Bobby Joe had agreed to one last condition that

Parr had remembered just in time: not to tell Gail that he was flying back to Memphis that same night.

"Yes. Thanks for coming in. I wanted to discuss a discrepancy in the records with you. I just signed up to get the phone bills online. Seems like some of them have disappeared. You're usually so conscientious about that."

She dialed down the sexy pose, sitting up straight. "Anyone can make mistakes."

"You made a big one." He held up the printout of the online phone bill and pointed to the line he'd marked with yellow highlighter. "You knew I'd recognize my mother's landline number if I happened to look at the monthly bill. You only used your work phone—which I pay for—that one time. Guess you didn't have your personal cell with you, but it's not like I'm invading your privacy."

She watched him warily, tapping the toe of one high heel on the floor.

"No doubt you noticed that my mother's house phone doesn't have a number screen. In fact, it's so old it doesn't have anything but a rotary dial."

"I don't remember. That was months ago."

"Doesn't change the facts, Gail. You called to speak to Bobby Joe, hoping he'd pick up, and he did. You lured him out of the house after Mary Beth's birthday party."

"I wouldn't use the word *lured*. Your baby brother is hot to trot, like, all the time."

"Which begs the question of what you see in him. Used to be you didn't like competition, Gail."

Silence.

"I just wanted to confirm that Bobby Joe ditched her to go see you at the motel."

"Boo hoo. Poor little Mary Beth."

"What you did wasn't right."

"Well, I'm not going to jail for it either," she pointed out.

"No."

"I do want to say that it's very sweet of you to take such good care of her, Parr."

"Bobby Joe doesn't," he said in a level voice. "I can't check his phone records, but I'm sure you're not the only one he pursued. But that's beside the point."

"Is it? Is Mary Beth going to come after me screaming and clawing and carrying on? I won every catfight I ever started."

"Get over yourself," Parr said with disgust. "I don't think she cares one way or another about you."

"Oh. Okay. I won't worry. I'm fired, right? I'll apply for unemployment tomorrow."

"You do that. Get your stuff and go. I'll wait here so you can give me back your key before you go."

He watched her walk away. He knew she didn't have much in or on her desk and it wouldn't take long for her to pack.

"One more thing," he said as she stepped over the threshold. "Why'd you do it? Why go after Bobby Joe when you could have just about any man you wanted?"

Gail thought it over, taking several extra seconds for theatrical effect. "Because I couldn't have you. But I didn't do it out of spurned love. Spite is more like it."

Parr shook his head and concentrated on his paperwork again as his former assistant walked out of his
office and out of his life.

Parr handed over the white box to Mary Beth. She
accepted it hesitantly, looking around the restaurant
he'd chosen. No one knew them here and the tables
were miles apart.

Just as well on both counts, because Parr's explanation of how he'd gotten the necklace back was difficult
for Mary Beth to listen to. As far as Bobby Joe and
Gail, she did think it was a shame they couldn't be
faithful to anyone at all, ever, because they richly deserved each other.

But she'd thought it all through and made up her
mind before Parr had called her and got her to come
here. Sometimes you had to be a little bad to get a
good man, and not care what people might think. As
it had turned out, most had been rooting for her and
Parr all along.

"I had it fixed. Nothing to it. Then I hung on to it
because it sure as hell didn't belong to Bobby Joe and
I didn't know if you wanted it."

She opened the box. The ruby pendant caught the
fire of the flickering candle on their secluded table. The
delicate gold chain shimmered as she lifted it out. It was
back to its original length. The other chain she'd added
to it to hide it from prying eyes had been removed.
"Thank you, Parr. I do want it. You know I do."

He glanced at her slender fingers, bare of rings.
She'd been happy to give those back to her former

fiancé. Alma and Howard seemed more relieved than anything else once they'd been informed of the bare facts.

She wasn't out for revenge. Neither was Parr. The past months seemed like a bad dream—but they were over.

"So what now?"

Mary Beth rose and went over to his side of the table and sat on his lap. "Would you mind putting it on for me?"

"Not at all."

She bent her head forward, smiling as the fine chain tickled her neck. He fastened the clasp and pressed a kiss to her nape.

She turned gracefully and returned the favor, right on his lips.

"The waiters are watching," he murmured.

"I don't care," she said.

Epilogue ...

They'd gone to Jackson just to get out of Iminga and have some not-married-yet fun away from the parents. True, Mary Beth had a hidden agenda. She'd wanted to visit a bridal boutique famous for southern charm and one-of-a-kind dresses.

"Don't make me go in there, Mary Beth."

She had just come out. Parr was seated on a wrought-iron bench on the sidewalk, between two planters of moon-white flowers.

"Brave men do it all the time. Why not you?"

He didn't seem bothered by her affectionate joke. "Why can't your gown be a beautiful surprise?"

"It will be. I haven't even decided on the style. I just wanted to ask you about colors." She held up different swatches in her hand.

"What if I pick the wrong one?"

"Parr, please pay attention. The maid of honor— that's Eve—and her daughter, Carrie, the flower girl, and Amanda, the flower baby, will wear a coordinating shade, but first I have to pick mine."

She riffled through the swatches.

"They all look the same to me."

"They're not. Snow or vanilla? Sugar or milk?"

"Are you eating it or wearing it?"

"Funny. Come on. Which?"

"The one on the right looks nice."

"That's cream. Not quite white," she said mischievously.

Parr grinned. "I would say cream as in strawberries and cream. Because you are one delicious dish, Mary Beth." He pulled her down beside him before she could go back in the boutique. "So am I done? Is that the choice?"

"I'm not sure."

"Okay. No cream then. All I ever wanted is one sweet strawberry and that's you. I love you more than I can ever say. Now do you love me?"

"You know I do!"

"Prove it, girl."

Mary Beth threw her arms around his neck and let the swatches fly away.